Run Into Trouble

by

Alan Cook

AuthorHouse™
1663 Liberty Drive, Suite 200
Bloomington, IN 47403
www.authorhouse.com
Phone: 1-800-839-8640

First published by AuthorHouse 1/19/2009

ISBN: 978-1-4389-2350-5 (sc)

Library of Congress Control Number: 2008911731

Printed in the United States of America
Bloomington, Indiana

This book is printed on acid-free paper.

ALSO BY ALAN COOK

Gary Blanchard Mysteries:
Honeymoon for Three
The Hayloft: a 1950s mystery
California Mystery:
Hotline to Murder
Lillian Morgan mysteries:
Catch a Falling Knife
Thirteen Diamonds
Other fiction:
Walking to Denver
Nonfiction:
Walking the World: Memories and Adventures
History:
Freedom's Light: Quotations from History's Champions of Freedom
Poetry:
The Saga of Bill the Hermit

ACKNOWLEDGMENTS

I appreciate the assistance of my running consultants, Mike, Phil, and Brian, who provided me with information and anecdotes about running. Mike read a draft copy of the book and made good suggestions. Any errors, of course, are mine.

DEDICATION

To Andy, a freedom fighter

CHAPTER 1

They that can give up essential liberty to obtain a little temporary safety deserve neither liberty nor safety.

—Benjamin Franklin

If the Communists took over, I'd go to them and say, "What do you want me to do?"

—Young woman at a party in the Hollywood Hills, December 1961

ꕥ

THE TAXI DRIVER SUDDENLY SWORE, CAUSING DRAKE TO SNAP OUT OF his reverie. He glanced at the back of the head in front of him. The man appeared to be looking in the rearview mirror. Drake spun around in the backseat, and an identical expletive escaped his lips. A truck was overtaking them at a high rate of speed. It couldn't pass them on the narrow road without crossing into the opposing lane of traffic, and the driver apparently had no intention of doing that.

"Step on it."

Drake's order came too late. He instinctively ducked his head an instant before the collision, which drove his face into the thinly padded seat back. The noise sounded like an exploding bomb, and he thought he was back in the army.

Then all was silent. Drake wondered whether he was dead, as he always did after a similar occurrence. He heard a noise. The engine of the truck was revving. He raised his head in time to see the truck backing up. Was the driver planning to hit them again? Probably not.

He would have to drive into the field where the taxi had landed after being momentarily airborne. The truck swerved onto a side road. It skidded to a stop and then lurched forward, accelerating back toward Interstate 5.

The rear end of the taxi had telescoped, and Drake realized that a few more inches and he would have telescoped along with it. Through the broken rear window he saw liquid spilling out of what had once been the gas tank. Gasoline. He had to get out of here.

He heard a moan. He realized for the first time that the driver was lying in the backseat beside him. His seat back had broken during the collision.

"Are you all right?"

An answering moan told him that he would have to get them both out. Drake shoved at the mangled door beside the driver, not bothering to look for the door handle, which was surely non-functional. The door was jammed. He tried the door on the other side with equal lack of success. He reached across the driver into the front seat and found the handle on the driver's side door. Although that door didn't look as bad, it didn't respond to his pressure.

The easiest way out was through the rear window; the glass was already broken. Drake knocked out several loose pieces of glass that were still clinging to the window frame. He grabbed the shoulders of the driver who was lying on his back, his body partially on the errant seat back, and tried to lift him. He was greeted with a full-fledged groan.

No time to be gentle. Drake hefted the driver up, ignoring louder groans, and shoved him head first through the window. He stopped for a second to collect his energy and realized he was panting. With a supreme effort, he pushed the body after the head. The driver rolled off what was left of the trunk and hit the ground with a thump.

That had used most of Drake's strength, but he had to get himself out. He forced his muscles to move. He got his head and shoulders through the opening and became stuck. He couldn't go any farther. It would be easier to stay here and let things take their course. Which would involve him burning up in a fiery inferno, like the suttee he had seen in India.

You candy ass, he told himself. You've gotten yourself out of worse jams than this. Just not recently. You're out of practice. Do this one thing and you can rest. He wiggled his body slowly through the opening, but when most of it was through, he didn't have strength enough to stop himself from rolling off the remains of the trunk, just as the driver had done.

He felt pain for the first time as his chest landed on a rock. But he was finished. No, not quite. They weren't safe yet. He smelled gasoline. He struggled to his feet and grunted as he lifted the driver under his arms near the shoulders, dragging him away from the car into the dirt of the field, which, fortunately, had nothing planted in it at the moment.

He stumbled backward, slowly, the earth and the legs and butt of the driver creating friction, noticing the sweat rolling down his face, his lungs feeling as if they would collapse. How far did they have to go?

A fireball whooshed into the air in all directions; Drake felt the heat from it, even though they were now a safe distance away. He dropped the driver and hit the ground himself, watching in awe as the car was consumed by angry red flames. He hadn't seen a fire this spectacular in a long time.

How was the driver? Drake sat up and looked at him. His eyes were open.

"How do you feel?"

"My neck hurts."

Whiplash. He also had some cuts from the broken glass. Drake took out a handkerchief and wiped them off, but they weren't bleeding badly. If those were the extent of his injuries, he was lucky. He noticed the driver staring up at him.

"You're bleeding, man."

Drake put his hand to his face, and his fingers felt the red liquid gushing out of his nose. He had been unconsciously licking it off his lips. He pressed the handkerchief against his nostrils to stanch the flow and jumped as pain radiated through his head. His nose was broken. What else? He needed to take inventory. In addition to the cuts he had suffered from the broken glass, his back hurt. Of course. His body had been twisted when the collision occurred.

He became aware of a car heading toward the still burning taxi, traveling at high speed, coming from the direction of the beach. It must be associated with the race he was supposed to be entering. The car stopped fast, not far from the taxi, and two men jumped out. They got as close to the fire as they could and appeared to be looking for something.

Signs of life, Drake thought grimly. Well, don't keep them in suspense. He laboriously stood up and waved his hand. They still didn't see him. "Over here." Shouting made his head hurt.

∽

The one thing Drake insisted on was that the taxi driver get the medical treatment he needed and a brand new car, even if Drake, himself, had to pay for it. Why should he suffer when he hadn't been the target of the attack? He was collateral damage, as the military liked to say.

"It's all being taken care of."

Fred Rathbun had introduced himself as the race coordinator while he and his assistant, a man with a name that sounded like Peaches, helped Drake and the taxi driver into their car and drove them to a hospital in Chula Vista. After spending a lot of time on a pay phone in the lobby, Fred joined Drake in the emergency room where he waited for his x-rays to be developed.

"Giganticorp is going to cover all his expenses and pay him a salary while he recuperates. And we'll buy him a brand new taxi. Of course, we're also covering your expenses since you're a participant in Running California."

Was a participant. Giganticorp, the sponsor of the ambitious race from the Mexican border to San Francisco, had been difficult for Drake to obtain information about. It was privately owned but apparently wealthy enough to easily afford the million dollar prize that would go to the winning team. That was enough information for Drake who was a capitalist at heart. He viewed free enterprise as a good thing. He had been working as a real estate agent for several years.

Fred wore a business suit, white shirt, and tie. His clothes made him look more like an IBM sales rep than a race coordinator. He smelled of some kind of aftershave. As an employee of Giganticorp, he was first and foremost a businessman, but race coordinators, in Drake's experience, usually looked as if they could run a race. Fred looked like the conception of an artist who liked circles. His body was round, his face was round, even his short haircut was round.

"Do you have any idea who hit you?" Fred asked.

The question was phrased in an interesting way. Not "Did you get a look at the truck?" or "Did you get a look at the driver?" How much did Giganticorp know about him? Probably not as much as he imagined.

"It was a pickup truck. I didn't get a look at the driver. I don't even remember the color. It looked pretty much like any other pickup truck, except that I caught a glimpse of the front bumper before it hit us, and it appeared to be larger than usual—perhaps reinforced."

"Hmmm." Fred wiped his sweating face with a large handkerchief. "So you don't have any idea who it was?"

It occurred to Drake that he'd better be careful in dealing with Fred. He might look like Humpty Dumpty, but looks could be deceiving. "I'm not on any list that I know about."

"I understand that you used to work for the government on some sensitive projects…"

Fred made it an incomplete sentence that Drake would feel he had to complete. He resisted the impulse.

"Yeah. That was a while ago."

"Do you want to file a police report?"

Drake hadn't gotten that far in his thinking. The taxi driver was being taken care of. He was being taken care of. He wouldn't be able to give the police enough information to help them find the culprit. If this were the work of a former enemy, the police would be powerless, anyway. But why would they come after him now? Because the race would undoubtedly generate publicity? Because his name might be in the papers? It didn't make sense.

"I don't think talking to the police would accomplish anything."

Fred nodded. "The red tape would hold up the race."

A thought tugged at Drake's brain. Something about the collision. Just before he had ducked his head, he had noticed something about the truck. Or heard something. That was it. The noise of the engine had lessened. The driver had backed off the gas pedal—perhaps even put on his brakes. He hadn't hit the taxi as hard as he could have.

What did that mean? Drake decided not to mention it to Fred.

"Isn't the race supposed to start in…" Drake looked at his watch "…about an hour?" By some miracle, his watch was still working. It was coming up on noon. As he recalled, the race was scheduled to start at one.

"The start has been postponed until tomorrow morning. Casey is with the other runners now, explaining it to them."

The race was already being delayed because of him. "I'm sorry I screwed it up. Are you going to be able to replace me?"

"Replace you? Of course not. You're going to be in it."

"Fred, perhaps you haven't noticed, but I'm in no condition to run a race. Especially a race of six hundred miles."

Fred sounded enthusiastic. "You'll be fine. I just talked to the doctor. The glass cuts will heal quickly. The bruise on your chest is temporary. He'll put a splint on your nose to hold it in place and protect it."

"What about my back pain?"

"The x-rays show nothing but a little scoliosis."

Curvature of the spine. "I've had that all my life."

"That's what the doctor suspected."

"But what about the pain? I can hardly walk."

"We'll bring in physical therapists, massage therapists, whatever you need."

"I couldn't stand for anyone to touch me right now."

"The doctor's going to give you a prescription for morphine."

"How come you know all this before I do?"

"Here comes the doctor now to tell you."

CHAPTER 2

As Peaches, or whatever his name was, drove Drake and Fred to the Hotel del Coronado where the runners were going to spend the night, Drake reflected that he looked like a classic hood instead of a businessman. His conservative suit didn't hide his bulging shoulders, and Drake was certain he had a gun concealed beneath his jacket. His only expression was a perpetual scowl. Drake decided that he needed to be as wary of Peaches as Fred, but for a different reason.

The most impressive thing about the Hotel del Coronado wasn't the gleaming white expanse of the building located on the beach, or the contrasting red roofs, but that it had been in business since the nineteenth century and had played host to "presidents and princes," as the brochure Drake read stated. If this was typical of how the runners were going to live during the race, he wouldn't fight it.

His room didn't have an ocean view. That was a concession to economy. It cost more to see the sea. The room was in the Victorian Building, the oldest part of the hotel, and was labeled quaint, meaning that it wasn't large and the furniture was old. It had the odor of quaint.

Drake still wasn't convinced he wanted to be in the race, especially if it were going to get him killed. He hadn't figured out why anybody wanted to kill him for running the California coast, but somebody must not like him.

He had an out. The person who had recruited him by phone, whose name he had forgotten, had told him that his teammate had already been picked. The recruiter couldn't tell him who his teammate was, for reasons Drake didn't understand. Both members of a team had to cross the finish line before both members of each of the other teams, in order to claim the million dollar first prize. He had reserved the right not to participate if he didn't like his teammate.

Fred wouldn't tell him who it was on the way to the hotel. "You'll find out when you get there."

Why the mystery? Well, he was at the hotel, and he still didn't know. He was being given a few minutes alone to "freshen up." He didn't have any luggage—that had been burned in the taxi—so freshening up consisted of washing his hands to get rid of the hospital smell. And noticing in the bathroom mirror how ugly he looked with two black eyes and the tape that covered his nose and much of his face.

He did have a new shirt and pants. Peaches had purchased them for him while he was at the hospital, because the clothes he had been wearing were covered with blood. Fred had promised that underwear and more clothes, and even a toothbrush and razor, would show up at the hotel. He had yet to see them.

He did one other thing. He opened the bottle of morphine tablets that the doctor had given him, swallowed one, and flushed the rest down the toilet. He knew from his training that morphine was one of the most addictive drugs in existence, and he wasn't having any part of it, even if it cost him a lot of pain. He wouldn't be controlled by anything or anybody.

There was a knock on the door. Drake opened it and saw a pleasant-looking man wearing a colorful sport shirt, glasses, and a concerned expression on his face. Youngish, but with a touch of gray in his otherwise dark hair that was neatly in place and cut with precision.

He extended his hand. "Casey Messinger. I'm very sorry to hear about your accident. Terrible thing. I'm looking into it."

"Nice to meet you." Drake was surprised at the strength of his grip. His name sounded familiar. "Are you by any chance the CEO of Giganticorp, Mr. Messinger?"

"Call me Casey. And yes, Oliver, I am."

"Call me Drake."

They both laughed. Drake immediately liked him. Not just his manner, but he was the first Giganticorp employee Drake had met who might actually be a runner.

"I understand you postponed the start of the race just for me."

"Yes, but it's not a problem. We'll start tomorrow morning at Border Field State Park and still be here in time to cross the Coronado Bridge in conjunction with its grand opening tomorrow afternoon."

"I take it there'll be publicity."

"Lots of press and brouhaha. Yup."

Drake had to phrase this carefully. "I have a concern. The accident...may not have been an accident."

"I get your drift. You're under my protection. As long as you're part of Running California, you have nothing to fear."

Big words. Confident words, but, somehow, Drake almost believed them.

"I'm not really going to be in shape to run tomorrow."

"That's all right. The first day is ceremonial. Everybody will run together in a group and be given the same time. It doesn't matter how fast you go."

Drake hadn't gathered that from the information about the race. He guessed that the Golden Rule came into play here—he who owns the gold makes the rules.

"May I ask you one more question?"

"Anything."

"Why are you doing this? Not just the race, itself, but the million dollar prize. I'm sure you could have offered much less—"

"We think big at Giganticorp. This will be great publicity for the company and for the state of California. And for the runners. I know that in the past you've avoided the spotlight, but you might get to like it."

Drake wondered. "I almost forgot. Who's my partner?"

"Wait here."

Casey gave Drake an enigmatic smile and left the room.

ᘓ

"You look terrible."

Drake stumbled backward from the doorway. His headache suddenly doubled in intensity. He would recognize that face and musical English accent anywhere, even though the words were far from musical. It was Melody. Or her ghost.

"Aren't you going to invite me in?"

"Come…come in."

She was approximately the last person in the world he had expected to see, this apparition that walked lightly into the room, almost without leaving footprints, and closed the door behind her.

"If it's any consolation, I'm glad you weren't killed today."

She still looked the same, her slim body hidden inside a warm-up suit, belying not only her curves but the strength within, both physical and mental. The sandy hair caught in a ponytail, ready for a run; the pert nose framed by a sprinkling of freckles on the small face.

"Do I have to carry this conversation all by myself?"

"Sorry." Drake sat down hard on the bed. His legs would no longer support him. "I…I didn't expect to see you here."

"Don't feel like the Lone Ranger, as you yanks would say. They didn't tell me about you, either, until they were forced to by the accident. All the other runners had partners, except me. When they finally divulged the secret, I almost walked out, just the way you did six years ago. For some reason that I can't attribute, I waited around to see whether you were alive or dead. I must say, you look more dead than alive."

"I'll recover." At least from the collision. "I guess I owe you an apology."

"You owe me a lifetime of apologies. Let's see. You leave me with no message and no explanation. I'm frantic, thinking that you're dead, or at the very least a prisoner in a Soviet Gulag camp. Finally, after months of searching and talking to everybody I can think of, a sympathetic bloke at your embassy does some checking and lets me know that you're all right but doesn't know where you are. I wait for word—and wait. For six years I've waited. In vain."

"I had no choice." Drake felt miserable. "I was ordered to secrecy."

"Yeah, I remember bloody government secrets. Your government and mine. Don't let the right hand know what the left hand is doing. But I take it you've been out for several years. Why did you quit?"

"It got to the point where I had a hard time telling the good guys from the bad guys."

"I know the feeling. Would it have hurt you to drop me a line?"

"I didn't think you wanted to hear from me. And I didn't know where you were."

"Poor excuses for excuses. You could have written my mum in Rotherfield."

"How long have you been in the U.S.?"

Melody sat on the edge of the bed beside Drake and appeared to deflate, like a balloon.

"Two years. Our little island became too small for me. I knew where too many bodies were buried, literally and figuratively. So I came to the land of the free and the home of the brave. I may even become a citizen someday."

"Where are you living?"

"Denver. Running at high altitude is great conditioning for running at sea level. I'm working at a Jack LaLanne health club as a fitness instructor and running the occasional marathon, when I can find one that accepts women. What about you? Tell me your recent history in two sentences or less."

Nonstop physical activity. That sounded like the Melody he knew. If anybody were in shape for this race, she was.

"I resigned four years ago. I've been living with my sister and brother-in-law in Idyllwild, which is about a hundred miles from here. It's also in the mountains, a mile high, same as Denver. I've been selling real estate and working out. I ran Boston last spring."

"Fancy that. We're both running marathons. I'm planning to run Boston next year. We might have run into each other, sometime, if you'll excuse the little joke. Except for your face, you look fit. Well, I guess the first thing we have to decide is whether we're going to quit while we're behind or have a go at this."

"What did they tell you about the collision?"

"That it was an accident. Your taxi was rear-ended, I believe."

"It was no accident. The truck driver hit us deliberately."

Melody caught her breath. "What else do you have to tell me?"

"Actually, that's it. I haven't had any contact with the agency for four years. I don't know why anybody would want to eliminate me. I doubt that any of our Russian friends care about me any longer. I don't want to expose you to any more danger. The one thing I was happy about when I left you was that you would be safe. You were, weren't you?"

"I didn't suffer any physical repercussions, if that's what you mean. Only emotional. I was reassigned. But we were in it together, Drake. We were both professionals. I knew what I was doing."

"Okay, but this is different. You're a civilian now."

Melody turned and looked into his bloodshot eyes with her green ones. When she did that, Drake was sure she could penetrate his brain and his very soul. Slowly her expression changed, and a smile lit up her face.

"To tell you the truth, life has been a bit boring since you left. The year I spent with you was a lot of things, but it was never dull. I don't know what chance we have of winning the million, but it might be a lovely adventure."

"Then the first thing we have to do is get me in shape to run."

Melody's manner became brisk. "Tell me about your injuries. I assume your nose won't be a problem, except that it may spoil your pretty-boy looks if it ends up misshapen. That may be a good thing. I won't be tempted to shag you."

"I have a few minor cuts, as you can see. Other than that, I have a bruise on my chest…"

Melody began unbuttoning his shirt. When Drake protested, she said, "I'm a certified fitness instructor. Hold still. I'm not going to rape you."

She pronounced his chest satisfactory. He told her about his back.

"Take off your belt and lie on the bed on your stomach."

That was easier said than done because the act of lying down was painful to Drake. When he finally got comfortable, she pulled his shirt up and examined his back. She also pulled his pants down a little. His back hurt when she touched it.

"I prescribe an ice pack. You can put ice cubes in a towel. I'll get you some. Have you got any aspirin?"

"The doctor gave me morphine, but I flushed it down the toilet."

"That sounds like you. I'll get you some aspirin. That won't kill you."

"There's something bothering me." Drake laboriously rolled over onto his back. "You and I being matched for this race is far too great a coincidence."

"I was thinking the same thing. Giganticorp knows a lot more about us than is good. What we did together was top secret. Especially what we did when we were off duty."

Drake smiled at the thought. "We need to keep our eyes open."

"And our mouths zipped. Loose lips sink ships."

"Seriously."

"Seriously. Of course you're right. You were always right."

"Thank you." He didn't mind sarcasm coming from her. "I know we're supposed to meet for an introductory dinner, but I can't make it."

"Quite right. I'm the doctor, and I'm prescribing bed rest. Alone. Fortunately, you and I have the only single rooms. The other nine teams are all lads, and teammates have to room together. I'm the lone girl in the race."

"I'd rather have you for a teammate than any male runner I can think of."

"Flattery is nice, but it won't get me into bed with you. I've learned my lesson on that score. I'll be back with ice and aspirin. And I'll have dinner sent up to you."

CHAPTER 3

Border Field State Park marks the United States side of the border with Mexico. The route for Running California starts here and wends its way north along the beach past the Oneonta Slough. Some wading may be necessary. The route continues along Imperial Beach and then across the narrow isthmus that separates the Pacific Ocean from San Diego Bay. It may be easier to run on Silver Strand Boulevard (Route 75) than the sand here. Stay on Route 75 and continue to the entrance to the San Diego-Coronado Bridge.

ഗ

THE OFFICIAL GIGANTICORP BUS WAS bright green with "Giganticorp" written on the side in large orange script. Below the company name the words "Running California" were painted on it in purple. The whole scene would have been impossible for Drake to miss, even if Melody hadn't been standing beside the bus waving frantically at him. He limped over to her.

She looked at him, not trying to hide her dismay. "Where were you? I rang your room, but you didn't answer."

"Good morning to you, too. My first problem is going to be getting up these steps."

The initial step, especially. He'd had enough trouble negotiating a few much lower steps. Drake tried to lift one foot, but the pain in his back stopped him well before it reached the level of the step. If the bus had been able to pull up to the curb in front of the hotel, he might have had more success. The extra nine or ten inches of height from street level was a killer. He did no better with the other foot. His run of the California coast might end right now.

"Could we have a boost here?" Melody called to Peaches who was sitting in the driver's seat.

Peaches got up and stomped down the steps. Without saying a word, he positioned himself behind Drake, grabbed his elbows, and lifted him up to the first step with about the same effort that it would take most people to lift half a dozen hardcover books from a table. It hurt to be lifted, but Drake squelched a groan. The other steps were lower, and Drake managed to escape further humiliation; he pulled himself up by grabbing the handrails and putting most of his weight on his arms.

Ignoring the stares of the other runners, he stumbled along the aisle and fell into an empty seat.

"Move over—if you can."

He laboriously moved over to the window seat as Melody sat down beside him. In contrast to his elephantine moves, she was so graceful that it almost looked as if she sat on air just above the seat. Peaches shifted into gear, and the bus started rolling.

Melody looked at him. "I didn't think you were going to show up. Maybe it would be better if you hadn't. You're fit for nothing but lying in a bed of pain."

"You always did have a way with words. But to answer your earlier question, I was on the floor stretching, and I couldn't get to the phone when it rang. The pain woke me at four, and I spent the next three hours alternately icing my back and trying to stretch without killing myself."

"Did you eat?"

"I had room service bring me breakfast. I figured if Casey could afford a million dollar prize, he could afford that. Tell me about the dinner last night."

"I met the runners I didn't meet yesterday afternoon. Naturally, they're completely discounting us."

Drake shrugged. "They're not used to seeing women runners. That would work to our advantage, but because of the shape I'm in, they're quite correct to discount us."

"There's another thing." Melody lowered her voice. "I'm the only one not from California."

Drake pondered that. "I think we have some questions to ask Casey. Did he make a speech?"

"Actually, he did. He's quite the orator. He talked about the glorious adventure we were embarking on and how much good it was going to do for the great state of California."

"Did he mention the million dollars?"

"He managed to toss that in. And he emphasized the tax free part. Although I'm not sure how he's going to manage that. One thing I've learned since I've been in the States is that taxes are inevitable, just like they are in jolly old England, and just like it says in the saying."

"I suspect he's going to pay additional money to the winners to cover the taxes. Although, if he does that, the additional payment becomes taxable, and he'll have to give more money to pay those taxes. And then—"

"I get your point. It goes on forever. Well, I'll let you be the calculator for our team. You always were more calculating than I was."

ᔓ

"We missed you at dinner last night."

The man avoided looking at Drake's bandaged face.

"I heard it was a lot of fun."

He shook hands with the eighth or ninth runner he had just met. He thought this one called himself Glen. The names and faces blurred together, although he realized that their body types were similar—thin and not too tall. Not one was over six feet, and the shortest had only an inch on Melody who stood about five and one-half feet. In contrast, Drake cleared six feet by a couple of inches and had a stockier build.

One of the runners had a name that sounded familiar: Tom something-or-other. Drake mentioned this to Melody who was standing beside him, also trying to learn the names.

"Tom Batson. He's the only Californian ever to win the Boston Marathon."

"I should know that."

"After what you've been through, it's a wonder you remember your *own* name. These are serious runners. Even if you were healthy, we wouldn't stand much of a chance."

Peaches had brought them to Border Field State Park. Drake didn't know it until he swung himself off the bus using mostly his arms, but Casey had ridden on the bus with them. He was wearing runner's clothes, and he was going to run with them today. Fred had driven separately. There were no reporters here at the boundary between the United States and Mexico.

Fred herded the runners over to the Mexican Border Monument, a marble obelisk proclaiming the friendship of the United States and Mexico, and took pictures of Casey and the runners. The ugly metal and wire border fence extended on either side of the monument and into the ocean. Drake could see a section of Tijuana through the fence, complete with a bullring, which contrasted to the barrenness on the U.S. side.

Casey addressed the group. "I realize that this is an inauspicious start to a grand enterprise, but you'll receive a proper sendoff this afternoon at the Coronado Bridge. So let's get going. We're going to run up the beach for awhile before we hit the road. There may be some swampy places, but we're runners, and we don't mind getting our feet wet, right?"

Everybody echoed, "Right."

"Okay, follow me."

Casey set off along the sand at a moderate pace. The runners, all wearing shorts and singlets with Running California printed on them, easily kept up with him. Drake's clothes had been delivered to his room by the taciturn Peaches. Only his running shoes were his own. Fortunately, he had been wearing them yesterday. If by some miracle he was able to continue, he would have to buy at least one more pair of shoes and break them in as they went.

Drake and Melody started behind the others. At first, Drake could hardly walk, let alone run, but after a while he loosened up a little and accelerated to a slow trot. Melody floated effortlessly beside him.

She watched him closely. "You're looking a little better. How do you feel?"

"Like somebody is sticking pins into my voodoo doll."

The cloudless sky proclaimed that it was a California August—summer at its peak. How could anybody feel bad on such a beautiful day?

Surprisingly, within a few minutes Drake felt better. The movement helped. Running elevated his spirits, as it often did. Producing endorphins, or something. They sped up to a jog. He and Melody chatted about inconsequential things. His problems seemed to melt away. He almost forgot that someone might be trying to kill him.

They splashed through shallow water as Oneonta Slough lazily joined the ocean, but wet feet were par for the course for marathoners. Running on sand didn't jolt his back as much as running on a hard surface, but the tradeoff was that it required more effort because the sand gave beneath his feet. That slowed them down, but speed was the least of his worries.

Soon they were passing a row of houses that were right on the beach. Piles of dark rocks formed a wall in front of them—a breakwater, evidently to ward off extra-high tides. Casey was sitting on one of the rocks. Had he given up already?

He rose as they approached and fell into stride beside Drake. He didn't look winded at all. He was wearing dark glasses against the August sun.

"I'm worried about you."

"Nothing to worry about. Either I can do it or I can't. I figure today's run is the equivalent of perhaps half a marathon. Challenging but not conclusive since we're going to be running daily marathons soon. We put a man on the moon in July. This can't be any harder than that."

Casey laughed. "Giganticorp helped create the technology for the space program. Fred is setting up an appointment with a chiropractor for you after you cross the bridge. We should be able to get you one every day as long as we're in the populated area of Southern California."

"Thanks, but it's going to take more than a chiropractor, I'm afraid. Like rest."

"Rest is the one thing I can't promise you, although you'll get a day off from time to time." Casey grinned at Drake. "But I know you'll stick it out. You've done harder things in your life."

From the other side of Drake, Melody said, “Why should we stick it out if we have no chance of winning the money?”

Casey’s face had a look of surprise, whether real or feigned Drake didn’t know. “I don’t believe that for a minute. You’ve got the experience and persistence the others don’t have. They can run a single marathon, but can they run a marathon day after day without burning out? Do they know how to pace themselves? I figure you two should know how to do that. When they start to fade, you’ll eat them up.”

Right. What did he mean about experience and persistence? That Drake was the oldest entrant and thus had more life experience? Age wasn’t a plus here. He had other questions. “Why teams? Running is an individual sport.”

“Practical considerations. A lot of the California coast is pretty desolate, and we don’t have the manpower to keep track of every runner all the time. We figured that you have an incentive to stay with your teammate and make sure he’s okay.”

“I understand that all the runners are from California, except Melody. Why did you pick her?”

“Don’t you like having Melody as a teammate?”

That was a non-answer. Drake and Melody glanced at each other.

Casey must have seen the look. He turned on his ingratiating smile.

“I heard somewhere that you two already knew each other and figured that you might like to run together.”

Drake and Melody exchanged another look. Casey was in effect admitting that he had access to classified information. Either that or he knew somebody who had known them in England. Whatever the truth, they couldn’t probe without being in danger of violating their personal secrecy prohibitions. They couldn’t even admit they had known each other before yesterday.

Drake pulled a canteen from a small pouch strapped to his waist and took a couple of swallows of water without slowing down. He decided to change the subject. “I’m concerned that whoever hit the taxi yesterday—”

“May try again. Don’t sweat it. As long as you’re part of Running California you’re under the protection of Giganticorp. You’re safe.”

It was the second time he'd said that. Melody moved over so that she was on the other side of Casey. "You just said yourself that parts of the California coast are desolate, and you don't have enough Peaches clones to patrol them."

"I'll tell you what. If either of you gets injured in any kind of attack, I'll give you a million dollars. How's that for a guarantee?"

Drake smiled. "My sister will love it. But it won't do me any good if I'm six feet under."

"You're not chickening out, are you? After the firefights you survived in Korea?"

Giganticorp had investigated his military career. Found out about Melody. Now Casey was appealing to his manhood. He really wanted Drake on this run. Why? Something to think about. He changed the subject again.

"I wonder if a really high tide ever reaches those houses we passed."

Casey took in the entire beach around them with a sweep of his hand. "This belongs to everyone. Nobody should be allowed to build houses on the beach."

"You mean because of the danger that they'll be washed away?"

Houses on Malibu Beach, north of Los Angeles, were periodically damaged during storms.

"Because the beach belongs to everyone."

Casey was repeating himself. Drake decided to test him. "According to California law, the part of the beach below the mean high-tide line does belong to everyone. The part above that is private property where it isn't a government-owned recreation area."

"The boundary line between public and private property should be at least an eighth of a mile inland."

Melody laughed. "Based on my observations so far, I would say it's a little late for that."

Casey looked up as if searching the heavens for some kind of truth. "Is it?"

Casey stayed with them as they ran along the isthmus between the bay and the ocean. They ran on the silky white sand instead of the pavement of Silver Strand Boulevard because the softer surface was easier on Drake's back.

"Unidentified vehicle at nine o'clock."

The other two followed Melody's pointing arm and saw a jeep coming across the sand at an angle to cut them off. She turned to Drake. "Do we need to take evasive action?"

Although what evasive action they could take without weapons, in the middle of the beach, Drake didn't know. They certainly couldn't outrun the jeep. They stopped running and watched it approach. Melody moved away from Drake so that they wouldn't present an easy target. Casey watched the jeep too, but didn't seem to be alarmed.

The driver wore a fatigue uniform, and Drake concluded he must be a naval officer. He relaxed a little. As far as he knew, the navy didn't have anything against him.

The jeep stopped beside them, and the officer bid them good morning. When they responded in kind, he said, "There may still be unexploded shells on this part of the beach from training exercises. For your own safety I recommend that you run on the road."

"No problem." Casey smiled at the officer. "We'll do that. We don't want to get blown up."

The officer thanked them and drove away.

Casey turned his smile on Drake and Melody. "False alarm. I told you I'd protect you."

Drake noticed that he took a large handkerchief out of his waistband and wiped the sweat from his forehead.

CHAPTER 4

The San Diego-Coronado Bridge opens today, Sunday, August 3, 1969. It has a distinctive curve and soaring sweep and is the first structural conquest of San Diego Bay, joining the Island of Coronado and City of San Diego. The bridge is 2.1 miles long and has a vertical clearance of approximately 200 feet, so that the tallest ships can pass beneath it.

ංඉ

A CROWD HAD GATHERED IN the park near the entrance to the San Diego-Coronado Bridge to watch the opening ceremony. A platform, covered with red, white, and blue bunting, was set up with seats for Coronado and San Diego city officials. They took turns praising themselves for constructing this magnificent structure.

Fred had herded the Running California group into an area near the platform. Drake, who wasn't much for speeches, tuned out the droning from the platform and looked at the other people. Many of them were dressed in shorts and T-shirts. The first traffic allowed on the bridge would be pedestrians—runners and walkers. After several hours, the bridge would be closed to pedestrians and opened to vehicle traffic. Drake thought it was a shame that a walkway hadn't been included on the bridge so that pedestrians could use it all the time.

Drake's attention was brought back to the platform because the speaker mentioned the name Casey Messinger. He said that Casey had been instrumental in arranging the run/walk that was to take place before the bridge opened to vehicle traffic. He called Casey up to the platform. Casey bounced up the temporary wooden steps to cheers and applause from the enthusiastic crowd, still in his running uniform, shook hands with the official who had introduced him, and went to the microphone.

With a big smile on his face, he raised his arms, as if proclaiming a great victory. "Isn't this a glorious day?"

Affirmative shouts accompanied more cheers and applause.

Casey waited for the noise to quiet down before he started speaking again. He said how pleased he was that the bridge had been built. Although he didn't take credit for building the bridge, he had a way of speaking that made it sound as if the whole thing had been his idea. He talked about how everybody here would get to know the bridge personally by covering it on foot.

Then he talked about Running California. "This is the perfect day to start a run of the California coast by going over our brand new bridge. I'd like you to meet the ten teams competing for the prize of a million dollars. Will the runners please come up on the stage?"

Drake hadn't expected this. Apparently the other runners hadn't either. They looked at each other, each one unwilling to lead the way. Finally they started toward the steps.

Melody put a hand on Drake's shoulder. "I expect we'll have to get used to this sort of thing. Casey wants to get as much publicity as possible."

In their former lives together they had shunned the spotlight and lived in the shadows. This was a big change. Melody went up the steps behind the other runners, followed by Drake who went slowly and tried to keep the pain of the ascent from showing in his face. He wondered what the crowd thought about the bandage on his face and the cuts on his arms and legs. He heard enthusiastic cheers.

Casey spoke again after the cheers died down. "We hope to do this run every year. Perhaps in the future some of you will be part of it. I won't take the time to introduce all the runners by name, but I'd like to mention two of them. The first is Tom Batson, the only Californian to ever win the Boston Marathon."

More cheering. Tom raised his hand.

"The other person I'd like to mention fought in the Korean War. He was awarded the Silver Star for gallantry in action. Since that time he has been working to preserve our freedom in a capacity that I can't talk about here. Rest assured that he is a real hero. Oliver Drake."

He pointed at Drake. Drake saw this coming when Casey mentioned the Korean War. He didn't want to be cheered for being a hero. He was just doing his job. But the crowd was yelling. He felt awkward and wanted to hide.

"Raise your arm and smile," Melody hissed in his ear.

Drake reluctantly raised his arm as cheers engulfed him. Photographers snapped his picture. The Korean conflict, although not widely popular, at least had the advantage of being over, something that couldn't be said about Vietnam.

Again, Casey waited for the cheering to subside. "Incidentally, Drake—he likes to be called Drake rather than Oliver—didn't receive his broken nose in combat."

Titters from the audience.

"He'll be fine in a few days. I have one more announcement, and then we'll cut to the ribbon cutting ceremony."

More titters.

"I think this is the ideal time and place for me to announce that I am going to be a candidate for the United States Senate from the great state of California, running as an independent."

∽

Hundreds of runners and walkers thronged the bridge. Drake and Melody hadn't started with the first group of runners, because Drake knew he couldn't keep up with them. Now they were trapped within a large mass of slower joggers. This was fine with Drake, whose back hurt from the effects of the day's exertions. He wanted nothing more than to be flat on his bed at the hotel.

They didn't speak until the space around them grew large enough so that they were able to talk without a dozen other people hearing every word.

Melody spoke first. "Surprise, surprise. Yon Casey is ambitious. I *thought* he had a lean and hungry look."

"I think you're misquoting your bard, but in any case, I don't like the implication that Tom and I are supporting him."

"And the reference to your secret activities was out of bounds. He could get us into trouble."

"This whole thing smells like rotten fish."

"Do you want to drop out now?"

Drake considered. "There's something going on here that's below the surface. I'd like to stick around and try to find out what it is, if possible. Let's see if I can still move in the morning. Are you game to continue?"

"Always."

CHAPTER 5

From the San Diego-Coronado Bridge the route of Running California heads north on Harbor Drive. Follow it around the bay, south of the San Diego International Airport. Turn right on Lowell Street and jog right on Nimitz Boulevard. Turn right on Sunset Cliffs Boulevard and left on Mission Bay Drive. Continue north along Pacific Beach. It's all right to run on the road next to the beach here rather than on the sand. Cliffs and rock formations prevent running on the beach through La Jolla. Use the cliff path whenever possible. Otherwise, run on the adjacent streets. North of La Jolla run on the beach. A race official will record the time of each team where the run ends on the sand at Torrey Pines Beach. Please obey all traffic laws when running in populated areas. Race officials will observe the runners at various checkpoints and provide water. Runners taking shortcuts will be penalized by having time added. Any runners not covering the entire distance will be disqualified. Fred Rathbun has final judgment on penalties.

ᔕ

WHEN DRAKE TRIED TO GET out of bed the next morning, he knew he was in trouble. He couldn't even sit up because of the pain in his back. He had spent most of the night in one position, not daring to move. He lay still for several more minutes, wondering whether he could lie there until his back got better. At least he wasn't in pain when he didn't move. The pressure on his bladder banished that thought.

He knew that if he could roll over onto his side, there would be less pull on his back when he sat up. He finally managed that because he had no choice, but the pain almost overwhelmed him. He rested for another minute and made it to a sitting position on the edge of the bed. He grabbed the aspirin bottle from the nightstand and swallowed several of the white pills without benefit of water, ignoring the acidic taste.

He wondered whether he could lift his legs high enough to pull on his pants.

ഗ

Several of the other runners were already eating breakfast at the Hotel del Coronado's outdoor Boardwalk Café overlooking the blue ocean when Melody arrived there. Drake wasn't among them. The air was still cool, but the sun was bright. It would get warm—perhaps too warm for marathon runners. It was a good thing they were running near the water where the temperature was always significantly cooler.

She sat down at a table next to a slightly built man named Aki—she thought he might be Japanese—and ordered a light breakfast.

Aki grinned at her. "Good day for running. I hope it doesn't get too hot."

"I hope not."

The heat was the least of her worries, of which the major one was Drake's fitness to continue. He had retired early last night, complaining of pain and fatigue. Million dollars or no million dollars, there was no point in torturing him. If they didn't have a chance, why not pack it in?

"Good morning, Melody. Morning, Aki."

Casey had a big smile on his face as he sat down beside Melody. He was wearing a conservative business suit with a tie this morning—Melody had to admit that he looked like a businessman—and radiated good humor.

Melody studied his bright red tie. "I take it you're not going to run today."

"Nope. Gotta get back to work."

"Where's your office?"

"Giganticorp's headquarters is in San Jose. I'll grab one of the shuttle flights that tool up and down the coast all day. They're also going to make it easy for me to keep tabs on how you're doing."

He ordered coffee from a hovering waitress, glanced at the menu, and then turned to Melody.

"What do you hear from your teammate this morning?"

"Nothing."

"Well, I'm sure he'll be down in a few minutes. He looked strong yesterday. He appears to be recovering remarkably fast."

Casey was either a cockeyed optimist or trying to convince *himself* of Drake's good health.

Melody drank her orange juice while she contemplated a reply. Did she dare challenge the mighty Casey—CEO and self-proclaimed senatorial candidate?

"I don't think it's a good idea for him to continue. He might injure himself permanently."

When Casey didn't immediately say anything, Melody turned to look at him. The intensity in his blue eyes told her that he was fighting to hold back an outburst. He took a deep breath and a sip of coffee.

"He has to continue. He can't quit now, not at the start. A lot of time and expense has been put into Running California. He has no choice."

"Doesn't he?"

Melody and Casey turned around and saw Drake who had come up behind them silently. Part of his expression was covered by the bandage, but his lips were set in a grim line, and an unusual scowl creased his smooth forehead. He wasn't dressed in running clothes. He sat down laboriously in the seat next to Casey.

Melody broke the silence. "How do you feel?"

"Don't ask. At least I'm up and walking, which is more than I could say twenty minutes ago."

Drake ordered breakfast from the menu. Aki looked uncomfortable, excused himself, and left the table. Casey didn't say anything. He appeared to be unnaturally subdued. Melody couldn't think of anything more to say. She thought her point had been proved.

Drake managed a smile. "Did I walk in on a funeral? If so, I'd like to know who died. Not me. I'll be fine. I just need a little rest."

Casey found his tongue. "You're right, of course. But you're in excellent condition, overall. I think if you start slowly and get some more chiropractic treatments, you'll work your way out of it. To show you my heart's in the right place, I'll give you—you and Melody—a thousand dollars just for completing today's run. Five hundred apiece. Just don't tell the others."

Melody bristled. "It isn't about money."

Drake smiled for the second time. "Maybe it is about money. All right, we accept. A thousand dollars just for today."

ꕥ

"Tell me again why you wanted to continue."

Melody sipped water from her canteen and watched Drake as he sat on a rock beside the La Jolla caves and attempted to bend over and touch his feet. He was trying to get the kinks out of his back.

The sweat on Drake's face wasn't just from the warm sun.

"I can't remember. Oh yes, I said it was for the money. Well, the money's nice, but there's something more. It's a feeling I have."

"Intuition?"

"Intuition is what women have. But something doesn't feel quite right. Why is Casey willing to pay us a thousand dollars a day to stay in the run? That's a lot of money. He wants us really bad."

Before flying to San Jose, Casey had upped his monetary offer from a single payment to a thousand dollars a day—payable when they finished the run.

"Compared to the million dollar prize, a thousand dollars a day isn't a lot of money. It's also very clear that he doesn't want me; he wants you. I'm just your partner. Here to provide you aide and comfort. Although I'm not providing the kind of comfort that Casey probably envisions."

"I'm not capable of enjoying it right now, anyway. I saw the article about the opening of the bridge in the San Diego Union this morning. Casey got a lot of publicity for his announcement that he's a candidate for the Senate. There's a picture of him with us in the background. I have a feeling he's going to milk this run for the publicity value."

"What gave you the first clue, Sherlock? That's not a crime, is it?"

"Not yet. I also keep going back to the accident that wasn't an accident. Who and why? I don't have any enemies in the U.S. government that I know of. And it's a bit late for a foreign government to eliminate me. I'm harmless."

"Maybe it's somebody closer to home. Are any of your mates pissed at you?"

"I don't have many mates. One thing I remember—the driver of the truck slowed down just before he hit the taxi. He didn't hit it as hard as he could have."

"He felt sorry for you."

Drake struggled to his feet. "Right. Well, if we're going to finish today's run—and I use the word 'run' loosely—before midnight, we'd better get our bodies moving."

ග

"How far behind the others do you think we are?"

Melody wondered why Drake cared how far behind they were.

"We've only been doing this for a few hours, so we can't be more than a few hours behind."

"You're so reassuring. I'm glad we're partners."

"I try to look on the bright side. Hey, that man isn't wearing any clothes."

"This area is called Black's Beach. It's clothing optional."

"You didn't warn me about it."

"I like to surprise you."

"It's a surprise, all right. But…" Melody looked around as more optional men came into view. "Not necessarily a bad one."

"Where are the girls? There are supposed to be girls here."

Melody patted Drake on the back. "Aw, poor Drake. No naked birds to ogle. In your body's present state it's probably just as well. We don't want to place any extra strain on it."

Drake glared at her. He had already been going slowly and was now moving at what could only be described as at a labored walk.

"It's not worth it. I've been watching you all day. The money isn't worth your pain and anguish. Let's call the whole thing off." Melody repeated her last sentence, singing it to the tune of the song with the same name.

"You always were the sensible one. All right, we'll tell Fred as soon as we get to our motel, or wherever we're staying tonight. We'll leave Casey alone to play whatever game he's playing."

❧

Although Fred wasn't wearing a tie, he still looked like a businessman with his pressed pants, expensive shoes, and sweater worn over a white shirt. Because the day was too warm for the sweater, his face was red and wet, and he mopped it with a large handkerchief. Casey had done the same thing. Were plus-size handkerchiefs standard issue at Giganticorp? Fred drove Drake, Melody, and a young woman they hadn't seen before to their motel near the campus of the University of California at San Diego.

The woman, who was dressed more casually than Fred, in shorts and a Running California shirt, had met Drake and Melody on the beach where the day's run officially ended. She clicked her stopwatch as they came up to her and introduced herself as Grace Harbison, a Giganticorp employee. She must be one of the race officials mentioned in the written briefing they had received that morning concerning the day's route. She called Drake Mr. Drake.

She led them up a steep hill from the beach. Grace and Melody climbed it effortlessly, or so it seemed to Drake, but it almost did him in and increased his resolve to quit the race. After they had registered at the motel, Fred escorted them to Drake's room and asked them both to go inside with him.

He closed the door, sat on the bed, placed an attaché case he was carrying on his lap, and clicked open the metal latches. He raised the top and extracted two bank passbooks, handing one to Melody and one to Drake.

"We have opened passbook savings accounts for each of you at our corporate bank in San Jose. After you finish each day's run we'll deposit five hundred dollars in each of your accounts. You can phone the bank to verify your balance and get your passbook updated when you are in the San Jose area. The money becomes yours as soon as you finish the race. Needless to say, don't discuss this arrangement with any of the other runners."

"How did you get the passbooks so fast?" Melody asked. "Casey just made us the offer this morning."

Fred's already large mouth expanded when he smiled. "We work fast at Giganticorp. If you must know, Grace flew down from corporate this afternoon and brought them with her."

"I'm impressed." Melody looked at Drake, waiting for him to speak. He was bending down to stretch his back, his face contorted. When he didn't say anything, she said, "We appreciate your, ah, generosity, Fred, but Drake has something to tell you."

Drake didn't picture himself as a quitter. Telling Melody he was going to quit was one thing; telling Fred was entirely different. It was difficult for him to get the words out of his mouth.

"The situation is this. Running the equivalent of a marathon every day is very hard on an athlete's body, even an athlete in splendid condition, which I'm not at the moment. I…well I can't do it. I'm going to have to drop out. We'll forfeit the money for today."

"Nonsense." Fred's smile never wavered. "I've got an appointment with a chiropractor for you in…" he checked his watch, "…one hour. Peaches will drive you. In a week you'll be as good as new. You've got a few challenges, but you've overcome worse problems."

Melody frowned. "How far ahead of us are the others?"

Fred shrugged. "Don't worry about it. We're paying you to stay with Running California. You add a lot of color to the program. The others all look the same, even Aki. They run the same, like robots. They ran in a posse today, and all nine teams finished within fifteen minutes of each other. We need you two—Melody, because you're an exceptional woman, and Drake, because you're a hero."

Drake was torn. He didn't feel as bad as he thought he might. Of course, they still weren't running marathon distance.

Melody apparently didn't have any conflict. "I'm sorry, Fred, but he can't do it. We're through."

Fred rose from the bed. "There's a reporter in the lobby who wants to talk to you. This is a good time while you're still sweaty and have your running clothes on. We want the press to appreciate what you're doing."

He ignored Melody's words of protest and led them out the door.

CHAPTER 6

On the section from Torrey Pines to the Oceanside entrance to Camp Pendleton, we will run on the beach the whole way. Because this is a populated area, it is safer and sometimes faster to run on the beach. You're used to beach running by now, and it should be no problem. You will be passing through a number of lovely beaches, including Del Mar, Solana, Cardiff by the Sea, Encinitas, Leucadia, Carlsbad, and Oceanside. If the beach is difficult to negotiate at high tide, you can temporarily run on the road.

ꕥ

THE RINGING TELEPHONE WOKE DRAKE from a dream in which he was attempting to run somewhere, but large rocks and other obstacles kept getting in his way. He opened his eyes. A rosy glow behind the thin curtains told him that the sun was almost up. Should he try to answer the phone? It had been easier for him to turn over during the night than it had the night before.

When the phone kept ringing its persistent double brrrr he couldn't think of any excuses to ignore it. He reached out his arm and lifted the receiver.

"This is your wakeup call. It's six a.m."

Drake growled something back at the too-pleasant voice and dropped the receiver on the cradle. He stretched, trying to get a reading on his back. The pain was still there when he moved. What were they doing today? Oh yes, he and Melody were quitting Running California and going home. They had talked about spending a couple of days together first—on holiday, as she phrased it, but nothing had been settled.

Fred had not only refused to accept their resignations, he had made them talk to the reporter just as if they were still in the race. The young man was a sports reporter by trade and had wanted to talk about the athletic aspects of the race. Drake had played down his injuries while they discussed how one prepared for and maintained conditioning during ultra-marathoning, a term used by the reporter.

It would be fun to be alone with Melody for a few days. Just like old times, hopefully. Drake rolled onto his side, sat up, and headed for the shower.

ꝏ

"Mr. Drake?"

Drake turned and saw the middle-aged woman at the reception desk. Her voice sounded like the voice on the phone. He was meeting Melody here. They were going to the café next door to eat a real breakfast. The continental breakfast served by the motel wouldn't sustain them.

"I have an envelope for you."

"For me?"

"You are Mr. Drake, aren't you?"

"Yes."

How did she know? It wasn't difficult. He was the only guest at the motel with a bandage on his face. Somebody must have told her that. He took the proffered envelope, thanked her, and sat down at one of the small tables in the lobby area where a few early rising guests were drinking coffee and eating sweet rolls.

It was a white business-size envelope with "Oliver Drake" typed on the outside. It had been sealed but only at one spot in the center. Drake tore the envelope open and pulled out a sheet of standard typewriter paper folded neatly in thirds. He unfolded the paper and saw a typewritten note. As he quickly read the note, he got a sick feeling in his stomach. The English was broken and there were spelling errors, but the meaning was clear.

To: Oliver Drake
From: The Syndicate
You not know us but that no matter. We know you. We have great interest in Running California race. We see it as chance to make much money. Many people betting on race. People betting that you and Melody Jefferson not finish race. We bet that you finish race get exelent odds. But then you have acident. We think we know who caused acident but we not able to get out of bet. So you have to stay in race. We know where Melody mom lives in Rotherfield England. As long as you too stay in race she ok. If you quit race she in big trouble. Do you understand? Do not show letter to any one.

Shit. Drake almost said it out loud. He read the note a second time, more slowly. The meaning didn't change.

"Letter from home?"

Melody placed a hand on his shoulder and started to look over it. Drake's first inclination was to hide the paper, but he knew she had to see it. He reluctantly handed it to her.

"Brace yourself. It's not good news. I'll be right back."

While Melody read the note, Drake went to the reception desk. He fidgeted impatiently while the clerk took care of a man who was checking out. He finally got her attention.

"The envelope you gave me? Who gave it to you?"

"It was here when I came in at five. I think it came in on Peter's shift."

"Where's Peter?"

"He left at six."

"So he's home now?"

"Probably. He sleeps during the day."

"I need to talk to him. Can you ring him for me?"

The clerk looked dubious. "He might be asleep."

"He left less than an hour ago. He's probably eating breakfast or something. Please. This is very important."

People were lining up at the counter to check out. The clerk apparently decided it was faster to give in than to argue. She checked a list and dialed a number. After a pause she said, "Peter? Hang on. Mr. Drake wants to speak to you."

She handed the receiver across the counter to Drake. He put it to his ear. "Hello, Peter?"

"Yes."

"This is Oliver Drake. You were given an envelope to give me?"

"Oh…right."

"What time was that?"

"Let's see. Johnny Carson had ended. I was doing some paperwork. It must have been about midnight."

"Can you describe the person who gave it to you?"

"Not very well. He—or maybe she—I'm not even sure which, was wearing a sweatshirt with a hood and dark glasses. Jeans, tennies. Not too tall, slim build. I didn't see any hair, because it was covered by the hood. The face was smooth—young looking."

"Did he—or she—speak to you?"

"No. He came running into the motel like he was trying to catch a bus, handed the envelope to me, and ran out again without saying a word."

"Did you see a car or anything?"

"No. He disappeared. I was so surprised that I followed him to the door, but by the time I got outside, he was out of sight."

"You said the face was smooth and young looking. Like that of a young man or woman?"

"Yeah, either one."

"You didn't see any lipstick or anything?"

"Nope. I'm not saying she wasn't wearing lipstick. I didn't get a good look at the face. It happened so fast."

"Did you notice anything else about the person?"

"He sure could run fast. That's about it."

"Okay, Peter. Thanks for your help. If you think of anything more, could you call…Giganticorp—you must have their corporate number—and leave a message for Oliver Drake of Running California? Leave a number where you can be reached in the evening, and I'll call you back."

"After ten I'm usually at the motel. I work the night shift."

Drake said good-bye and hung up. He turned and found Melody at his elbow. He had been so absorbed in the call that he hadn't seen her approach. Her face looked ashen under her tan. They needed to talk, but not here with people milling around, including some of the runners.

"Let's go next door to the café."

He took her arm and guided her out of the motel. A few minutes later they were seated at a booth that promised some privacy as long as they kept their voices low. He ordered orange juice, scrambled eggs, and toast for Melody—she appeared to be in shock—and coffee and a bigger breakfast, including bacon and potatoes, for himself.

Melody, who had been clutching the piece of paper, laid it on the table. "Do you think this is a prank?"

"If so, the prankster has a lot of information about us, including where your mother lives. I think we have to treat it as real. The first thing we can do is stay in the run. By carrying out the instructions, we hopefully protect your mother."

And give Melody some piece of mind.

"I want to call my mum and see if she's all right."

"I don't know if we can make overseas calls from the motel. Fred should be able to set it up for us. If necessary, he can patch it through Giganticorp. We can tell him your mother's been sick. I don't think we should tell him about the note yet until we have some more information about who it's from. The writer said not to."

When they had worked together fighting Communism, they had operated on the premise that they couldn't trust anyone. That was probably a good approach to follow here.

"How are we going to get that information?"

"After we get to our next stop, I'll call a guy in D.C. I worked with, see if he's familiar with any betting syndicates. He's the only one still working there that I trust."

∽

"I wish we'd been able to reach my mum."

"She was probably out in her garden. She has such a beautiful garden. We'll try again this afternoon."

"Not too late. There's an eight-hour time difference. If we call at four it'll be midnight in England. She likes to get her sleep. If I wake her, she'll think I'm in trouble."

Drake was trying to keep Melody from worrying about her mother. Just because she didn't answer her phone didn't mean that something had happened to her. However, he wished that she had been home.

It was another beautiful day in Southern California. They ran close to the water because the sand was firmer where the high tide had packed it down. Drake's back had loosened up just a hair, and they were moving faster today than they had yesterday. Flocks of seagulls rose into the air as they approached, and sandpipers scooted out of the way.

They still weren't close to the other runners. After Grace started them at the bottom of the cliff—Fred had declined to walk down it—the other nine teams quickly ran away from them and eventually disappeared from view. They ran in a posse, as Fred had said, apparently content to stay together for the time being.

Melody glanced at Drake. "You look a bit more like your old self with the bandage off. Your nose is discolored and swollen, though. I don't know whether you'll ever be as beautiful as you were."

He had taken the bandage off before they started the run. "I was tired of wearing that damned thing. I felt like a cripple. That's a luxury I can't afford now. Just don't hit me in the nose."

"I really appreciate you not quitting. As least we're abiding by the terms of the letter. I hope it isn't too hard on you."

"I'll survive. I don't want anything to happen to your mother. Unfortunately, it's not a long-term solution. Either of us could twist an ankle at any time and not be able to run at all." Drake was silent for a minute. "One way to keep my mind off my body is to see what we can deduce. For example, the letter is full of grammatical and spelling errors. It was written by somebody whose English isn't great. A foreigner."

"Be careful how you speak about us foreigners. *Or*, it could be somebody who wants us to think he's a foreigner. Did you notice the incongruity? Even with all the errors, the typing itself is perfect."

"No typos except the spelling errors, which are consistent. No cross-outs. No evidence that the typist even used that white liquid they use to cover errors. An experienced typist did it, but not necessarily one who knows proper English. And it looks like it's been typed on a good typewriter, like an IBM Selectric."

"You mean the one with the bouncing ball?"

"Right. Most business offices use them."

"He knew where my mum lives."

"He knows a lot about you. He's got connections, whoever he is. He knows where we're staying. This is not a fly-by-night operation."

"What about fingerprints?"

"Well, yours and mine are all over the letter. Mine are on the envelope, and I even took notes on it. We didn't exactly follow good evidence procedure. There may be others, but we can't go to the police."

"What did you find out about the messenger?"

"Not much. Not even sex."

"Like yes or no?"

"Like boy or girl. Whoever it was was apparently young—and nimble. Got away before the desk clerk could note any identifying characteristics."

CHAPTER 7

Drake and Melody decided that if they were going to find out anything, they needed to get better acquainted with the other people associated with Running California. When they arrived at the motel—courtesy of Peaches, who met them, noted their time when they finished the run, and drove them to the motel, all without saying more than five words—the first people they saw were Tom Batson and his running partner, Jerry Kidd.

Drake invited them to have dinner with Melody and him. They accepted and agreed to meet after Drake had his appointment with a chiropractor. Thirty minutes later Drake returned to the lobby, having showered and changed his clothes. He was able to move a little better—he was becoming slightly less stiff. By the time they finished the run, he might be in the kind of shape he should be in right now—if it didn't kill him before then. Peaches, his driver, was sitting in the lobby reading a magazine about martial arts.

They walked out to the company car. Drake sat in the passenger side of the front seat. In a nod to the warm weather, Peaches was wearing a summer-weight suit with the jacket on to hide his gun, Drake was sure. Although not as tall as Drake, he was broader, with a bull neck and large head topped with short, dark hair. Drake decided to see if he could get Peaches to talk.

In a conversational tone he asked, "How long have you worked for Giganticorp?"

Peaches made a turn onto the street in front of the motel and glanced at Drake. "Long enough."

That wasn't a promising start. "Are you stationed in San Jose?"

"That's what it looks like."

"How many employees does Giganticorp have there?"

Peaches looked at Drake as if he thought Drake were trying to pry company secrets from him. Was Giganticorp so private that they didn't even release employment figures? What could he ask Peaches that wouldn't be considered confidential? He wanted to ask his real name, but that would sound like an interrogation.

"I guess Giganticorp is a good company to work for."

When Peaches didn't say anything at first, Drake wondered whether he had used up his quota of words for the day.

Finally, he said, "It's a job. Better than some, worse than others, but it keeps beer in the cooler."

Encouraged that Peaches had uttered more than one sentence at a time, Drake was going to try to keep the conversation going, but at that moment they arrived at the chiropractor's office. When Peaches drove him back to the motel an hour later, he had retreated into his shell and only grunted in response to Drake's questions.

ഗ

"Fred tried to call my mum at noon, but there was still no answer. That would have been eight o'clock at night her time. She should have been home."

Melody and Drake were waiting in the motel lobby for Tom and Jerry, the runners they were going to have dinner with.

"Did you try again from here?"

"It was too late. I don't want to call her in the middle of the night there. It would scare her to death. When I was working for the agency, although she didn't know exactly what I was doing, she suspected enough that she said what she feared most was that call in the middle of the night because something had happened to me."

Tom and Jerry appeared in the lobby, two runners cut from the same mold: medium height, skinny frame. They wore their hair down over their ears, but not long enough for them to be mistaken for hippies. More like the Beatles. Tom's was red and Jerry's was brown. It flopped when they ran.

"Do you want to go to an Italian place?" Tom asked. "Italian food's good for carbohydrates."

"There's one about two blocks from here." Jerry looked at Drake. "Do you think you can walk that far?"

"I don't have my cane with me, but I think I can make it." Drake used an old man's voice. "If not, you can carry me." He exaggerated a hobble as they started along the street. Young whippersnappers.

"Congratulations on being in first place." Melody was trying to direct attention away from Drake.

Fred had posted a typed listing of the teams on a bulletin board in the motel and written down the time of each team so far. Drake and Melody were so far behind that they didn't even try to figure out how far.

"Thanks," Tom said. "But we're only about five minutes ahead of three or four other teams. Not exactly a comfortable lead with so far to go. We've had to learn to pace ourselves. A couple of teams tried to break away today, but they ran out of steam and we caught them."

Jerry nodded. "They underestimate the difficulty of running on sand. It slows you down and takes a lot of energy, something they don't account for. They think they can run as fast on sand as pavement."

"I was in the race when you won Boston," Drake said to Tom. "I was a few hills behind you, however."

"So was everybody else." Jerry grinned at his teammate. "He blew them away."

"Jerry ran under two-thirty in that race," Tom said.

They were clearly the team to beat. They reached the small restaurant and were seated immediately at a square table for four with a red and white checked plastic tablecloth. It was noisy and friendly. Drake ordered a bottle of beer. Melody had iced tea. Tom and Jerry split a carafe of red wine. Each team had been issued two credit cards for food and incidental expenses.

"How did you two become teammates in this race?" Melody asked.

Tom looked surprised. "I was invited to enter and pick my partner. Jerry and I train together in Redding, so it was a natural. What about you?"

Evasion time. Drake signaled Melody with his eyes. "We didn't pick each other. Giganticorp picked for us. I guess that's why we're in last place."

Tom looked from one of them to the other. "Didn't you know each other before?"

How much had Fred let slip? "Only casually. We'd run into each other a few times."

Jerry laughed. "Run into each other. That's good. So the beanstalk boys picked you. We call Fred and Peaches and the others the beanstalk boys. Giganticorp—giant—'Jack and the Beanstalk.' Get it? You two must have been chosen to add color. A girl and a war hero."

"I'm not a war hero."

"We were chosen because we make a good team." Melody had the look in her eye that Drake knew meant that you better not underestimate her. "If Drake hadn't been hurt, we'd be doing much better."

"I don't doubt it," Tom said. "I've watched you run. You're the best female runner I've seen. And I've seen the women who've run Boston since they started letting them in."

Melody picked up male admirers wherever she went. It was obvious that Tom was among that number. Also that she was susceptible to his flattery. Something stirred inside Drake. He tried to squelch it. He'd had his chance and blown it.

Tom looked at Drake. "If you were in top shape I'd be watching over my shoulder for you two."

"Thanks. Maybe you'll still have to."

ഗ

Drake closed the door of the phone booth located at an intersection in downtown Oceanside, not far from their motel. He had walked back to the motel with the others. After they had said goodnight to Tom and Jerry, he had told Melody what he was going to do.

He had decided against making the call from the motel room. Years of covert operations had taught him that if you didn't want other people to find out what you were doing, you shouldn't leave a trail, however faint. With the phone booth door closed, nobody would hear him, especially with the traffic noise. He kept his hand over his mouth on the off chance that somebody might be watching through a pair of binoculars and trying to read his lips.

He lifted the black receiver and dialed zero.

"Operator."

"I'd like to make a collect call to..." Drake gave the long distance number to the operator. When she asked for his name, he said, "Drake."

He heard various noises while the operator put through the call and then the sound of a ringing telephone. He hoped Blade would be home.

After half a dozen rings the operator said, "Nobody is answering."

"Let it ring a few more times."

After about the eighth ring Drake heard the sound of the phone being answered with a brusque hello.

"I have a collect call from a Mr. Drake. Will you accept the charge?"

"Drake? Who does that bastard think he is?"

"Will you accept the charge, sir?"

"All right, all right, put him on."

"Go ahead, Mr. Drake."

"You took long enough to answer the phone."

"What do you mean by calling me collect?"

"Relax. I'll pay for it. I'm calling from a phone booth."

"Yeah, just like you paid for all those drinks you owe me. It'll be a cold day in hell... Speaking of hell, where the hell are you?"

"California."

"Since you flunked geography you wouldn't know that there's a three-hour time difference."

"You never go to bed before midnight, unless you've suddenly gotten senile. I need your help."

"That's not new. I bailed you out your whole career. What's the matter now?"

"I'm in a race called Running California. You ever hear of it?"

"Not a chance. It sounds crazy, just like you."

"It's being sponsored by a privately owned company called Giganticorp."

"I have a vague hit on that one. I think they supply military products to the government."

"I need more information on them and their CEO, Casey Messinger. He just announced he's running for senator from California?"

"You mean in nineteen seventy? That's more than a year away."

Drake heard a woman's voice in the background asking who was on the phone.

"Did you get married?"

"Hell no."

"Another thing. Somebody—or some group—may be betting on Running California." Drake filled him in quickly on the details, not mentioning the note or the demands. "I need any information you can give me on that."

"When I find out something—if I find out something—where can I reach you?"

"I'll have to call you. We're on the move."

"I supposed you'll call collect."

"Probably. Oh, and there's one more thing. Do you remember Melody?"

"How could I forget that babe? Although what she saw in you I'll never know."

"She's in the race. She's been having trouble reaching her mother in England, and she's worried about her. Do you think you could have an agent check up on her?"

"I'll see what I can do. Give me her mother's address."

Drake did that. "Thanks for the help. I owe you one."

"You owe me more than you can ever repay."

"Say hello to your squeeze for me."

"Go fuck yourself."

CHAPTER 8

We have obtained permission for you to run through Camp Pendleton on the beach. This is an isolated but beautiful area, and you should enjoy having the beach to yourselves much of the time. Near the north end of Camp Pendleton there is a bathing suit optional beach, but you should be used to this by now. You will have to go up to the road to detour around the San Onofre Nuclear Power Plant. We will post a race official on the beach at the path you should use to exit at the power plant. After passing San Onofre go back to the beach and continue to San Clemente State Beach. You will be leaving San Diego County and entering Orange County at this point.

ꕤ

DRAKE WAS UP BEFORE THE wakeup call at six, stretching his sore back muscles. Stretching through the lingering pain. If he were going to stay in this race, he wanted to do more than cover the distance; he wanted to compete. Even if they could narrow the time differential that the other teams were beating them by each day, that would make him feel he was accomplishing something.

His body felt a little looser. The good news was that after three days of running he hadn't suffered any new problems. Actually, to say that they were running was wishful thinking—their average pace hadn't been more than that of a brisk walk.

He put on his running clothes and then a sweat suit to ward off the morning chill. As he was about to leave the room, he noticed the note he had scribbled to himself in the middle of the night. Nighttime ideas disappeared like the stars when the sun rose. Now if he could only read it. He finally decided it was the letters BB. For "bulletin board."

He took the threatening note from the envelope in the suitcase Giganticorp had purchased to replace the one burned in the accident and went out to the lobby. He handled the paper with the sleeve of his sweatshirt, belatedly being careful to not leave more fingerprints.

Drake held the note beside the notice on the board that showed the elapsed time of each team. The names of the runners were typed with the times handwritten beside the names. He compared the typed letters of the two documents and noticed immediate problems. The sheet on the board was a Xerox copy, not an original. It had probably been typed in San Jose; copies had been made there. In addition, it had a different typeface than the threatening note. IBM Selectric typewriters had removable type balls. Each ball could have a different typeface. If the note he held had been typed on a Selectric, as he suspected, it might be almost impossible to find the actual typewriter that had done the job.

Melody appeared, also in sweats, looking unkempt, which was unusual for her. She had no makeup on, and her sandy hair had been hastily cinched in a ponytail, but loose strands stuck out of her head in several directions.

Drake tried to make a joke. "You look as bad as I did when you first saw me at Coronado."

"I couldn't sleep, worrying about my mum. Fred just helped me call her, but she still didn't answer the phone."

"Blade has an agent checking on her. I'll call him tonight to see if he's learned anything. The note said she'd be all right as long—"

"I know what the note said. Since we don't know who wrote it, how can we trust it?"

Good question. Melody was understandably upset. If they didn't receive any information by this evening, Drake was ready to call in the heavy artillery.

ᔕ

"Some researchers invented Gatorade for the University of Florida football team. It replaces carbohydrates and what they call electrolytes—stuff that you lose during vigorous physical exercise. Try it."

Drake took a swig of Gatorade, finished his banana, and watched Melody shove a mixture consisting of peanuts, raisins, and M&M's into her mouth.

"I have no problem trying Gatorade, but just be thankful that I suggested we carry the bananas and gorp in our pouches, along with drinks. You whined that it would add too much weight. Aren't you glad now that we're all alone away from civilization that we've got the food?"

The pouches were held in place by straps around their waists and weren't really that inconvenient. Some people called them fanny packs, but because "fanny" was a dirty word in England, referring to the female genitals, Drake was careful not to. Liquid was the heaviest thing in a pouch, at a pound for every pint they carried. The food didn't add that much weight, and Drake was thankful that Melody had insisted they carry it, but he wasn't about to admit it. He had struggled through marathons before without eating anything and drinking only water. This race was teaching him that it was smart to refuel along the way.

He was also glad that Melody's mood had improved after they started running, as it almost always did. He was worried about her mother just as she was, but there wasn't much they could do about it at the moment.

They had picked up their pace today, and the stop to eat and drink was momentary, although Drake did a few bends from the waist to try to keep his back loose. If it weren't for the pain that still radiated down his legs from his back, on occasion, his legs would be in good shape. His feet hadn't suffered at all, aided by the fact that much of their running had been on the beach. Melody didn't seem to have any physical problems. Drake couldn't recall that she had ever complained about ailments when they ran together in England.

They finished their snack and set off again, upping their pace a little more. The lapping of the waves on the beach and the squawking of sea birds provided background noise, so they didn't feel completely alone. Drake enjoyed the isolation, however. After some of the things he'd seen human beings do, he appreciated having breaks from most of them. Memories flitted through his brain, but softly, not having the power to stir his emotions at the moment.

Melody broke into his train of thought. "It looks like there are a couple of blokes on the beach ahead."

"Maybe marines on their day off."

As they drew closer, they saw that the two people were indeed men. They appeared to be wearing shorts, unremarkable on the beach. Melody, whose eyes were sharper than Drake's, gave an exclamation.

"They're two of our runners. One of them has a problem."

Drake could see that one of the men had his shoe off, and both of them were examining his foot. Melody spoke again.

"That's Aki, the Japanese lad. The other one must be Mike, his partner."

Drake and Melody came up to them and stopped.

Drake asked, "What's the matter?"

Aki looked up from his sitting position on the sand. "I cut my foot."

Drake could see blood on the bottom of the foot. Aki's sock, which was lying on the sand, was soaked with blood. He had twisted his leg to get a good look at the foot, as if he were a contortionist. He was in a position Drake could never hope to emulate.

Melody dropped to her knees to inspect the wound. "What happened?"

"I stepped on a sharp rock. It came right through my shoe. I kept running, hoping the pain would go away."

"He slowed way down," Mike said. "He was favoring that leg. I knew he'd never last, running like that. Finally, I told him he had to stop."

Melody pulled a small first aid kit from her pouch, another weight addition that Drake had opposed. She cut a piece of gauze from a roll with a miniature pair of scissors, poured a little water on it from her canteen, and wiped the blood off the cut. Then she took another look at it.

"It probably needs stitches."

"Shit." Aki sucked in his breath. "Sorry. But if I take the time to go to a doctor, it'll take hours, especially in this God-forsaken place. I'll never finish today's run. We'll be eliminated."

"I'll tell you what I'm going to do." Melody reached into the first aid kit and pulled out a roll of adhesive tape and a foam pad. "I'm going to cover the cut. That will protect it and should reduce the pain."

She squeezed some disinfectant from a small tube onto a gauze pad, which she placed on the cut. She covered the gauze with a foam pad and taped it firmly to Aki's foot.

"Wait ten minutes for the bleeding to stop. Then put on your sock and shoe. Start running slowly. If the pain is bearable, you can speed up. That should hold you for today. If we get to San Clemente before you, we'll arrange for you to see a doctor."

"Thank you." Aki looked gratefully at Melody.

Mike said, "Most of the runners wouldn't have taken the time to stop and help us."

"It's a long race," Drake said. "We need to help each other. Good luck."

He and Melody started running along the beach. After they had gone a hundred yards Drake looked back at the pair. They were still sitting on the sand.

"This is the first time we haven't been in last place during a day's run. And you've acquired a couple of new admirers. It's a good day."

"It will be a good day if we find out that my mum is okay."

ᔕ

"I'm actually glad you called."

Blade's voice sounded upbeat. Drake suspected that he didn't have a woman with him tonight that he had to impress.

"I take it you've got some information for me."

"One of our girls tracked down Melody's mother. I like Melody, so I gave it a high priority. Tell her that if she ever wants to come back, the agency has a place for her. And if she just wants to live the life of a princess, she can live with me. I'll take care of her. Tell her that."

"Fat chance. What about her mother?"

"Blondie went to her house; she wasn't there. She went next door and talked to a neighbor. It seems that Mrs. Jefferson is off visiting a friend in Sheffield. Blondie got the number and called her in Sheffield. She's having a jolly good holiday, as she said."

Relief flooded through Drake. He had been more worried about her than he had allowed himself to believe. Mona Jefferson had befriended Drake when he had been stationed in England. She had cooked scrumptious meals for him. Melody had complained that he liked Mona more than he liked her. Drake copied down the information about where she was.

"I appreciate you doing that."

"I know you do, you bastard, but I did it for Melody, not you. I did, however, out of the goodness of my evil heart, make a minimal effort to find out some information about Giganticorp."

"Shoot."

"Big G, as it's called in government circles, develops and manufactures a variety of electronic equipment and other stuff for the military. They have a sweet deal going. Some of their contracts weren't put out for bidding. They're privately owned, and I haven't seen the figures, but a contact at the IRS told me that they are immensely profitable."

"Ike's military-industrial complex in action."

"Looks like it. Casey Messinger, the CEO, is rolling in it. He owns several houses, including one on the Riviera. He's married to his second wife, a former Miss Galaxy, or something like that."

"It's funny that I haven't heard much about Giganticorp."

"Nobody has. They keep a low profile. When you've got it as good as they do, you don't want to spoil it by having people ask too many questions. Some generals and admirals own part of it. It's true that your Casey has filed for the U.S. Senate, but there hasn't been a lot of publicity about that yet. He's made his money, so now he wants to become a do-gooder and bask in the love from the proletariat that he deserves."

"The universe save us from do-gooders. All that is very interesting, but did you find out anything about betting on Running California."

"Ah, the race. An attempt by the humble Casey to publicize the great state of California—but also himself. He's been quoted about it in every major newspaper in the country, including the *New York Times*, *Washington Post*, et cetera. I even saw Oliver Drake, the military hero, mentioned. It brought tears to my eyes, and I found myself humming 'God Bless America.'"

"Save it. What about betting?"

"*Nada*. Zilch. The boys in Vegas couldn't care less."

"What about an international syndicate?"

"This is small potatoes for them. Nobody cares, Drake. Except me. I've always cared about you. Look how many times I've gotten your ass out of a jam—"

"I'll remember you in my will. Do you have any other information for me?"

"You don't care about me; you only care about what I can do for you."

"I'll call you again in a few days to see if you've learned anything more."

"I'll wait here—all alone by the telephone—pining for your call."

Drake hung up. Good news about Melody's mother. Bad news about the threatening note. It must be some sort of inside job. But inside what? And why?

CHAPTER 9

Today's run goes through some of the richer areas of Orange County. It starts out on the beach at San Clemente State Beach. Stay on the beach past the private homes that are built on the sand. It will be low tide, and you should have no trouble getting by them. At San Juan Creek in Doheny State Beach get on Route 1 and follow it for the rest of the run. You will pass Dana Point, commemorating Richard Henry Dana who wrote "Two Years Before the Mast," and Laguna Beach, the home of many artsy people and the annual "Pageant of the Masters." After passing through Corona Del Mar you will enter Newport Beach. The run ends at MacArthur Boulevard (Route 73). Please observe all traffic laws when you're running on Route 1.

ꟿ

"MAYBE I SHOULD FEEL THANKFUL to the person who wrote that note. Without it, I probably wouldn't have stayed in the race."

Drake and Melody were running through Laguna Beach on Route 1, past art galleries and other touristy buildings. A horde of shorts-clad tourists competed with them for sidewalk space, often slowing them down.

"I'm glad you're feeling better, but don't push it. The note said we had to finish the race. My mum was rather shocked when I called her, by the way. She wanted to know how I found out where she was."

"She always struck me as being very independent."

"Too independent. I'm trying to talk her into coming to the U.S. and living close to me so I can keep an eye on her, but she won't hear of it. She says she would miss her friends too much."

Drake looked behind him. "I wonder how Aki and Mike are doing. I haven't seen them since we got off the beach."

"They'll be okay. Aki said the doctor didn't think the cut was too bad. He just told him to stay off his feet for a few days."

"Which of course he isn't going to do."

"When did runners ever pay attention to what doctors say?"

"At least we're not in last place today. There's someone in worse shape than I am. I'll be happy when we're not in last place overall."

"As I said, don't rush it." Melody put a hand on his shoulder. "I feel your competitive fire returning, which isn't a bad thing. I'm glad to see the old Drake. However, you've got to last a few hundred more miles. There'll be opportunities. In a race this long, things are bound to happen."

"Like stepping on rocks. And getting rear-ended."

"I keep seeing signs about the Festival of Arts and "Pageant of the Masters." What's that about?"

"The Festival of Arts is an art festival. Ouch."

Drake recoiled as Melody punched him in the shoulder.

"Well, what did you want me to say? If you're going to hit me, I won't tell you about the 'Pageant of the Masters.'"

"This sounds like something out of Queen Elizabeth's time. The *first* Queen Elizabeth. Prithee, kind sir, tell me about the 'Pageant of the Masters.'"

"I went once. The folks who live here dress up like the people in paintings and sculptures and assume the same poses. They build sets for the backgrounds, and when you add the people and light it properly, you get a tableau that looks like the real thing. The models become the people in the paintings. It's amazing how they do it, and they've been doing it forever."

"That's brilliant. I'd love to see it."

"Well, since it's going on right now, maybe we can talk Freddy into taking us."

"Or steal the car and go ourselves. We have tomorrow off, so we don't have to worry about going to bed early."

"If it isn't sold out. It's very popular."

"Do they depict nude paintings like 'The Naked Maja'?"

"Sometimes, although if there are any men in them, they wear loincloths."

"That's all right. I've seen enough naked men on the beach. What about the women?"

Drake's smile told her all she needed to know.

ℰ

"May I say how beautiful you look tonight?"

"Thank you." Melody smiled at Fred.

"You know, it was my idea to invite you to participate in Running California. I'm certainly glad I did. You've been a breath of fresh air."

Drake reflected that this was the first time Melody had worn a skirt since Running California had started and wondered whether that had prompted Fred's attention to her. It was a short skirt—Mary Quant had introduced her minis into the States a couple of years back—but more of Melody's legs had been visible below the shorts she had been wearing every day. Somehow the skirt made her look more appealing, more feminine. In addition, she was wearing her sandy hair down without the ponytail. He began to rue the agreement between Melody and himself that they would sit on either side of the round and rolly Fred.

Melody, who was expert at manipulating men, made it sound to Fred as if they were trying to get to know him better. Which was certainly true, as far as it went. Fred had surprised the runners by producing a ticket to the "Pageant of the Masters" for each of them. Peaches drove them back to Laguna Beach from Newport Beach on the bus.

The Irvine Bowl was an outdoor amphitheater with tiers of seats rising gracefully in an arc from in front of the stage. It reminded Drake of a Roman theater he had seen on the island of Cyprus. It also bore similarities to a Greek Odeon, such as those at the Acropolis of Athens. Like the ancient theaters, there wasn't a bad seat in the place. Not everything of value had been invented in the last hundred years.

The show couldn't start until dark—about 8:30. It gave them a chance to talk to Fred. Drake decided it was time to change the direction of the conversation from how good Melody looked.

"How long have you been with Giganticorp?"

"Fifteen years. I joined right out of college."

Melody said, "The Company must have been small then. I'm trying to remember when I first heard of it."

"It was started in the late forties by a group of retired military officers and scientists who wanted to make sure that the U.S. stayed on the leading age of weapons and war technology. In some ways we got caught flat-footed by World War Two."

It had grown rapidly and become very large, all in twenty years.

Drake had a question. "Since it started small, as most companies do, how did it get its name?"

"That was a joke. You know how military men are with their big egos. They decided that if they were going to start a corporation, it was going to be a big one. In reality, it started in an old warehouse not much larger than a garage. It was just Casey and half a dozen scientists."

"How did Casey get involved?"

"His father was a lieutenant general in the army and on the original board of directors of Giganticorp. He died a few years ago. Casey was a senior at Stanford, majoring in business. They were working on a shoestring and needed somebody they could get cheap to head it. They pulled Casey out of school and made him president. I suspect they were planning to bring somebody in over him if they were successful."

Melody spoke above the murmur of the voices of hundreds of theater-goers, chatting as they drifted toward their seats. "It sounds like Casey was so successful they never replaced him."

"That's it in a nutshell. He proved to be good at getting military contracts—although, of course, the connections of the stockholders helped. The corporation grew faster than any of the founders had dreamed."

"I take it you've grown with the corporation over the years." Melody kept a straight face, not looking at Fred's waistline. "What's your position?"

"My official title is Vice President of Marketing Operations." Fred pulled two business cards out of a pocket of his sport coat and handed one to each of them. "I get involved with a lot of special projects."

"Like Running California."

"Precisely. Although I have to admit that was Casey's idea. He runs almost every day. I'm not a runner, but I admire people who can do that sort of thing."

Fred was smiling at Melody as he said this.

"Are you going to help Casey with his Senate race?" Drake asked.

"He hasn't asked me. I was as surprised as anybody when he made the announcement. He doesn't have an organization yet."

The sun had set, and the show would start soon. Drake still had a couple of additional questions. He watched Fred's face closely. "Are you aware of anybody betting on the outcome of Running California?"

Fred looked genuinely shocked. "Betting? You mean betting on who will win?"

"Or who will finish and who will drop out?"

Fred shook his head so vigorously that the flab on his cheeks shook.

"No. This is a clean race. It's strictly on the up and up. If you introduce betting, you have all sorts of possibilities—such as runners being tainted by the offer of money to do certain things. Why? Have you been approached?"

"No." At least not in the sense Fred meant. "Just curious. Of course, the prize for the winning team is so much that it might be difficult to tempt anybody to throw the race who was in the running to win."

Fred laughed. "That was Casey's idea, too. There's nothing like giving away a million dollars to get people's attention."

"But Giganticorp can afford it."

"Yes, Giganticorp can afford it."

The lights went out, and the audience hushed.

Melody spoke, her voice sounding unnaturally loud in the sudden silence. "One more question. Are you married?"

"Yes. Since we have a day off tomorrow, I'm flying to San Jose to see my wife and three children. I have two girls and a boy."

The orchestra started playing. Drake looked up at a million stars twinkling above them and hoped that the rest of the race would be as peaceful as it was here tonight.

ശ

While the players were depicting a painting that Melody was sure she had seen in the Louvre in Paris, Fred put his hand on her bare knee. A friendly gesture. From a man who had a wife and three children. Why did men like Fred think they were irresistible to women?

When the hand started to move up her thigh, Melody could almost hear his thought process: "Women are docile; she won't make a scene in a stadium packed with people."

She gave him a chance to reconsider his folly. When he started to go under her skirt, it was time for action. She laid her hand on top of his fat one. A friendly gesture on her part showing that she was enjoying his attention. She felt for his chubby little finger, giving him some sensory pleasure. She got a firm grip on it.

Slowly she started to bend his finger back. For the first few inches he might have seen it as an enjoyable form of sadomasochism. But she kept going. He tolerated it longer than she thought he would. Did she have to break his finger? Suddenly he snatched his hand away and rotated his body toward Drake. He didn't look at her during the rest of the show.

ശ

Drake didn't have his pants completely off when the telephone rang. He made the mistake of trying to hop to the phone with them around his ankles. A spasm in his back caused him to trip and fall forward. His nose hit the top of the nightstand, and he roared in pain. He sat on the floor with his back against the bed, trembling as he waited for the almost unbearable spears shooting through his nose and back to subside.

The phone continued to ring. He'd better answer it. Was he able to talk? He fumbled for the receiver and picked it up.

"Drake."

"Are you all right?" Melody's voice sounded frantic.

Drake cleared his throat and tried to speak above a mumble. "Yeah, I'm okay. Just had a little accident."

"Is somebody there?"

"No."

"Drake, somebody went through my things while we were at the show."

He was now fully alert. "Did they take anything?"

"No, nothing's missing."

"Money? Jewelry?"

"I didn't leave any money in the room. The jewelry I have with me is worthless. Nothing was nicked. What about your room?"

Now he understood what she was driving at.

"Just a minute."

Drake set the telephone receiver on the nightstand and crawled across the threadbare rug on his hands and knees to his suitcase. His pants were still around his ankles, but he didn't know whether he could stand yet, anyway. The suitcase was sitting on the floor against the wall of the motel room where he had left it. It took him a few seconds to open the latches because his hands were still shaking from the pain.

The differences were subtle, but he could tell that somebody had been in his suitcase. He arranged his clothes in a certain way from habit, left over from the days when he never knew who would be spying on him. Whoever had looked inside the suitcase had taken pains to cover his tracks, but he hadn't done quite a good enough job.

Drake crawled back to the phone. "Somebody's been in my things."

"I'm coming over."

"Wait..."

A click told him that Melody had hung up. She was only three doors away, so she would be here in a few seconds. Drake didn't want her to see him like this. He struggled to a sitting position on the bed and pulled up his pants. He didn't have his fly zipped or his belt buckled when there was a knock on the door.

"Just a minute."

He made it to his feet, zipped his fly after fumbling a bit, and put the tongue of the buckle through the first hole in the belt. He tried to walk to the door without limping. He opened the door and saw Melody, clad in a green bathrobe and barefoot.

"You look terrible."

Drake realized how contorted his face was and tried to smile. "That's become your standard greeting."

Melody pushed past him into the room. "It doesn't look as if you had a spat with anyone. What happened?"

"My own stupidity. I fell and hurt my back and nose."

"Are you all right?"

"I don't think I exacerbated anything."

"I'll exacerbate you if you did. Did anything get taken from your room?"

"Not that I can tell. I have one more place to look."

Drake tried to lift the only chair in the room, thought better of that plan, and ended up dragging the chair over to the wall by the window. He carefully stood on it, trying not to let Melody see how much it hurt him to lift his leg. Maybe he had reinjured his back. He pulled a dime out of his pocket and unscrewed the screws that secured the ceiling vent. After he removed the vent, he reached up and pulled down a brown paper bag.

He handed it to Melody and replaced the vent. "Don't touch them, but are the envelope and letter there?"

Melody looked inside the bag. "Yes, still here. Do you think that's what whoever it was was looking for?"

"Wouldn't doubt it. Maybe they suddenly realized that we might be able to trace them."

"We couldn't get a typewriter match, so it must be fingerprints. Of course *our* prints are all over them."

"We won't add any more."

"How can we get them checked for prints without raising all kinds of alarms?"

"I'll call Blade. There must be a local agent who can help us." Drake went over to the phone.

"Drake, it's three in the morning in D.C. Blade isn't going to be happy to hear from you."

"So what else is new? At least he'll probably be home. Unless he's sleeping over at his girlfriend's."

Drake got a long distance operator and called collect so that nobody from the motel could determine what number he had called. Blade was even grouchier than his usual self, if that were possible, but he accepted the call and listened as Drake told him what he needed. He promised to have an agent contact them the next day. Drake hung up.

"Whoever did this was a pro. Or at least a semi-pro. No forced entry. Nothing messed up—at least not very much."

"If we were normal people, we wouldn't have known about it—unless the thief had gotten the letter."

"I don't think you should sleep alone. Whoever it was may come back."

"Is this your sneaky way of getting me into bed with you?"

"Melody, I'm serious. I'm also in no condition to do anything. Maybe we can swap our two rooms for one with two beds."

"No." Melody thought for a moment. "I'm not afraid. I don't think anybody is going to risk being identified. It's interesting that they know our room numbers. It certainly looks like an inside job. Which means that they could have taken the letter when it was on the bus with our luggage."

"That would prove it's an inside job. We would go directly to Casey."

"Maybe we should, anyway."

"Not yet. We'd have to talk to him in person. I have a feeling we'll be seeing him soon."

"Give me one of your razor blades. If somebody comes into my room, I'll give him something to remember me by."

Drake went into the bathroom and came back with the requested blade.

"Be careful."

"I will. I know how to use this." Melody gave him a quick hug. "There's another reason why I can't stay in the same room with you. I might be the one who couldn't resist; I might jump your bones."

She opened the door just wide enough to slip through the crack and closed it behind her.

CHAPTER 10

THE RINGING TELEPHONE WOKE AN irritated Drake out of a sound sleep. Why was Melody calling him? They had agreed that this was their morning to sleep in. The light streaming through the partially opened curtain told him that it was broad daylight outside, so it couldn't be too early. Better answer the phone. His back gave a twinge as he reached for the receiver, but it wasn't as bad as last night.

"Drake."

"Blade asked me to contact you."

The voice was resonant, like that of a radio announcer. Drake uttered something in reply.

"I'll meet you and Melody this morning at ten at a coffee shop on PCH. It's about a mile from your motel. Here's the address."

Not "Can you meet me?" He'd better write down the address, but he didn't have pen and paper handy. Drake asked the man to repeat it. He did, his voice showing impatience. Then the line went dead before Drake could find out his name and how they would know him. A typical spy operation. Drake had been out of the business for too long. He had no desire to return to it.

ઌ

"PCH?"

"Pacific Coast Highway."

"I thought I was catching on to American English, but you Californians have your own brand."

"So do other sections of the U.S. Just like your beloved UK. Although I think in the UK it's more of a class difference."

Drake began whistling "Why can't the English teach their children how to speak?" from *My Fair Lady*.

Melody grabbed Drake's arm to keep him from crossing a street as the light turned red.

"I could make some comments about class in the U.S. Or ethnic groups. Or what some people call race, although last time I checked we're all members of the human race."

Drake was glad they were walking and not running. It allowed him to stretch his muscles without abusing them. The day off would be very helpful to him. He was already planning to take an afternoon nap. It was another cloudless day of California summer, and Melody had insisted they put on sunscreen, just as if they were going to be out running all day. Even with the sunscreen, their faces and limbs had grown several shades darker since the start of the race. In Drake's case, it helped hide the bruise on his nose. When he looked in the mirror, the image he saw looked almost like he pictured himself.

Drake spotted the coffee shop, which looked a lot like small restaurants everywhere. It was far enough from the motel that they were unlikely to see anybody connected with the race. They walked in at one minute to ten and looked around. Before Drake saw anybody who resembled an agent, Melody nudged him. She directed his gaze to the booth in the corner. A man sat with his back to the junction of the two walls wearing mirror sunglasses. He gave an almost imperceptible nod in their direction.

As they made their way to the booth, Drake spoke under his breath. "Those shades make him look like a California Highway Patrol officer."

"No remarks. Remember, he's doing us a favor."

"At least he knows how to keep his back to the wall—unlike Wild Bill Hickok."

"Enough."

They came up to the booth.

Melody extended her hand with a smile. "Melody."

He shook her hand briefly. "Slick."

As Drake shook his hand he wanted to say, "I'm sure you're slick, but what's your name?"

They sat down opposite him. With his short-sleeved sport shirt he looked like any other tourist except for the bulging muscles in his arms. Even his iron-colored short hair contributed to his look of hardness.

A waitress in an ugly brown uniform immediately bustled up, so Drake ordered coffee and Melody ordered iced tea. Slick was sucking on a tall glass of Coke through a straw. After the waitress filled their cups, there was silence for a minute while Melody put a spoonful of sugar in her glass.

Melody spoke first. "Thanks for helping us."

"Blade said you were good people and to do whatever you asked."

It was the same mellifluous voice that Drake had heard on the phone. That was Drake's cue to open the top of the brown paper bag he was carrying and show Slick the contents.

"The envelope and note may have fingerprints on them. Well, we know they have our prints, but they may have others. We're hoping you can connect them to people in the government files."

Slick opened an attaché case he had on the seat beside him. He placed the bag in the case and pulled a couple of items out.

"Since your prints are here, I'm going to fingerprint you now. I know we've got your prints on file, but it's always a pain to look them up, especially since they're not stored here. This way we can eliminate them from the evidence before we send it back east."

Drake wasn't keen on being fingerprinted, but as Slick said, their prints were already on file, so it didn't make a lot of difference. He and Melody rolled each of their fingers on the inkpad and left their prints on a card, being careful not to smudge them. Because they were in a corner booth, nobody saw what they were doing.

Drake tried to wipe the ink off his fingers with a napkin. "Please don't share the contents of the note with anyone except Blade. You don't need to do anything about it. We're taking care of it."

Slick raised his eyebrows, as if questioning their ability to take care of the situation, but he didn't say anything. They agreed that Drake would call Blade to get the results of the fingerprinting. Melody asked how they could get hold of Slick if they needed to talk to him directly.

Slick gave them each a business card. The cards were for the Christian Bookstore and gave an address in Los Angeles.

"Call this number and ask for Slick."

As he pocketed the card, Drake wondered if it were somebody's idea of a joke, but he didn't ask. It was obvious that Slick wasn't one for small talk. Drake and Melody exchanged looks.

Melody said, "I need to go to the loo and wash my hands."

As Drake reached for his wallet, Slick said, "I'll take care of it."

Drake and Melody went to the restrooms. When they came out, Slick was gone.

ɞ

As the runners filed into his motel room, Drake inspected them for physical problems. The only times they had all been together in the past few days were during the morning ride in the bus to the starting point of the day's run, and that situation didn't lend itself to general conversation. With all of the Giganticorp employees off for the day, he figured it was a good time to find out how everyone was doing and ask some other questions.

Aki appeared to be favoring his cut foot, but he didn't grimace in pain. He and Mike had finished yesterday's run in last place for the day, but they had finished. The other runners still looked healthy. Drake had to admit that Giganticorp had done a good job picking them.

They sat on the bed and on the floor, chatting and joking. Some stood and leaned against the wall. Drake offered the only chair to Melody, but she eschewed it, preferring to stand beside him. He tried to count attendees. He raised his hand for silence.

"Is everyone here?"

Three of the runners said that their teammates were with their families for the day. Seventeen out of twenty were present. Not bad.

"What's the purpose of this meeting?"

Drake looked at the questioner who was sitting cross-legged on the rug. "I'm sorry. I still don't know everyone's name."

"Phil."

"And your partner is?"

"Brian."

The names rang a bell, but the bodies were interchangeable.

"Let's have each of us give our name and indicate our teammate. I'm Drake and this is Melody."

"We know who you are."

General laughter. However, they did as they were told. That helped a little. Drake suspected that he was the only one, with the possible exception of Melody, who didn't know all the others.

"I thought we'd get together without the beanstalk gang to see how everyone is doing, any complaints, that sort of thing. Anybody want to lead off?"

"This running in sand is for the birds," Brian said.

"Especially when we have to run through a flock of seagulls," someone else cut in.

"I'm serious. It's hard work and slows us down."

"It slows everybody down equally."

"Except those who cheat."

All eyes looked at the speaker who Drake identified as Glen.

Feeling the stares he continued, "I'm not naming names, but several teams have been running on the street when they were supposed to run on the beach."

"One team got penalized."

That was common knowledge, because any penalties, in the form of minutes added to their times, were posted along with the rankings. Drake remembered that it was the team of Harrison and Danny.

Harrison stood up. He had black hair, and his body had a darker tan than most. "We weren't the only ones. Others did it too, but they weren't caught. Fred showed us a picture someone took of us. We didn't see the photographer. They have people watching us we don't know about."

"Other than Fred, Peaches, and Grace?" Melody asked.

A five-minute discussion ensued, resulting in agreement that Giganticorp had plainclothes people along the route keeping an eye on the runners. Several of the runners thought they knew what a couple of them looked like.

Drake ended the talk by saying, "There's nothing in the rules that says they can't do this. They're trying to make sure *we're* abiding by the rules."

"Speaking of rules, what about the rule that says we have to share a room?" Phil looked at Drake and Melody. "Apparently it doesn't apply to you two."

"He thinks you two should be sleeping together."

Brian winked at Melody while the other runners broke up.

Phil wasn't laughing. "Melody could room with Grace. Drake could room with…"

"Peaches?"

More laughter.

"We'll draw straws to see who rooms with Grace."

"And Melody."

Drake wanted to keep the meeting from degenerating into a bull session. "Another subject. Has anybody had any security problems? Losing things out of rooms, suitcases, et cetera?"

The room quieted down.

Danny said, "Why do you ask?"

"No special reason. Security can be a problem when you're traveling, especially in a group as large as this one."

"We have Peaches to protect us and our things."

The mention of Peaches seemed to provoke hilarity. Nobody admitted to losing anything or mentioned that their belongings had been disturbed.

Drake had one more question. "Has anybody been approached to…alter your running in any way and either been threatened or promised something?"

When the resulting buzz died down, a man Drake recognized as Winthrop said, "Are you saying that someone is betting on the race?"

"I'm not saying anything. I'm just asking."

Nobody volunteered any information. Drake didn't want to make an issue of it.

"I have a complaint about the prize money."

All eyes looked at Mike, Aki's teammate.

"There's only one prize. It's winner-take-all. What does the team that finishes second get?"

"A case of Rice-A-Roni."

"An all-expense-paid tour of the California coast."

"Tom and Jerry aren't complaining."

Their lead had increased to over fifteen minutes.

Tom spoke up. "It's a long race, guys. Anything can happen. You know, we're taking it one day at a time."

Cliché city, but it made him a few points. A vigorous discussion ensued. Drake argued that having one prize fostered competition. His argument lost some force, at least for himself, because he and Melody were being paid to run. It was a good thing the other runners didn't know that. He rationalized it by telling himself that it was an appearance fee, like some elite runners received for entering marathons. Although why he and Melody deserved an appearance fee he didn't know.

One thing everybody agreed on was that the publicity would help them with their running careers. It was also a great vacation and beat working for a living.

CHAPTER 11

Today's run starts at MacArthur Blvd. on Route 1. Follow the road through Newport Beach and across the Santa Ana River, being careful to obey all traffic laws. Run on the beach starting on the far side of the river, through the long and beautiful Huntington Beach, then Bolsa Chica State Beach, and Sunset Beach. Return to Route 1 at the far end of Sunset Beach and follow it into Seal Beach. Jog left on Marina Drive and follow it across the San Gabriel River into Los Angeles County. The run ends at 2nd Street.

ᘓ

DRAKE AND MELODY ACTUALLY HAD several other teams in sight as they crossed the Santa Ana River. In addition, Mike and Aki were behind them.

"There's Grace to make sure we get on the beach here." Melody's sharp eyes recognized her first.

"I'll bet, from what we heard yesterday, that Fred has cars driving up and down PCH making sure we stay on the beach."

As they approached Grace, standing on the other side of the bridge, it struck Drake for the first time that she was a very good looking young woman. Clad in shorts and a Running California sleeveless top, she looked like a runner herself. Her long dark hair was in a ponytail, like Melody's, and her legs were well defined, although she didn't have the runner's calves Melody had.

Grace smiled at them as they came up to her. "Congratulations. You're within five minutes of four other teams. Keep up the good work."

They stopped momentarily and gulped water in paper cups that Grace had set on a tray. Drake took an extra cup and poured the contents over his head. They waved to her and scrambled down from the highway onto the sand. When they regained their strides on the beach, Drake spoke.

"There's something about Grace. You know, I don't think she's wearing a bra."

"It took you long enough to figure that out. I think I can say with certainty now that you're back to being the old Drake. That's a relief."

"It must be the hippie influence. I'm sure she doesn't dress like that when she's in San Jose. She'd better be careful, or the guys will be all over her."

"The runners? They're pussycats. I'll tell you who she has to worry about."

"Who?"

"Fred."

"You're kidding me."

"No I'm not. During the Pageant he put his hand on my leg."

"I didn't see—"

"You were engrossed with what was happening on the stage. It was okay; I've faced down men bigger than Fred and ten times as vicious. I took hold of his little finger and bent it back until he decided that his hand would be better occupied elsewhere."

"You could have broken it."

"I considered doing that, but the crime didn't justify that punishment. I think he's learned his lesson. However, Grace doesn't know the tricks I know. It might be a good idea if we got to know her better."

"I agree."

ೞ

They took Grace to an Italian restaurant.

When they were seated, Melody said, "I hope you like Italian food. We eat Italian a lot because it's easy to get both protein and carbohydrates in dishes like spaghetti and meatballs."

"I love it. In fact, I love almost all food."

"It doesn't show on you. You have a marvelous figure."

"Oh, thank you. I like to run—of course not as far as you two. I was on the track team in college. That's one reason I got to work on the race. I wish I were as thin as you, though."

"No you don't. You only get this thin by running fifteen or more miles a day. When the race is over, I'm going to become a glutton and weigh three hundred pounds."

The waitress came and took their order. Melody ordered iced tea, and Grace ordered a glass of red wine. Drake ordered the darkest beer they had, which wasn't very dark. He had gotten used to drinking Guinness Stout in England.

Drake knew that if he didn't assert himself, he might be shut out of the conversation.

"Grace, tell us about your ancestry."

She had the kind of complexion with a perfect balance between too light and too dark that you don't get out of a bottle or under the sun, although he wasn't about to give her another compliment and sound like one of the girls.

Grace laughed. "I'm a mixture of just about everything: white, black, Japanese. I even have some Indian blood—Apache, I think. What about you, Mr. Drake?"

"Please call me Drake."

Melody put on what Drake knew as her sarcastic smile. "He's very humble."

"Oh…sorry…Drake. What's your ancestry?"

"Most of the European countries, if you go back far enough. With emphasis on English, Scottish, Irish, and German."

Melody said that she was primarily English, Dutch, and French. Drake wanted to steer the conversation to Giganticorp. He asked Grace how long she had worked for them.

"Almost three years now."

"You joined right out of college?"

"Yes."

"And you love it." Melody said it as a statement, not a question.

"It's a wonderful place to work. I've learned so much."

The way Grace gushed made it sound like a conditioned response.

"How do you like working for Fred?"

Grace hesitated. "In San Jose he was several levels above me. I didn't see him very much."

"But here you're working directly for him."

"Yes."

Several expressions fought for control of her face, none of them happy. It appeared that Melody was onto something, Drake thought. Better that he didn't interfere.

When Grace didn't speak for several seconds, Melody spoke again. "Let me tell you a little story. The other night at the 'Pageant of the Masters' I sat beside Fred. During the show he touched me inappropriately."

A look of fright had gained control of Grace's face.

"I was wondering if anything like that had happened to you."

Grace remained silent for long seconds. Then she spoke in a pleading voice. "I don't want to lose my job." She looked at Drake.

Melody saw the look. "You can talk in front of Drake. He's safe. Nothing you say leaves the table."

Grace's expression changed to one of determination. "Several nights ago when I was in my room there was a knock on the door. I asked who it was. It was Fred. He said he had something to tell me. When I let him in, he said something inconsequential. Then he said how good the Running California shirt looked on me. He began to trace the letters on the shirt with his finger. I jumped back."

Grace stopped to gain control of her voice. "He told me not to be afraid. I let him trace the letters, hoping that was all he was going to do. But then he put both hands under my shirt."

She stopped, shuddering.

Melody prompted her. "What did you do then?"

"When I couldn't stand it anymore, I told him I was going to scream. He told me not to scream and that he was just being friendly. Then he left the room. I felt dirty. I took a long shower."

"That does it," Melody said. "Starting this minute, you and I are rooming together."

Grace's scared expression returned. "No. Fred wouldn't like that."

"I'll handle Fred. I'll tell him I'm afraid of the dark. Don't worry. He'll agree to anything I say."

Drake saw that Grace was wavering. "When Melody is determined, she's like a bulldozer. Nobody can stand in her way. I know." He smiled ruefully.

"Well..."

"There won't be any repercussions for you. Your job is safe. We guarantee it." Drake smiled an empathy smile. "You're too good a person to have bad things happen to you."

"Thank you. Oh, there's one thing. Sometimes I have to get up at night to run errands for Fred. I might disturb you."

It was Melody's turn to smile. "As long as the errands don't involve him feeling you up, you won't bother me. I sleep like a stone."

Grace looked from one of them to the other. "You're such good people."

"Don't let it get around," Drake said with mock concern. "You might ruin our reputations." He saw the waitress approaching with their plates. "Something smells delicious. Let's eat."

CHAPTER 12

Today's run is being split into two parts. All of it is on hard surface. Start on 2nd Street and head west into Long Beach. Jog left on Livingston Drive. Jog right on Ocean Boulevard. Follow Ocean west along the beach. Although you are permitted to run this section on beach paths, Ocean is more direct, and if you stay on the left or beach side of the street, you shouldn't have a problem with cross traffic. You will be able to see the Queen Mary at her permanent dock. Continue on Ocean through downtown Long Beach and across the Gerald Desmond Bridge to Terminal Island. On Terminal Island, Ocean changes to Seaside Avenue. Stop at the entrance to the Vincent Thomas Bridge where your time will be recorded.

The Vincent Thomas Bridge is normally not open to foot traffic, but we have received a special dispensation to have it open it for 30 minutes from 10 to 10:30 a.m. All runners must cross the bridge during this time period. Your time will start again when the bridge opens for us. After crossing the bridge, head south (left). Jog west to Pacific Avenue or Gaffey Street and continue heading south. It is also okay to run on the smaller streets until you get to 25th Street. Turn right (west) on 25th. You must be on 25th Street when you cross Western Avenue. 25th Street becomes Palos

Verdes Drive South. Circumnavigate the fabulous Palos Verdes Peninsula on Palos Verdes Drive South and Palos Verdes Drive West. You will pass Marineland of the Pacific with its orcas, dolphins, and seals. Palos Verdes Drive West becomes Palos Verdes Drive North near Malaga Cove. Jog left on Palos Verdes Boulevard and follow it to Pacific Coast Highway in Redondo Beach where the run ends.

ఌ

Drake was surprised at how well he was adapting to running almost every day. He was controlling his back pain with chiropractic sessions, lots of stretching, and baths that Melody had talked him into taking when they stayed at a motel that had bathtubs in the rooms. Being English, Melody was used to taking hot baths, but she said that for running, a cool bath was better than a hot bath—in fact, the colder the better.

It took Drake a while to become convinced of that, but he found that in fact a cold bath after running was good not only for his back, but also his legs and feet.

When the wakeup call came at 6 a.m., he felt chipper enough to wish the caller a good morning.

"Mr. Drake?"

"Yes." He was surprised that the desk clerk was still on the line.

"I have an envelope for you at the desk."

Drake suddenly felt as cold as if he were taking one of those baths.

"Don't touch it. I'll be right there."

He pulled on some clothes and raced out to the front desk, surprising the meek-looking man with glasses who, he was certain, hadn't expected him so fast.

"Show me where the envelope is, but don't touch it."

The man looked scared. "I've—I've already touched it, I'm afraid."

"That's okay. I…I think it's a prank. I don't want a dragon to pop out at you."

Slightly mollified, the clerk pointed to the envelope, which was sitting on a table on his side of the counter. He opened the door for

Drake, who took a handkerchief out of his pocket, stepped behind the counter, and carefully picked up the envelope by its corner. He smiled at the clerk.

"I have this friend who likes to play practical jokes."

With his free hand, Drake reached into another pocket and pulled out his wallet. Using dexterity fueled by long practice, he extracted a dollar bill from the wallet using only the one hand, and handed it to the clerk.

"Thanks for notifying me so fast."

"Oh, the envelope came an hour ago."

"Did you see who delivered it?"

"It must have happened when I stepped away from the counter for a minute. I had to go to the men's room. When I returned, it was sitting right here."

Drake thanked the clerk again and hurried back to his room. He sat on the bed and inspected the envelope. It was a white, business-size envelope and had his name typed on the outside, just like the first one. The printing looked different, however. Several of the letters were slightly smeared, as if from dirty typewriter keys. They had been typed on a manual typewriter, not an electric.

The envelope was sealed in one spot, just like the first one. Drake took the small Swiss Army Knife he carried and slid a blade under the flap to unseal it, being careful not to touch the envelope with his fingers. Holding it with the handkerchief, he opened it and extracted the white sheet of paper inside, using a different part of the handkerchief. He unfolded the paper and read it.

To: Oliver Drake
From: The Syndicate
So far good. You have recovered nice from acident. Good news. Now that you back in top shape we need you to do one thing more. Win race. You long shot, exelent odds. Good for both of us. You get million dollers, we get big money to. You have to start working harder. Maybe we help you. Dont forget Melodys mom. Dont show letter to any one.

Win the race? Why not ask him to fly to the moon without a rocket? The stakes were being raised. Shit. Drake retrieved his wallet and found the card that Slick had given him. He picked up the phone and called the number listed for the Christian Bookstore, not expecting an answer this early in the morning. The call was answered on the second ring by a female voice.

"Christian Bookstore."

"This is Drake. I need to talk to Slick."

"He'll call you back in five minutes, Mr. Drake. May I have your number?"

Drake gave her the number and hung up. He debated whether to tell Melody about the new letter immediately. He decided not to for a couple of reasons, including the fact that he didn't know Grace's room number. He opened his suitcase and, using the blade from his Swiss Army Knife, carefully reopened a slit in the lining that he had made after his room had been searched.

He had sewed it up again using the sewing kit his mother had put together for him when he left for college. Fine stitches, just like she had taught him. Even a person experienced in finding things wouldn't spot them during a fast search. He pulled a copy of the original note out of the space behind the lining. Now he could verify the similarities and differences between the two notes.

He would also make a copy of the new note before he gave it to Slick. If he were careful, he could do it without damaging any fingerprints. The motel had a copier; the clerk at the desk would help him.

ᔓ

"We're running faster today. Are you sure you're up to it?"

Melody's question brought home to Drake what effect the letter was having on him. It scared the hell out of him. All the runners were in a tight group as they navigated east Long Beach. Of course, if he and Melody wanted to actually win the race, they had to be ahead of the others, not just with them. Way ahead. They were many hours behind Tom and Jerry overall.

"Let's drop back ten yards. I need to talk to you."

"We'll catch them again if they have to stop for a light."

"I haven't noticed that they pay much attention to mundane things like traffic lights."

It was true. The runners tended to keep moving in these urban areas, regardless of traffic, crossing streets against lights, endangering themselves. It was amazing what the carrot of a million dollars did to one.

Drake and Melody dropped back as they turned onto Ocean Avenue. With the beach now on the left, there was little cross traffic, and it was less dangerous and easier to talk. Drake filled Melody in on the letter, trying to keep his voice calm. He watched her face and saw the strain there, but she didn't interrupt him. He mentioned that he had talked to Slick.

She pulled a bottle of Gatorade from her pouch and took a swig. "How are you going to get the letter to Slick?"

"He told me he'd meet us somewhere along our route. I gave him the route and approximate times."

"So you have the letter with you."

"Inside the envelope, inside a paper bag, inside my pouch. I haven't touched it with my fingers."

"The desk clerk's prints will be on the envelope."

"We're covered on that. I asked him to give me a piece of paper to write a note on. I had him pick a sheet from the middle of a pile of typewriter paper, so the only prints on it will be his and mine. I even got him to hold it with both hands. I'll give that to Slick too."

"Sometimes I'm amazed at your cleverness. What time was the envelope delivered?"

"About five. The desk clerk was away from the desk and didn't see who brought it."

"Drake, Grace's alarm clock went off at quarter to five. I pretended to be asleep, but I watched her out of one eye. She threw on some clothes and went out of the room. She returned a few minutes after five and got back into bed."

"If she was under orders, they probably came from Fred."

"She got a phone call about 8:30 last night. She didn't say who it was, and I didn't ask, but she set her alarm after the call."

"I take it you didn't talk to Fred about your new sleeping arrangements."

"No. If it was Fred on the phone, he didn't know I was there."

"Just out of idle curiosity, did you sleep in the same bed?"

"Yes, since there was only one. Before you get any prurient thoughts, it was a big bed, and girls can sleep together easier than lads. Hey, now that the mist is lifting, I can see the Queen Mary. You stole it from us."

Drake saw the great ship, too. It was impressive, even at a distance. "As I recall, you didn't want it anymore."

"What an excuse. Since Casey is meeting us at the bridge, we have to figure out what we're going to tell him."

"I don't think we can tell him anything right now. He'd want the letter, and I'm giving that to Slick. I don't want him to know about Slick and Blade. We can't trust anyone related to the race. If worst comes to worst, we'll get Blade to help protect your mother."

"Cold comfort. However, I think we have to grill Grace. If we scare her enough, she might not tell anybody we talked to her."

"She may be the weak spot that helps us penetrate the impregnable fortress. We have to take the chance of what she might do."

ᔕ

The runners all arrived at the Vincent Thomas Bridge together. The rules stated that times were only recorded to the minute, not the second, and that runners finishing a segment in a group without gaps would receive the same time. Although Drake was glad that he and Melody had not lost any time to Tom and Jerry so far today, it wasn't enough.

The Cat and Mouse duo, as they were called, were smart runners. Their strategy was not to lead but to stay in the lead pack, so that nobody could gain time on them. They were wise to the occasional team that tried to break away from the pack at an unsustainable pace and didn't try to go with them. Those teams tired and were later caught by the other runners.

As advertised, the bridge was closed to vehicle traffic at 10, and the runners were started on their run over it. Several photographers took pictures. Since it was Sunday, a number of other runners and walkers who had read about the closure joined them. The Running California group was given a head start of several minutes so they didn't have to run in a crowd.

As Drake and Melody ran up the ramp, Casey appeared beside them in his running clothes. "Mind if I run with you?"

"Happy to have you along," Melody said, "but I must warn you that we're going a wee bit faster than we were the last time you saw us."

"I think I can keep up with you for the length of the bridge. Then I have to go to a meeting. For some reason I'm drawn to running over bridges, especially bridges that aren't usually open to foot traffic."

"How did you manage to get permission to have it closed?" Drake asked.

Casey smiled. "I don't know if you've been reading the papers, but Running California is generating a lot of great publicity for the state. I was able to convince the powers that be that letting us run over the bridge would be good for the local economy, including the shipyards—both Long Beach and Los Angeles."

Drake shook his head. "It's a shame they didn't provide a pedestrian walkway when they built the bridge. I said the same thing about Coronado."

"If I were in charge, they would have." Casey was puffing with the uphill climb to the top of the arch. "Say, you are running faster." He took a look at Drake. "I can't believe how well you're doing. No limp, and your face looks almost like the picture of you I saw when we were recruiting. I remember thinking I want this handsome guy to be part of Running California. I figured the photographers would love you."

Melody frowned. "Don't compliment him. He's conceited enough already."

Casey laughed. "I assume that you two have no more doubts about staying in the race."

"As long as Tom and Jerry remain in good health, we have about as much chance of winning as I, a non-citizen, have of being elected president."

Casey looked around to see where the other runners were. He spoke in a low voice. "That's why I'm paying you."

That triggered something in Drake's brain. "Why do you care so much whether we stay in the race? If I continue to improve, we'll probably move up a few places because of problems like Aki's having, but Melody's right about our chances of winning."

"First, because you're the only woman in the race." He nodded at Melody. "We talked to several other women we thought could stick it out, but they weren't able to commit the time. Second," indicating Drake, "because you're a war hero."

"That's bullshit. I'm no more a hero than hundreds of other guys. Why didn't you pick somebody younger who fought in Vietnam?"

"Vietnam's not a popular war. You're the one we wanted."

"One more thing. Putting Melody and me together is too much of a coincidence. How did you know we knew each other?"

Casey smiled. "Do you know who's on our Board of Directors?"

Generals and admirals who had access to top secret information.

CHAPTER 13

"This road is daft with its patches and rollercoaster ups and downs. It looks as bad as some of our country lanes in the backward areas of England."

"This is a slide area. A lot of houses were destroyed here a few years ago. The slide is ongoing. They have to keep rebuilding the road. You can see that the sewer pipes are aboveground."

They were running on Palos Verdes Drive South with the dry brown hill of the Palos Verdes Peninsula on the right and a cliff heading down to the water on the left. A few lonely houses remained on the nearby hillside, some held in place with jacks. They ran past the slide into an area called Abalone Cove. A black Porsche was parked in a turnout ahead. A man was leaning against the car, staring out to sea.

He looked familiar to Drake. "Is that who I think it is?"

"It's our old friend, Slick. What shall we do, run past him and then stop?"

"Sounds good, although I hate to waste the time when we're doing so well."

"We'll make it short."

They were still with the pack of runners and didn't want their rendezvous to be noticed. Casey had long since left them. They ran fifty yards past the turnout where Melody spoke for the benefit of the other runners.

"I've got something in my shoe."

Melody and Drake stopped and let the other runners pass them. They walked back to the turnout where Slick was still looking out to sea as if pining for a shipwrecked lover.

"Aren't you a long way from home?"

Drake's greeting purposely had an edge to it. After all, Slick hadn't exactly exhibited much warmth toward them.

"Good day for a drive."

Slick finally turned and looked at them. He was dressed in tight jeans and a colorful sport shirt and was wearing his trademark mirror sunglasses. Drake wondered what Slick's eyes looked like. He suspected Melody was wondering the same thing. She went for tall, good-looking men.

Drake took off the pouch and opened it. He pulled out the bag with the envelope and note. It also contained the page with the desk clerk's fingerprints. He quickly explained the contents of the bag to Slick.

Melody took a bite of banana. "Have you found any prints on the other note?"

He frowned at them, disapprovingly. "Both your prints are all over the note and the envelope. There are other prints on the envelope, probably from two people. And some prints on the letter. From their position, we suspect they're from one person. They're the same as some of the prints on the envelope."

"The odd person on the envelope is probably the desk clerk at that motel." Drake thought for a moment. "So we've got prints from one unknown person."

"We sent the letter back east. They'll be checked against our files, including employees of Giganticorp. We've got prints on all of them because everybody at Big G has a security clearance."

Drake looked down the road. The other runners had disappeared over a rise. "Thanks for your help. We've got to run."

"Don't let me stop you. Don't sweat too much."

Drake and Melody started running at a pace they hoped would allow them to catch the others. In a couple of minutes the black Porsche roared past them in a low gear. Slick didn't even bother to wave.

ശ

Drake knocked on the door of the room being shared by Melody and Grace. Melody had just phoned him and hung up when he answered, their agreed-upon signal. Grace didn't know he was coming. Melody opened the door.

"Drake. Come on in." She made sure her voice carried back into the room.

As he entered, he saw Grace quickly cover her upper thighs with the short bathrobe she was wearing. She was sitting on one of the beds watching television. She looked startled.

"Mr.—I mean, Drake. I didn't know you were coming over."

Melody was also wearing a bathrobe. "We need to talk to you, Grace." She turned off the TV.

Drake felt uneasy. As Melody had pointed out, he had always been uneasy questioning female suspects, especially the ones who liked him. Melody said Grace liked him.

Drake said, "Yeah, like a father."

Melody had shaken her head. "Definitely not like a father. She asked me if you and I were…together."

"Did you tell her about our past?"

"She's not interested in our past, only our present."

They had agreed that Melody would be the hard-ass in the questioning, and he would be the good guy, instead of the reverse. Drake picked up a straight-back chair and positioned it so he could sit facing Grace. Since he was the good guy, he gave her a little smile. Melody stood beside her bed, assuming the dominant position in the room. Drake let her speak first.

"Where did you go when you got up early this morning?"

"I…nowhere."

"Where exactly is nowhere?"

Drake watched Grace's face closely. When they had talked about Fred, her face had given away her feelings. Now it might be registering fright.

"I…I was running an errand."

"For whom?"

Grace didn't answer.

It was Drake's turn. He spoke in a reasonable voice, as if it were obvious. "You were running an errand for Fred, weren't you? You said you sometimes run errands for Fred."

"I can't tell you."

She zippered her mouth and hugged her knees. Drake had been trained to read body language. Her actions showed her agitation—and her legs.

Melody spoke. "Let's see if we can reconstruct what happened. You received a call from Fred last night. He told you he needed you to run an errand for him this morning. You set your alarm for quarter to five. You went to his room and he gave you an envelope. You went out the side door of the motel, circled around, and went in the front door. You put the envelope on the counter and then retraced your steps. You returned to your room and went back to bed."

Grace had her chin on her knees, and looked as if she might be going to place her hands over her ears and make a noise to drown out Melody.

"You must have looked at the envelope, so you know who it was addressed to."

No answer, but Grace's eyes flickered briefly on Drake's.

"Did you see the contents of the envelope?"

"No."

She realized what she had said and shut her mouth again. It might be true that she was an unwitting accomplice. Drake decided it was time for a softer line. "The envelope contained a threat to Melody and me. The first one you delivered did also."

"I didn't know what was in the envelopes. I was just told to deliver them in such a way that I wouldn't be recognized. Nobody saw me this morning."

"But they did the first time. Where did you get the hooded jacket?"

"From Fred. It's his. He also gave me the dark glasses."

Melody said, "With all this clandestine behavior, didn't you feel that something was seriously wrong?"

Grace shrugged her shoulders. "Fred said to think of it as a game, just as the race itself is a game. He said it wouldn't hurt anyone."

"And you believed him?"

"I'm paid to believe him. He's my boss."

"So to recap. You went to Fred's room; he gave you the jacket, glasses, and envelope. You—"

"He didn't give me the envelope."

Melody waited for Grace to speak.

"I got it from a man in the parking lot. He was sitting in a car."

"Was it the same man both times?"

"I'm not sure. The car was parked in the dark, away from the lights. I couldn't see his face."

"It wasn't Peaches?"

"No. I would have recognized him."

"What about the car?"

"I think it was the same car. A Ford or something like that."

"Color?"

"In the dark all cars are black." Grace looked from one of them to the other. "Are you going to tell Fred what I told you? I don't want to lose my job."

"Did you touch the envelope with your bare hands?" Drake asked.

"Fred gave me a pair of gloves, too."

Melody broke in. "You must have known the gloves were to keep you from getting fingerprints on the envelope."

"I…yes, I guess so."

"So that makes you an accessory."

Grace looked scared again. "What are you going to do?"

She was naïve, and she wanted to keep her job. She had good reason to not like Fred. It was also evident that Fred wasn't the end of the line in this operation, so getting him out of the way wouldn't necessarily kill it. Drake had an idea. "Would you like a chance to redeem yourself and keep your job at the same time?"

She nodded.

"It involves keeping an eye on Fred and everything else that goes on. If you see or hear anything suspicious, let Melody or me know. By the way, do you, Fred, or Peaches have a portable typewriter?"

Grace shook her head.

"Do you know the other people who are helping with the race, the plainclothesmen, so to speak?" Melody asked. "Watching for violations, that sort of thing?"

"No. I know there are several of them. Fred deals with them directly. I suspect he feels I'd tell the runners who they are. I-I'm sorry I delivered the notes. What do they say?"

"It's better that you don't know," Drake said. "Not knowing will help keep you out of trouble." And reduce the chances of her speaking out of turn.

Drake and Melody spent the next half hour briefing Grace on the kinds of things she should be looking for and how she could do it without Fred catching on. Melody softened her tone, and Drake put on his instructor hat.

When they were wrapping up, Melody changed the subject. "After what I've done to you tonight, you may not want to room with me anymore."

"No, I do. I feel safer with you. With both of you. I'm not sure what's going on, but I get the feeling that you'll protect me."

Drake smiled. "We'll try. We're not sure what's going on either. I guess we're all in this together."

CHAPTER 14

Today's run is almost entirely on the beach. Run on the bike path or walking path where available. You will have views of surfers, volleyball players, chainsaw jugglers, piers, marinas, power stations, airplanes, and dolphins if you're lucky. Starting on Pacific Coast Highway in Redondo Beach, take Avenue I to the Esplanade. Head north and take the first available ramp down to the sand. Follow the bike/walking path to the Redondo Beach pier. Go through the parking structure and alongside the dock to Harbor Drive. Follow it past King Harbor and return to the beach at Herondo. Follow the walking path through Hermosa and Manhattan Beaches, and continue on the bike path through El Segundo Beach and Dockweiler Beach, which goes under the takeoff path from Los Angeles Airport. At the north end of Playa del Rey follow the bike path across the first channel. Turn right and then left on the path to Fiji Way. Follow Fiji Way, turn left on Admiralty Way, right on Via Marina, and left on Washington Boulevard back to the beach. Follow the beach paths through the kooky area of Venice Beach. Continue through Ocean Park, and you're in Santa Monica. Go through Will Rogers State Beach and Pacific Palisades to Topanga State Beach at the end of Topanga Canyon Boulevard. If this part of the beach is impassable due to high tide, run on Route 1 but watch for cars.

"Running on concrete is more jarring to the knees than running on asphalt."

Drake made this observation as they wended their way past the many souvenir stands of Venice Beach. Interesting characters of all ages and manner of dress threatened to slow them down, but by going single file, the runners kept up a good pace.

Melody did a double take at a man juggling several objects, including a whirring chainsaw, and hoped that his arm wouldn't be amputated in the process.

"When it's a choice of concrete or sand, like today, I pick concrete for speed, but, of course, sand is easier on the body, at least for short distances. Because of our new policy of staying with the leaders, when the others are running on concrete, we have to also."

They had been within sight of the leaders all day. So had Tom and Jerry, which meant that nobody was gaining on them. Drake felt twinges in his back, a result of their faster pace. He was sure that Fred had set him up with a chiropractor for this afternoon, probably in Pacific Palisades or Santa Monica. Fred had been very good about taking care of his needs. Thinking of Fred reminded him that they hadn't had a chance to discuss what if anything they should be doing about Fred.

They passed the Venice Beach crowd and were in a quieter area. The other runners were spread out enough so they could talk without being overheard. Drake voiced his thoughts. "Fred has taken such good care of us that it's hard to picture him as being part of this intrigue."

"Maybe the fact that he's taking good care of us makes it easier to picture him as a conspirator. If he wants us to win, he should be catering to our every whim. He asked me if I needed a chiropractor, a massage, or anything else. He's been very solicitous."

"He wants to get into your pants."

"If so, he's not acting on it. Ever since the pageant he's been the soul of politeness and respect."

"I've tried to think how we could confront him with the letters without all hell breaking loose and Grace getting fired."

"It could also endanger my mum. We can't prove anything. I have a feeling that Grace would not be a reliable witness. She'd cave under threats. Whoever's behind it, it's more than just Fred."

Drake grabbed a handful of gorp from his pouch and shoved it into his mouth. He pondered while he chewed and swallowed. "Do you think Grace will talk to Fred about our conversation?"

"I doubt it because she's afraid of losing her job. However, that fear might make her report things about us to him that don't implicate her."

"Making her a sort of triple agent. We have to be careful what we tell her. We can't trust anybody."

"Just like when we were working together. We should feel right at home."

"Now I remember why I left you. It was because wherever you went, trouble followed."

"Speak for yourself, John."

ꕥ

Drake's after-dinner regimen mainly involved getting himself ready for the next day. Since the routine included sleeping a lot, it didn't give him much time for night life. Up to now he hadn't felt like doing anything, anyway, but as his body healed, he began to have his old urges. So far he hadn't acted on them beyond wondering whether it was possible for him to patch up his relationship with Melody.

He had just emerged from a cold bath and was drying himself briskly with a too-small motel towel, trying to get some warmth back into his body. He couldn't take a bath right after they finished running because he'd gone to a chiropractor, but he had to admit that Melody was right and the cold helped, even if hot water was a lot more comfortable.

Sleeping, stretching, chiropractors, cold water. All necessary to keep his aging and damaged body moving. Once they got beyond the populated area of Southern California, daily chiropractic sessions would no longer be an option, so he had to take advantage of that opportunity while he could.

It wasn't even nine o'clock, and he didn't feel like going to bed yet. He pulled on pants and a shirt without much of a plan beyond perhaps wandering over to the room shared by Melody and Grace to see if they wanted to play cards or something. The corridor was empty and everything was quiet. Tired runners weren't noisy at night, so they didn't disturb the other guests.

Drake remembered that Melody's room was the first one along the hallway. He knocked on the door.

"Who is it?" It was Grace's voice.

"Drake."

The door opened.

"Is Melody here?"

"No, she isn't."

"Oh, sorry." He turned to leave.

"Would you like to come in?"

Drake turned back, surprised, and saw Grace's welcoming smile.

"Well…I think I'll—"

"I'm just reading a book. Come on in for a minute and keep me company. I'm lonely."

"Well, all right."

He was surprised that Grace was willing to be alone with him in a motel room. She pointed to a chair and sat down herself on one of the beds hard enough that she bounced. Lending credence to the probability that she wasn't wearing a bra under her Running California tank top. He asked her where Melody was.

"She went out with Tom and Jerry for a drink."

"Oh." He was surprised at what he felt. She was a big girl and could do what she liked. She certainly wouldn't break training. She was probably drinking club soda. "Why didn't *you* go?"

"Well, if you want to know the honest truth, I think runners are a little strange with their diets and all the things they do to keep fit. Kind of self-centered." She put her hand to her mouth. "Oh, I didn't mean you. You're a real person."

"Thank you, I think."

They both laughed.

Grace said, "I had a strange conversation with Glen. He told me that every morning he tapes his toes to avoid blisters and his ankles to avoid tendonitis. Then he puts Band-Aids on his nipples to avoid chafing. On a hot day he puts Vaseline on his armpits and crotch, and in what he called his nether regions. He gave a dissertation on how he prepares his bowels so he won't have to go during the race. If you want to make time with a girl, that definitely isn't the way to do it."

"I'll remember that."

They laughed again. Drake had an idea.

"Not to change a subject that fascinates me since I'm a runner, but do you think you could find out who the other people monitoring the run are besides you and Fred and Peaches—I mean without endangering yourself?"

"I think so. Fred keeps information like that in his attaché case. We have three vehicles: the bus, a van, and a car. I drive the car and the van, and I'm learning to drive the bus. Of course we have to carry our stuff from one place to the next, some in the bus and some in the van. Fred's attaché case is usually in the van. It's just a question of picking the right moment."

"Does he keep it locked?"

"Yes, but…" She reached into the pocket of her shorts and pulled out a key.

"How did you get that?"

"This morning I was helping him pack up. One of the keys dropped on the floor. I picked it up and put it in my pocket. I figured if I were going to be a spy—"

"Didn't he miss it?"

"He ranted and raved about it being lost, but he's got another one. He'll forget about it."

She was braver than he thought.

"Has he bothered you any more?"

"No." Grace smiled. "Not since Melody and I started rooming together. I think Melody scares the hell out of him."

Drake's thought was that Grace looked so good with her long black hair and dressed in shorts and a skimpy top that *she* was beginning to scare *him*. He stood up.

"Well, being a runner in training, I've got to do strange things like going to bed early."

She stood up, facing him, inches away, her voice soft. "Is there anything else I can do for you?"

He spoke quickly. "No, not tonight. See you tomorrow."

He edged past her, being careful not to touch her, and made a hasty exit.

CHAPTER 15

Today's run starts at Topanga State Beach and heads west to Leo Carrillo State Beach on the Ventura County border. You will complete the first part on the sand, which will give you the opportunity to get a seaside look at the mansions of the rich and famous who live on the beach at Malibu. Some of the houses are built close to the high tide line. Depending on the state of the tide, you may occasionally have to run around the columns supporting the structures. Try not to aggravate the owners or their guards. After going through Malibu, we will have somebody stationed to direct you to Route 1 for an easy lope along the road to the end of the day's route.

ᔓ

Melody didn't mention that she had gone out for a drink with Tom and Jerry. She also didn't say anything about Drake's meeting with Grace. Perhaps Grace hadn't told her. Or perhaps she figured talking about it would lead to a discussion of her own activities.

Drake decided that silence was the best policy on his part. He didn't have the right to quiz Melody, and he felt uncomfortable talking about Grace. Although he shouldn't. Nothing had happened between them. And, as a very old and very racist saying went: They were all free, white, and twenty-one. Except that Melody believed everybody belonged to the same race and that traits like color were a miniscule variation because of the latitude where one's ancestors had lived. In addition, Grace wasn't just white but a mixture. A mixture of latitudes. So what did that make her? Perhaps anything she wanted to be.

Drake reminded himself to quit following wisps of ideas that avoided the issue and net out what was important. Again. He had a habit of doing that. He had some sort of feeling for Grace, probably not wholesome, and he didn't want to discuss it with Melody. He was disturbed that Melody went out without telling him, but she didn't answer to him. So there. End of thought process. He chuckled.

"What are you laughing about?"

Drake's muscles contracted in a startle reflex as Melody's question brought him back to the present.

"I was just thinking that these houses are so close to the water that a tsunami from an earthquake like the one in Alaska in nineteen sixty-four would wash them all out to sea. That one uprooted redwood trees."

"That helicopter is flying awfully low."

Drake glanced up as the chopper went past them heading east along the line of the beach. He turned his head to follow its flight and could just barely make out Harrison and Danny who were trailing the pack of runners today. Danny had complained that his knee hurt, and Fred had sent him to a doctor who had taken x-rays and recommended that he not run for a while.

That wasn't an option, of course, and Danny was struggling to stay in the race. Drake wondered whether he and Harrison would be the first team to drop out. Knee problems could be serious, and they were usually not curable overnight.

The rest of the runners were within fifty yards of each other. Yesterday, Drake and Melody had finished within a couple of minutes of the four leading teams.

"We have to figure out how we can gain on Tom and Jerry. Maybe we should try to break away from the pack."

Melody looked sideways at Drake. "You know how that would end. Try not to worry about my mum. Something will turn up."

"I'll call Blade tonight to see if he's found out anything on the prints."

"Better give him a few more days."

"Fred has got to be part of this. I'm going to put him on the rack—"

"Not yet."

Melody was trying to keep him calm, even though she had more to lose.

The explosion behind them rocked Drake. He caught his balance and turned around in time to see black smoke rising from a beach house and several objects arcing their way toward the smoke from the ocean. His military experience immediately told him that they were shells of some sort.

Even as disbelief filled his mind, the shells hit houses in the vicinity of the one that had absorbed the first blast, sending smoke and debris into the air. Eerie silence followed. Drake glanced out to sea. He thought he saw something disappear under the waves, but he couldn't be sure. He realized that Melody was clinging to him.

"Bloody hell!"

Her grip was so tight it hurt his arm. The other runners had stopped, also, and were looking at the smoke with their mouths open. The assault appeared to have stopped. Other than half a dozen beachgoers, they were the closest people to the destruction. Drake started running back toward the houses. Melody and the other runners followed him.

Three or four houses had been hit. Anybody who had been inside one of the houses was probably dead. Flames started to shoot up from the wreckage. Whatever the shells hadn't already destroyed, fires would.

Melody asked the question that had just occurred to Drake. "Where are Harrison and Danny?"

"I don't see them. They must have been close to those houses."

The smoke, which had initially surged straight up, was being carried away from them by the prevailing wind. Drake could see the beach in front of the houses. Two men were lying on the sand.

"Look." He pointed toward the men.

"That's them. Harrison and Danny."

Drake and Melody ran up to the pair who were lying amid debris blown from the houses. They were close enough to feel the heat from the flames. Harrison lay face down with his arms and legs spread out at grotesque angles. He had been hit by a large chunk of concrete. There was no way he could still be alive. But Danny was lying on his back and moving. Drake dropped to the ground beside him. His eyes were open. They looked at Drake with fear and confusion. He was in shock.

Blood gushed from a wound in his leg. Melody was already pulling her first aid kit out of her pouch. She extracted a gauze pad, placed it directly on the wound, and pressed. Stop the bleeding. That was the first rule of helping wounded soldiers.

Drake looked at the burning mansions. They were ovens. Nobody could go in there, and nobody could have survived inside them. In the distance he already heard sirens. The local fire company was on the ball. The firemen would keep the fires from spreading to other houses. The paramedics would take care of Danny and get him to a hospital. It was too late for Harrison and anyone who had been inside the houses. Drake didn't see any other casualties on the beach. Tuesday was a workday and not a beach day. Luckily.

He had to get to someone higher in the hierarchy than the local authorities and tell them what he had seen. An older couple had come out of a house several doors from the conflagration. The man and wife watched in horror. Drake would use their phone to call Blade in Washington. In a few words he told Melody what he was going to do. She nodded and gave a terse response, indicating that she would take care of Danny until help arrived.

Drake rose and became aware of the other runners clustered around them. Phil and Brian had tried to assist Harrison and were shaking their heads in horror.

Drake said, "Danny's going to be all right."

As he headed for the house and a phone, he hoped he had spoken the truth.

∽

"Harrison's body is being returned to his parents in Riverside. I've talked to them and expressed our condolences. I know how badly you all feel. We'll take tomorrow off in his memory and hold our own memorial service."

"So you're not going to cancel the run?" The question came from Aki.

Casey looked surprised. "We definitely want to continue the run. I visited Danny in the hospital. He wants us to continue as a tribute to Harrison. I think it's important that we continue."

"How is Danny doing?"

"A couple of days in the hospital and Danny's leg will be fine. He lost some blood, but Melody's quick action prevented him from losing more. He'll be running again in a few weeks."

Casey smiled at Melody who was sitting beside Drake in a conference room of the motel. All the remaining runners were there, as well as Fred, Peaches, and Grace. Casey had magically appeared at the motel that afternoon, saying that he had been in the L.A. area on business.

Winthrop raised his hand, and Casey recognized him.

"Isn't there some…danger to us? Couldn't there be another… attack or whatever it was?"

Nobody seemed to know what had happened. Drake hadn't told anybody except Melody and Blade what he had seen. Apparently the others hadn't seen the shells in flight and possibly a boat like a submarine. He didn't plan to say anything until he had spoken to the military personnel who were converging on the spot. Coast Guard helicopters were already making flyovers of the Malibu area. He also suspected that naval vessels were cruising up from San Diego.

Casey spoke, carefully choosing his words. "I don't think there's any danger. If I did, I wouldn't allow the run to continue. Although we don't know what happened, we can be sure that the authorities are looking into it. As an incentive for the remaining nine teams to continue, Giganticorp will pay you a per diem of a thousand dollars a team, payable when you complete the race."

Drake and Melody were already receiving the per diem. Now all the teams would get it. Casey really wanted the race to continue. He talked about logistics. Today's run would not count. They would start again the day after tomorrow from the point where today's run would have ended if it had been completed.

A motel clerk came into the room and got Casey's attention. He said that a visitor was in the lobby for Mr. Drake. Drake rose and signaled Casey that he had to leave. It was probably somebody from the military. He strode down the corridor and into the lobby, expecting to see a man in a military uniform. Who he saw was definitely military—or more correctly, retired military. He was in civilian clothes. He was—Drake's father.

Drake was not easily surprised by most events, but this was a surprise. He hadn't seen his father for over four years. From around the time he quit working for the federal government. It wasn't that Admiral Justin Drake had disowned him. He just hadn't communicated with him. He rebuffed Drake's attempts at communication.

Drake saw his father before the older man saw him. He looked trim and fit as he sat ramrod-straight on the edge of a chair, reading something. Even his civilian clothes were worn with military precision, including a gleaming belt buckle. His short hair was snow white, and the wrinkles on his face had been earned by many years of service and sacrifice for his country.

Drake hated to disturb the peaceful scene, but he had no choice. "Hello, Father."

Admiral Drake looked up from the piece of paper he was reading. "Hello, Oliver."

They had always addressed each other formally. The admiral stood slowly, and Drake saw some strain in his face. He suspected his father had arthritis, but he would never admit that his body wasn't in top shape. He didn't smile as they shook hands. A hug was out of the question.

"I'm glad you survived the shelling today."

"I am too. One of our runners was killed."

"I know. I listened to the news on the way over here. There are four confirmed dead. The involved houses are still being searched for casualties."

A dozen questions competed with each other in Drake's head. He chose the least personal one. "How do you know the houses got shelled?"

"I got a call from Andy Anderson. He's on the board of Giganticorp."

Admiral Anderson. Drake knew that Anderson and his father had been in the same class at the Naval Academy. That also explained how his father had heard he was in the race. His father lived in Bakersfield, in the San Joaquin Valley. He must have hopped in his car and driven here as soon as he got the call from Admiral Anderson. Drake suspected that his main reason for coming was not to see his only son.

Drake knew the answer to his next question as soon as he asked it. "Why does Admiral Anderson think that the houses got shelled?"

His father looked surprised. "He said you saw shells being fired from a vessel."

Bad news traveled fast and became exaggerated as it went. Drake had called Blade. Blade had contacted the military. The military pipeline apparently included retired admirals, like Anderson, and now his father. Drake knew one thing for sure. When he made his official report, he would have to word what he had actually seen very carefully and sign a document to that effect, if possible. Wars had been started because of inaccurate intelligence.

Something else puzzled Drake. "Why did you come here?"

"Isn't the welfare of my son a good enough reason?"

No. It had never been before. Perhaps if he had followed in his father's footsteps and attended Annapolis instead of enlisting in the army as a private, he would have won his father's approval. As things stood, he was a failure in the old man's eyes.

They were still standing in the middle of the lobby with Drake facing the entrance. He saw Slick open the door, stick his head in the doorway, and give a nod to indicate that he wanted to speak to Drake. So Slick was going to debrief him. He didn't want Slick's presence here to be generally known, not even by a retired admiral.

"I have to go to a meeting. Are you going to be around for a while, sir? You can have dinner with Melody and me."

"Melody?" Admiral Drake smiled for the first time. "That's right; Andy said she was your running partner. Always did like that girl. She's got spunk. Unfortunately, I can't make it. Andy and some of the other board members of Giganticorp are coming here. I'm having dinner with them. Maybe we can get together tomorrow. I'm staying overnight."

Everybody was converging in Malibu. Events were getting curiouser and curiouser. Drake shook hands with his father and headed out of the motel. He saw a black Porsche sitting in the far corner of the parking lot and walked toward it.

ഗ

Drake was sitting on a bed in the room belonging to Melody and Grace who were sitting on the other bed. He had told them both what he had seen or thought he had seen.

Grace looked scared. "Do you think we're being attacked by the USSR?"

Melody patted her hand. "That's not likely. If they attacked us, they wouldn't just destroy a few houses."

"But it says on TV—"

"You can't believe everything you see on the telly. Unless…"

"Unless they want to get our attention," Drake said. "Show us how vulnerable we are."

"Why would they do that?" Grace asked.

"Negotiating ploy. We've been making noises about atrocities happening at the Berlin Wall. People trying to escape from East Germany getting shot. Maybe they just want to direct our attention elsewhere. Anyway, we've got destroyers sweeping the area looking for submarines. The marines have set up a machine gun on Malibu Beach and put out barbed wire."

"Will we go to war with them?"

Melody was the one who answered, saying that she hoped there would be no war. Before dark they had seen a couple of the gray naval vessels off the beach. It brought back memories of Korea to Drake.

He decided it was a good time to change the subject. "We had the two notes you delivered to me checked for fingerprints. There is one unidentified set of prints on the first note, but it doesn't belong to anybody at Giganticorp. The only prints on the second envelope are those of the desk clerk at that motel. The note doesn't have any prints on it at all."

"I'm glad my prints weren't on them." Grace didn't ask how they had gotten the prints checked. She looked conspiratorial. "I have some information for you."

She pulled a folded sheet of paper out of the pocket of her shorts and handed it to Drake.

"During the confusion today I was able to open Fred's attaché case and look inside. Fortunately, he's a neatnik, with all his folders labeled. I looked in one called 'Personnel.' It had three sheets in it, each one giving information about a man. I just had time to copy their names and telephone numbers and addresses."

Drake looked at the handwritten names and numbers to make sure they were legible. He would pass these on to Blade and Slick.

"Good work. Just be careful. We don't want you to get caught."

Grace beamed. "I was careful. By the way, Drake, I understand that your father's here. I've never met a real admiral. I've seen some at Giganticorp, but only from a distance."

"Maybe you'll get a chance tomorrow. He'll like you. He's got an eye for pretty ladies. Right now he's out with his buddies telling war stories." Drake realized he shouldn't compliment Grace apart from Melody. He said to her, "I forgot to tell you that my father mentioned that he wanted to see you. He said you had spunk."

"Better that than he said I stunk."

CHAPTER 16

Today's run is all on roads, so be extra careful to watch the traffic. It goes from Leo Carrillo Beach to Oxnard Beach Park in Oxnard. Start at Leo Carrillo Beach on Route 1 and run to Point Mugu. You will pass the Point Mugu missile display at Wood Road. Head north on Navalair Road and west on Hueneme Road. Along this stretch you will see many vegetable farms and fruit trees. Turn north on Ventura Road through the city of Port Hueneme and past the Seabee Museum. Head west on Channel Islands Boulevard and north on Harbor Boulevard to Oxnard Beach Park.

∽

The memorial service for Harrison had taken place as promised by Casey, but not all of the runners had attended. Some had used the day off to visit their families. Drake didn't blame them. He had barely known Harrison, himself, and although he attended the service, his main feeling was the "it could have happened to me" syndrome, which he had encountered in Korea when his buddies got shot. He didn't feel the guilt of "why was I spared?" perhaps because it all seemed so unreal.

Today they were racing again. The disadvantage of running on roads was that the runners had to be constantly alert and often had to run single file. This resulted in them being even more spread out than usual. When Drake and Melody were able to run beside each other, they tried to make sense of what had happened.

Drake's main questions concerned the response to the shelling. He took advantage of a wide area to pull up alongside Melody. "If you believe the commentators on TV, we're already at war with the USSR. And yet, I haven't heard that anybody saw anything more than I did, which was almost nothing."

"Grace turned the telly on first thing this morning to watch the news. The report said no trace of any boat has been found. Supposedly there are ships patrolling the whole west coast, both Coast Guard and Navy."

"Or at least a couple of destroyers. Since we're fighting in Vietnam, we're spread a little thin."

"There was also talk that the military might occupy part of the coast. They've already sent a force of marines to Malibu, as you know. That's in addition to the specialists combing the ruins of the houses for evidence as to what happened."

"The locals must love all the attention. They're always fighting to keep people off their beaches, and now they've got soldiers to contend with. They'd better lock up their daughters."

"The reporter said the residents asked for the troops. They're panicked and afraid that more shelling is going to occur. Or some sort of an invasion."

"Be careful what you wish for. Maybe the commies have a kayak navy out there ready to storm the coast of Malibu. My question is, why did my father show up?"

Melody put on her most concerned voice. "He came to see if his little boy was all right."

Drake snorted. "If I believed that, you could sell me London Bridge."

"Too late. Lake Havasu already has it. That's another thing you stole from us."

"If we 'steal' many more things from you, you'll be rich enough to buy back the colonies. As you'll recall, when he was able to fit me into his schedule yesterday, instead of talking to me, my father made time with you."

"And Grace. Who was thrilled out of her mind to meet a real admiral."

"The feeling was mutual. There must be a shortage of women in Bakersfield. Maybe things would have been better if my mother hadn't died."

Melody nodded. "It's hard to lose your spouse. Don't you think he came to see his old military buddies?"

Drake pondered that. "As far as I know, Admiral Anderson is the only one he knows from his years in the navy. I don't think they're that close. I've heard my father say derogatory things about him."

Melody took a drink of Gatorade while a semi rolled by; the noise from its powerful engine drowned out any attempt at conversation. Phil and Brian were running a few feet ahead of them. The wind stream that followed the truck blew the cap off Brian's head. Drake considered ignoring it and making Brian come back and pick it up, but one thing his father had done was to train him in good manners. He reached down and grabbed the cap.

Brian waited for Drake to catch up with him and took the cap from his outstretched hand. He thanked Drake who decided to ask him a question. "What's your take on what happened? Do you think it's dangerous for us to run on the coast?"

Brian loped easily alongside them. He was one of the youngest runners and obviously in top condition. He and Phil were in second place overall.

"Naw. Even if that happens again, the chances we'll be there when it does are infinitesimal."

"Lightning can strike twice—"

"Life is a risky business." Brian smiled. "Do you want to live forever?"

ꟹ

Casey had left for other climes sometime last night, according to Fred. Drake wanted to ask Casey about the meetings that had been held during the last two days. He was still trying to get a handle on what his father was up to. Why did he care? His father hadn't cared much for him after he had strayed from the straight and narrow path carefully laid out for him. Why should he care what his father was doing?

Drake decided to ask Fred his questions. He offered to buy him a beer at the local Oxnard pub. Drake used the word pub instead of bar because Oxnard sounded a lot like Oxford in England. Being around Melody brought back the English mannerisms he had learned. Fred drove them a few blocks to a bar that was practically deserted in the late afternoon heat. Drake purchased two draft beers and took them to a rough wooden table Fred had selected.

He didn't want Fred to know the extent of his estrangement from his father. That was none of his business. However, he could make a kind of joke out of it.

"I was wondering why my father was here meeting with your directors. He doesn't confide in me very much. You know how fathers are."

Fred smiled as he took a thirsty sip. "Actually, it wasn't an official directors' meeting since only four of the directors were present, including Casey. We're always looking for opportunities to serve our country."

"You're looking for ways to boost your sales."

"Same thing. The U.S. Government is our biggest customer."

"What can you sell the government to fend off an invasion by sea?"

"My, you are inquisitive. One would think that you're a stockholder."

"I'm a taxpayer. I want to know where my tax money's going."

When Fred laughed, he jiggled all over like a plate of aspic salad. "We've developed a mini submarine that could be used to patrol the coast. It's much less expensive to build and operate than a nuclear sub, of course, and only requires a crew of six. If there's an enemy ship out there, these subs could be used to find it."

"Have you sold any?"

"The Navy purchased a few to try out, but we're trying to sell them a whole fleet."

"What does my father have to do with all this? He's retired, or supposed to be. He's not a stockholder in Giganticorp, is he?"

"Giganticorp is privately held, and the names of our stockholders are confidential."

Drake faked a yawn. "Okay, you've given me the company line; now tell me the truth."

"My gosh, Drake, you're persistent." Fred's smile was meant to be conspiratorial. "All right, here's the scoop. No, Admiral Drake isn't a stockholder. He's a concerned citizen. He's also a good friend of Senator Leffingwell."

Drake didn't know that. Leffingwell was a senator from California. Drake had tried to isolate himself from politics the last few years. His knowledge of the senator was sketchy. A small shaft of light penetrated his brain.

"He must be the member of a key Senate committee for approving military purchases."

"You're not as dumb as you look. There's more. As you know, Casey is running for the other Senate seat next year."

"He wants Leffingwell's endorsement."

"Bingo. Give that man a silver cigar."

It made sense. Sort of. One thing still puzzled Drake. "How did you get my father to drive down here from Bakersfield on such short notice?"

"We told him what happened to you."

"Nothing happened to me. It happened to Harrison and Danny."

"No, I meant the accident with the truck. Of course, we also mentioned that you were close to the houses when they were shelled."

"Wait a minute. You're saying my father drove here because he was concerned about my welfare?"

"Yup."

"I don't believe you."

"He's your father, Drake. He loves you."

"He's got a funny way of showing it."

Drake went to the bar and came back with two more beers. He was trying to think of how to broach the next subject. Perhaps the introduction of his father into the scheme of things gave him some leverage. He lifted his glass. "To a successful race."

"Hear, hear."

Fred clicked glasses with him. They each swallowed a mouthful of beer. Drake put down his glass. "I'd like to talk about something else for a minute. Since the run started, I've received two anonymous letters delivered to motels."

Fred's eyebrows went up. "Anonymous?"

His expression looked innocent.

"Yes. Threatening letters."

"What did they say?"

"The more recent one says that Melody and I have to win the race."

"What have you done with them?"

"The letters say not to tell anyone."

"You've told me. Why don't you give me the letters, and I'll look into them?"

Drake no longer had the originals. Even if he had them, he wouldn't have given them to Fred.

"I've stored them in a safe place. If anything happens to me, they'll be turned over to the authorities."

Fred regarded him. "Someone wants you to win the race."

"You know how much chance there is of that."

"You've moved into ninth place. A few more attacks and you'll be in first place."

Drake stared at Fred.

"Sorry. Bad joke. Look, if there's anything I can do… I've tried to get you the best medical care, but I can't run for you."

"I just wanted you to know."

Drake tried to look into Fred's brain, but he was met with a bland expression that shielded his thoughts.

Fred spoke. "We're going to step up the pace a little. Each day's distance is going to be closer to a marathon. We don't want to drag this out too long. Everybody's reasonably healthy. I think you can handle it."

"It's not a problem for me."

Drake wondered whether Fred had been keeping the distances down to favor him, just as Casey had ordained that the first day's run wouldn't count.

CHAPTER 17

Today's run goes from Oxnard Beach Park to Carpenteria State Beach in Santa Barbara County. Start by heading north on Harbor Boulevard. However, beginning today we're going to let you decide when to run on the beach and when to run on a road. In some places along this stretch it may even be advantageous to run on the railroad tracks, but be careful of the spaces between the ties if you do this. Always watch for trains. The additional freedom should give more weight to individual tactics and make the race more competitive. Maybe we won't see so much running by committee.

ഗ

THE HANDWRITTEN SHEETS THAT FRED distributed to the runners each morning before they started bore the unmistakable flourishes of his big round hand. Whatever else you could say about Fred, he had beautiful handwriting. In addition, he wrote in distinctive green ink with a fountain pen, although you couldn't tell that from the black and white copies that were usually produced at the motel where they stayed.

The runners were gathering in front of the motel in the early morning fog, a magician that made the beach disappear, waiting for Peaches to produce the bus that would take them to today's starting point. Most wore sweatshirts over their running clothes that they would leave on the bus. They stretched and moved around, trying to get warm and loose. The other runners, including Melody, could stretch their bodies in ways that Drake could never hope to emulate. He was just trying to relax his back muscles so he wouldn't have spasms.

Since it was only a few blocks to their starting point, they could easily have walked the distance, but Fred insisted that everybody be treated the same so they would get a fair start. Fred was all about fairness, thought Drake. Or was he? Wasn't this change designed to help Melody and him? Give them an opportunity to break away from the pack by taking a different route? Of course it could backfire if they chose the wrong route. Drake shared the sheet with Melody, wanting to get her reaction.

"I'll bet Tom and Jerry are in a funk about this."

Drake was surprised. Only Tom and Jerry? He had been thinking too narrowly. It was true. The new rules were opening the door to all the other teams. Tom and Jerry could no longer guarantee their leading margin by staying with the pack, if the pack split up and went several different ways. The race could get more exciting.

ග

"Isn't that Peaches?"

"Where?"

Drake looked past several of the runners who were ahead of them and over to the side of the road where Melody was directing her gaze. They were running on the road because it was faster than running on the beach. The beach along here got very narrow at times with houses and rocks blocking the way. These beach houses, like the ones at Malibu, were vulnerable to any kind of an attack from the sea. That was crazy thinking. Who was going to attack beach houses? And yet it had happened. It almost seemed like a dream. A beach setting was too idyllic. Maybe it hadn't happened at all.

Drake finally picked out Peaches. Seeing him here was not unexpected, because he and Grace were often stationed along the way to make sure that everyone was following the correct route. Routes were no longer designated, apparently, but the two still were needed to supply water at places all the runners were bound to pass and check to see that they were all right. Peaches appeared to be in his own world.

He wasn't even looking at the runners. He had his jacket off and was moving in circles. Drake was amazed at how gracefully he moved.

"What the hell is he doing?"

"Correct me if I'm wrong, but he looks like he's dancing."

"Maybe he's practicing a new form of karate."

"No, look. He's got an invisible partner. His right arm is around her waist. His left hand is holding her hand. He's waltzing. One two three, one two three…"

The other runners gawked at Peaches as they gulped down cups of water he had set out. A couple of them were brave enough to make joking comments as they ran by, comparing him to Fred Astaire. He ignored them. The taciturn man who always looked somewhat ominous had a radiant glow on his face as he whirled around to music that only he could hear.

Drake and Melody grabbed the paper cups without stopping, and spilled water dripped off their chins as they drank. Melody was mesmerized by Peaches. "He's a lot better than some of the blokes who used to step on my feet."

"You used to dance?"

"When I was young. Before I met you."

"I never knew that."

"Pardon me, but you never struck me as being the dancing type."

That was true. He had gone to dances when he was in school because that's where the girls were, but he had never been any great shakes on the dance floor.

Melody was musing out loud as they started running again.

"That's a new side of Peaches we haven't seen before. I'm going to try to get to know him better. He might be useful to us in trying to figure out what's going on here."

"Be careful. You don't know anything about him. He might be a…"

"A harasser? Grace says that he's always treated her with respect. You're thinking of Fred. I let *you* deal with Fred. By the way, he didn't admit to anything, did he? We still don't know what his connection is with whoever is sending the notes."

Peaches was a sealed box to Drake. Although he had been alone with him several times going to appointments with a chiropractor, the man hadn't opened up to him at all.

"If you're going to talk to Peaches, I'm going to be with you."

"You've talked to Peaches. He hasn't told you anything. Now it's my turn."

❧

"We may have hit the jackpot here."

Drake was surprised at the animation in Blade's voice. He shifted the motel room phone to his left ear so that he could take notes with his right hand. He no longer bothered to find a phone booth when he called Blade. "How?"

"One of the guys whose names you gave me has his prints on file with the FBI. They match the prints on the letter."

"I didn't know you talked to the FBI."

"We do when we have to. Your Malibu incident lent a little impetus to that. His name is Dennis Sterling, aka Dennis the Menace Woodbury, aka lots of other names. The name you gave us was Sterling, so we checked the prints on the letter against the prints for that name on the FBI file. They matched."

"I'm glad to see that you're doing some useful work. Tell me about this guy Sterling."

"He's not your usual hood. He's got a degree from a revered eastern university I hesitate to mention by name because you'll make derisive comments. He's served time for extortion and blackmail. He's got connections in Las Vegas."

Drake made a couple of notes. "Before, you said that Las Vegas didn't care about Running California."

"We're revising our thinking on that and doing some checking."

"What about the other two names we gave you?"

"We came up blank on them. It doesn't mean they don't have records. They may be using aliases we don't know about."

"Aliases? Why didn't I think of that?"

"Okay, smart ass, here's one for you. Apparently, you're the only living person who saw what actually happened in Malibu. Can you think of a scenario that would involve the Vegas mob in that?"

"You're trying to tie Malibu to my letters? Sounds like a stretch."

"We're stretching as far as we can, son. Moscow has made an official denial that they had any part in this. We have no evidence to prove otherwise. There aren't too many other loose cannons in the world. Germany and Japan have been peaceful for years. We don't think North Korea has the capability. Everyone here's going berserk."

"The marines have invaded Malibu. Destroyers are cruising off the coast."

"That's my point. We're acting like World War Three has started, and we don't have an enemy."

"That never stopped the military before."

"Here's something to think about. It's a lot easier for governments to grab power during a crisis. It doesn't matter whether the crisis is real or invented, as long as people think it's real."

"Would you like to repeat that for the record?"

"No. If you quote me, I'll deny it, and you'll be shark bait."

"I'm trembling in my boots. Was Sterling born in the U.S.?"

"Yes, in Minnesota."

"So his English is probably better than what's in the letters, even though his education isn't proof of that. Does he have any connections with the commies?"

"None that we know of."

"Give me a description of him, in case he's still around."

"I'll do better than that. I'll give you a description and also have Slick deliver a picture of him to you. Call Slick and tell him where you are."

☙

Drake had borrowed the Giganticorp car and was driving himself into Santa Barbara for his appointment with a chiropractor. That meant Peaches would be free after he delivered the runners to the motel in the bus. All the runners had finished within a few minutes of each other. There had been no spectacular breakaways. They had followed the same route. As far as Melody knew, there had been no changes in position. She and Drake were still in ninth place.

In spite of what she had said to Drake about getting to know Peaches better, she didn't have any idea of how to go about doing it.

She had made sure that she was the last person to get off the bus. She stopped beside Peaches, who was still in the driver's seat.

"Uh, Peaches, I was wondering whether you could help me with something."

"What can I do for you?"

At least he hadn't rebuffed her.

"Look, can I buy you a drink or something?"

"I don't drink."

That was a surprise.

"I don't drink much either. How about a Pepsi or a Coke? Or even a cup of coffee?"

Peaches smiled, the first time Melody had seen that expression on his face. It made him look a lot less formidable. "You don't have to buy me anything. Meet me in the lobby in ten minutes."

ᔕ

They sat on a small patio in the back of the motel overlooking the sea. While she was running, Melody rarely thought about how beautiful the ocean could be, especially when it was calm, like an endless field planted with a blue crop. The few ripples were not unlike those caused by windblown grain. Not far offshore, the Channel Islands beckoned, promising romance, much as Bali Hai promised romance for Lieutenant Cable in *South Pacific*.

Melody had made herself a cup of tea from the motel's supply of hot water and tea bags. It wasn't English tea made in a pot, but she had learned to accept what passed for tea in the U.S. She didn't doctor it with large quantities of milk and cream like many of her fellow Brits, so she could actually taste the tea. Peaches had settled for a glass of water, in spite of her attempts to get him something more.

Peaches was silent after they sat down, seemingly as enrapt with the view as she was. He was wearing a short-sleeved white shirt, having taken off his jacket and tie. As far as Melody could tell, he wasn't carrying a gun. She decided it was up to her to start the conversation. "May I ask what your real name is? Peaches doesn't seem to fit you, somehow."

Peaches smiled for the second time. "My name is Robert."

"So where does Peaches come from?"

"One of Fred's daughters came to work with him one day. She saw me eating a peach and referred to me later as the peach man. Fred got a kick out of that and started calling me Peaches. It stuck to me like a burr in the woods. That man has a weird sense of humor."

"But you don't mind?"

Peaches shrugged. "As long as they pay me, they can call me anything they like."

Melody didn't want it to sound as if she were interrogating him. She decided to ask one more question. "When you're in San Jose, do you work for Fred?"

"No. He's not over security there. Why do you want to talk to me?"

A little of his gruffness had returned. Melody was correct in stopping the questioning. But how much could she tell him?

"I want to talk to you about Fred. He strikes me as being a very competent person. He's doing a good job of running the race. But he seems to have a thing about…women. Both Grace and I have had a problem with him."

Peaches didn't say anything, but Melody saw a muscle twitch in his jaw, as if he were clenching his teeth. Well, she had gone this far. "I can take care of myself, but I don't want anything to happen to Grace."

"Grace is a good girl. I'll take care of her."

The statement had finality to it.

"Thank you."

She couldn't think of anything to add on that subject. She was aching to ask him one more question. She might not get another chance.

"We know that Fred is using several men to help him with the race. Men that we haven't been introduced to, for reasons I can't comprehend. I was wondering if you had any contact with them."

Peaches stiffened visibly. He appeared to be choosing his words carefully. "What Fred does is his business. I will do what he tells me, as long as it isn't shady. I am not involved with any people in connection with the race other than those you've met."

That ended that discussion. But Melody didn't want to end the meeting like this. "I wanted to tell you that I used to do some dancing when I was young. I wasn't great but I had fun. You looked very graceful today."

Peaches smiled for the third time. "We had something called Cotillion when I was in school. My mother made me go. I told her I was a football player, not a dancer, but I secretly enjoyed it. Later I went with a girl who liked to dance."

He gazed toward the islands, so close and yet so far. Melody wondered whether he was yearning for his personal Bali Hai.

CHAPTER 18

Today we're going from Carpenteria State Beach through the city of Santa Barbara to a point on Hollister Avenue west of Goleta. Don't underestimate the run as it is close to marathon distance. Remember that the beach heads east-west here. This is an opportunity for each team to use its skills at picking a route because there are many ways to go. The best route may be some distance inland. For starters, we suggest that you don't try to follow the beach directly west of Carpenteria, because you'll run into a marshy area. Go inland to Carpenteria Avenue. You young studs may be tempted to go through Isla Vista to ogle the luscious lovelies on the bathing suit optional beach near the University of California at Santa Barbara. If you do, you'll get bogged down in sand and dead ends, and it may cost you a million dollars.

"This is where we separate the men from the boys."

Drake was feeling better than he had at any time since the race had started. Not only physically but his face was almost back to normal. Practically gone were the black eyes and discolored nose. He had to look closely in the mirror to tell that his nose was permanently enlarged and had a slight hook to it. He told himself that he had never been vain about his appearance, but it was nice that the visual reminders of his injuries were disappearing.

Melody chuckled. "This life seems to agree with you. I've never seen you acting so youthful. Perhaps your aging clock is rewinding, and you're getting younger."

"That would be nice, to a point. Right now I'll settle for gaining on Tom and Jerry."

They were running an inland route carefully picked out by Drake who had acquired a map of Santa Barbara. One thing he had learned in the service of his country was map reading, and he figured that gave them an edge over the other teams.

Melody looked around her. On a summer Saturday the locals and tourists were heading for the beach or shopping. The sidewalks weren't crowded.

"I don't see anybody else. We haven't been this alone since the first few days when everybody ran away from us. Hopefully, that isn't happening today."

"We'll be doing quite a stretch on Hollister Avenue. We should find out how we stand then."

Grace had eaten dinner with them last night. After dinner, Drake had gone through his routine of getting ready for the next day, including taking a cold bath. That hadn't given him time to talk to Melody alone. "I take it that you and Peaches are buddy-buddy now."

"Not even matey-matey, but he did open up to me a little. I got the impression that he's not a member of the Fred fan club and won't play his silly games."

"So he's not part of the threatening letter team."

"Not if we can believe him. He also said he'd take care of Grace."

"I heard you tell her that. Although I think she considers you to be her biggest protection."

Melody laughed. "Well, I did do a little finger twisting. Speaking of mates, how did your chat with Blade turn out? I take it that he's the one who put you on to this bloke Sterling."

Drake had told Grace to be on the lookout for Sterling and had given her his description without telling her where he had obtained the information. She hadn't asked. He filled Melody in on what Drake had said about Sterling.

"I may be able to get Peaches to help look for him."

"Be careful doing that. Do you trust him?"

"We have to trust somebody. Did Blade have any other words of wisdom?"

"He says the military thinks we're in World War Three, but not the president. There's a difference of opinion. Hopefully, the president can retain control of the military, like he's supposed to. But some people, in and out of government, are trying to influence public opinion in favor of war."

"That's scary."

ೲ

When they spotted the Giganticorp bus parked on Hollister Avenue marking the end of the day's run, Drake and Melody still didn't see any runners in front of them. As they drew closer, they saw Peaches standing beside the bus, presumably holding a stopwatch, but he appeared to be alone.

"Where is everybody?" Melody asked. "Do you think they're inside the bus?"

Drake was afraid to speculate. Either he and Melody were very late, or just perhaps… As they came up to Peaches, he had a smile on his face. It was the first time Drake had ever seen him smile.

"Congratulations. You're the first team to finish."

As Peaches wrote their time down on a clipboard, Melody gave Drake a big hug. Memories of how good her hugs felt flooded back. They waited for the other teams to finish. And waited. It was a good five minutes before the next team came into view. The two runners approaching weren't Tom and Jerry. Or Phil and Brian, the overall second place team.

It took forty-five minutes before all the other teams straggled in. Drake and Melody stood on either side of Peaches, peering over his shoulder at the clipboard as he wrote down times, comparing them to the teams' overall times, which were also on the clipboard. He didn't seem to mind.

When the dust settled, Drake and Melody had not only gained on all the other teams, they had passed Mike and Aki and were now in eighth place. They hugged again.

ೲ

Drake wasn't a fan of speechmaking by politicians. He remembered being in a stadium full of Eisenhower supporters when he was in college. A member of Eisenhower's campaign staff had the crowd chanting "I like Ike," louder and louder, whipping them into a frenzy. Drake, who didn't participate in the chant, felt like an observer from another planet. The ability of one man to bend the crowd to his wishes scared him. It reminded him of what he had heard about Hitler's hypnotic power over audiences.

The reason he wanted to hear this speech was because of the events that were taking place around them—and the fact that the speaker was Casey, making the first big campaign speech of his Senate race, right here in Santa Barbara.

The other runners had passed on the event, feeling that their sleep was more important. Fred apparently had already been with Casey all day. Melody invited Peaches who declined to come. Grace produced the keys to the company car and sat in the backseat.

"It's curious that Mr. Messinger is giving a speech here in Santa Barbara just as the runners are coming through."

Grace was the only one who called Casey Mr. Messinger. Melody turned her head around from the passenger position in the front seat.

"Everything in politics is curious, but you can bet your knickers it's all carefully planned."

"Knickers?"

Drake, an expert at Brit-speak, laughed. "She means panties. Casey will undoubtedly mention Running California in his speech. I just hope he doesn't try to get us on stage like he did at the Coronado Bridge. We'll sit in the back and be inconspicuous."

Judging from the number of cars parked in the lot beside the auditorium, it was a popular event. As they walked up the steps, Drake realized he was getting some looks from people wondering how he deserved to have a beautiful woman on either side of him, each dressed up in a short skirt and sheer silk blouse, as if they had consulted each other. They undoubtedly had. He had even taken some care with his own appearance. At least they didn't look like runners.

They found seats in the back as the crowd filled much of the auditorium. When the lights dimmed and a man appeared onstage to introduce Casey, it turned out to be none other than Fred. The three exchanged looks as Fred launched into a mercifully short introduction.

When Casey appeared, he received a generous round of applause. Drake and Melody went through the motions of clapping; Grace was more enthusiastic.

Casey was a good, if not great, public speaker. He touched on some of the usual subjects: prosperity, jobs, crime, taxes. Then he mentioned Running California. The runners had just come through Santa Barbara. They were a good advertisement for California and would promote tourism.

Unfortunately, one of the runners had been killed in the Malibu incident. Of course this had been featured in all the media, and when he told a story about Harrison's parents saying that the race must go on, he received a round of applause. This allowed him to segue into the security of the California coast.

Casey talked about the troops in Malibu and the patrolling naval ships, but he said that more had to be done. Drake was beginning to nod off when Casey said that people living on or near the beach were in danger from any attack. Something in Casey's tone brought Drake to full alertness. Casey continued to speak.

"The California beaches have always belonged to the people. They always will belong to the people."

Applause.

"As the law stands now, beaches are public property below the mean high-tide line. That has allowed houses to be built on the beach at Malibu and other places."

Other places close to Santa Barbara.

"The time has come to return the beaches to the people."

The crowd cheered. Drake saw an appalled expression on Melody's face that must have matched his own. There were undoubtedly some beach landowners in the crowd. What must they be thinking?

Casey went on to explain how creating a buffer zone between the water and any buildings would enhance security, and, at the same time, allow the people, as he called them, better access to the beach. His speech was a rousing success.

ᔕ

"Wasn't Mr. Messinger great?"

Grace was bubbling with enthusiasm for Casey. Drake glanced at Melody sitting beside him in the car, hoping that she would offer a response to Grace, as he didn't want to be the one to stick a pin in her balloon. Melody turned her head toward the backseat.

"Do you think it's a good idea to take away the property of people living near the beach?"

"If it would make them safer."

Drake couldn't remain quiet. "How do we know it would make them or anybody else safer when we don't know who made the attack? Casey didn't say how wide the buffer zone should be, but it would undoubtedly include thousands of homes throughout California. Where would the money to compensate the homeowners come from?"

"The state would buy them."

"With your tax dollars. Even if the state has enough of your money to do that, do you want government arbitrarily gobbling up private property based on unsubstantiated fears? A basic tenet of a free society is the right to own property without the government being able to confiscate it arbitrarily."

"But these are rich people, and they're blocking access to the beach."

Drake was about to respond, but Melody interrupted him.

"So far we haven't had any trouble getting to the beach. True, we've had to run around columns holding up houses a couple of times at high tide. But even if access could be better in places, that doesn't justify kicking everybody off the beach."

Drake cut in. "Isn't it interesting that Casey is making this a class issue, based on income, when he clearly could own all the ocean front homes he wanted?"

Grace spoke softly, almost to herself. "Wouldn't it be great being married to a senator?"

CHAPTER 19

The route from Hollister Avenue near Goleta heads west on Hollister to El Capitan State Beach where you will meet Route 101. Take Route 101 west. Even though it's a freeway here, you can run on the left shoulder, but watch out for traffic. Route 101 turns inland at Gaviota State Beach. Be sure to stay on the road as we won't be going through Vandenberg Air Force Base. Take Route 1 where it heads toward Lompoc. The day's run ends at the top of the first hill on Route 1. There's no good alternative to these routes, so we won't have any independent thinking today. Just remember to have plenty of water and/or Gatorade with you for the final push up the hill on Route 1.

ഗ

"Did you hear about the music festival that's going on in New York at a place called Woodstock or something like that?"

Tom asked the question of his partner Jerry, as well as of Drake and Melody. They had been running together since Route 101 had turned inland from the beach and started climbing steeply. Now they were on narrow Route 1, running single file and climbing even more steeply.

"I saw pictures on the news this morning," Melody said. "They estimated that half a million people have showed up. How do they all get fed?"

"I guess if they stay stoned, they don't notice how hungry they are."

Jerry was laboring and sweating profusely and not laughing.

"Fred's directions said hill, not mountain."

It was also a lot hotter here than along the beach. The double whammy of heat and the steep climb had left the other runners somewhere behind them out of sight. Tom, who was also sweating, took a drink of whatever was in his bottle.

"This is the first real hill we've seen. The Boston Marathon doesn't have hills like this."

Drake's chuckle was strangled by his heavy breathing. "Nobody would run a marathon that had this kind of a hill."

It was interesting to Drake that he and Melody seemed to be handling the climb better than the other runners. They had both been training in the mountains, which had ups and downs, and the thinner air had increased their lung capacity. Drake was bothered some by the heat, but he had brought enough liquid with him to keep from being dehydrated.

Melody's sleeveless Running California top was plastered to her body with sweat, which might be appealing if the men had the energy to notice, but she kept running, slowly but steadily. She passed Tom, who had been leading, and started pulling away from him. Drake was her partner; he should be staying with her. He made an extra effort and also passed Tom.

ꕥ

They were spending the night in the picturesque Danish community of Solvang. Melody took a cold bath and a cold shower. She had a rest. These activities restored her body to something resembling normalcy. She sipped a cold drink as she got dressed and then went out to the lobby of the motel to join Grace in a tour of the quaint shops. Solvang was made for shopping.

Grace was sitting at a small table in the lobby with Peaches. That didn't surprise Melody since they were both employees of Giganticorp, but they were talking softly with their heads close together. Melody hadn't seen any previous signs of intimacy between them.

She went over to their table, prepared to make a comment about them plotting the overthrow of the world when Grace motioned for her to sit down.

"Peaches has information for you."

Melody sat in the third chair and declined Peaches' offer to get her a drink. He took a sip of what was evidently a glass of water with ice cubes before he spoke again. "That fellow Sterling that Drake found out about?"

She'd told Peaches about Sterling the day before and showed him his mug shot, hoping that he might spot him, without going into detail about why they were looking for him. It was obvious from the photo, however, that he'd been in trouble with the law. Melody nodded, waiting for him to continue.

Grace beat him, whispering conspiratorially. "Peaches found him."

Melody had also told Grace about Sterling. Her heart gave a leap, and she turned back toward Peaches.

"You did?"

Peaches nodded. "He's staying at a motel just down the street."

"How do you know?"

"His car. I've seen the same car over and over again since we started the race. I drive along each day's route, keeping track of where everybody is. This car has been doing the same thing. At first I thought it was just different cars that looked alike. After you talked to me, I wrote down the license plate information the next time I saw it. Today I saw the car on Route 1. It was easy to spot now that we're out of the populated area. It had the same license."

"How do you know it's Sterling?"

"He's brilliant." Grace couldn't contain her enthusiasm. "Just like a real detective."

Peaches shrugged. "Grace actually found it. When we didn't see the car in the lot here, we went to the nearby motels and checked all the cars. She spotted it."

Grace continued the story. "Peaches picked the lock. I didn't know he could do that sort of thing. I was scared that Sterling might suddenly show up, but he didn't. Anyway, the car is registered to Dennis Sterling. So what happens now?"

"Now?" Melody hesitated. "First, thank you both very much. You've been a big help. Don't tell anybody else about this. Don't take any other action. I have to find Drake."

ꟹ

"Here's the car, right where they said it would be."

Drake looked where Melody was pointing.

"What can we deduce from the fact that the car hasn't moved?"

"Either he walked to a restaurant, or he hasn't eaten dinner."

Drake looked at his watch. It was 8:30. The sun had set. "Who in his right mind doesn't eat dinner? Anyway, we know he was here a half hour ago."

"Thanks to me."

Melody had called the motel, pretending to be Sterling's sister, and charmed the desk clerk into giving her his room number. When the clerk rang the room, she handed the phone to Drake. When Sterling answered, Drake said, "Sorry, wrong number," and hung up.

The motel was a boxy, two-story affair with an outside stairway to the second floor where Sterling had a room. They climbed the stairs and quickly found his room. The window curtain was closed, but a light shone on the curtain from inside. They could hear muffled sounds coming from a television set.

Drake looked around to see if anyone was in sight. The motel parking lot was deserted. He knocked on the door.

In about ten seconds they heard a male voice. "Who is it?"

Sterling was being cautious. They had prepared for this. Melody imitated an American accent when she spoke.

"It's the maid. I need to check your towels."

A click warned them that the door was being opened. As it came ajar, Melody moved aside enough so that Drake could shove one of his size twelves through the gap. He smelled the acrid odor of cigarette smoke. Sterling had a cigarette dangling from his lips. He also had a look of surprise on his face and tried to shut the door, but Drake's foot stopped it. Drake shoved the door all the way open and walked inside, pushing Sterling backward.

The bed was right behind Sterling, so Drake gave him an extra shove and sent him sprawling onto his back on top of the blanket. As he bounced, Sterling's look changed to anger.

"What the hell is going on here? I'm going to call the police."

"If you do, the FBI will be right behind them."

That shut him up. The cigarette had come out of his mouth and was threatening to light the sheet on fire. Melody closed the door and moved to the other side of the bed. Blade's description of Sterling had been accurate. He was a paunchy, middle-aged man, and Drake thought he looked more like an academic than a crook. His gray hair stuck out at odd angles and needed to be cut. He was dressed in boxer shorts and an undershirt. Drake saw some bones on a small table and smelled chicken from the local KFC.

"Were you planning to seduce the maid?"

Sterling didn't answer. Melody looked as if she were suppressing a laugh. Drake moved close to the bed.

"You know who we are. You've been tracking us since the start of the race. Put out that cigarette."

"Fred hired me to do that."

Sterling ignored the cigarette. The sheet under it was changing to a brown color.

"Did Fred hire you to write threatening letters?"

Sterling didn't answer. Melody had been looking around the room.

"There's a typewriter on the table."

Drake saw the gray, modernistic cover of an Olympia portable.

"Open it up."

Melody lifted the cover revealing the sleek machine underneath. Drake turned back to Sterling, who had assumed a more dignified sitting position on the edge of the bed. He picked up the cigarette and stubbed it out in an ashtray on the bed table.

"Where's the typewriter paper?"

"It's in my suitcase." Sterling indicated the piece of luggage sitting on the floor beside the bed.

"Give a sheet to Melody."

Sterling slid along the bed and opened the suitcase. He reached his hand inside. Drake's view was momentarily blocked, and he realized he'd made a mistake. Melody whistled four quick notes and dove across the bed. Drake was closer and got to Sterling first. He grabbed Sterling in a bear hug, pinning his arms to his sides, and threw him onto the bed for the second time.

Melody pulled the gun out of the suitcase.

Sterling rolled over, and, back on his back, stared from one of them to the other. "Fred didn't tell me you two were professionals."

Drake laughed sourly. "You didn't have a need to know—until now." He turned to Melody. "Type the same sentence in small letters and then in all caps. 'The quick young fox jumps over the lazy brown dog.'"

Melody retrieved a piece of paper from the suitcase and set out to do that. Drake sat beside Sterling on the bed. Sterling apparently decided he was safer lying on his back. He didn't try to get up. Drake looked down at him.

"Tell me about the betting operation."

Sterling didn't speak for a few seconds. The dialog of a TV movie droned in the background, punctuated by the click of typewriter keys.

Drake said, "Do I have to call my friend Slick? I bet he could get you to talk."

Sterling appeared to be examining his alternatives. He came to a decision. "It's run in Las Vegas."

"Did you contact them or did they contact you?"

"I contacted them. It was after the race started. I was already working for Fred, but just to see that the runners obeyed the rules."

"So you got the bright idea of a bet on the race. You contacted your buddies in Vegas and wrote the first letter. Why, for God's sake, did you bet on us? I was barely moving then."

"It wasn't quite like that. The first letter came before the bet."

"Huh?"

"Fred asked me to write it. He said he needed to make sure you two stayed in the race. He figured a threat against her mother would do it."

He motioned toward Melody, who had finished typing and was listening intently.

"So Fred told you to put in the part about my mum."

Sterling nodded. "I don't know your mother from Winston Churchill. Fred wrote the letter. I just copied it."

Drake said, "What typewriter did you use?"

"I borrowed one from the hotel I was staying at. I didn't want to use my own."

"But you used your own for the second letter."

Sterling looked wily. "You tell me. You've been gathering the evidence."

"Never mind that. When did you initiate the bet?"

"The first letter got me thinking. I called a friend in Vegas and told him the situation. He did some checking and said they could get terrific odds betting on you two. He cut Fred and me into the action."

"You have to admit that it still looks like a horrible bet."

"Not at all. All you have to do is stay in the race. The boys from Vegas will take care of the rest."

"You can't tell me that the Malibu incident was caused by Las Vegas hoods."

"That? No, that was an act of God. Or maybe the Soviet Union. But it's a long race. If necessary, accidents will happen to the other teams."

Drake and Melody stared at him. They hadn't expected anything this sinister. Drake took hold of the soft tissue at the top of Sterling's shoulder and squeezed.

"Ouch. You're hurting me."

"Give me a name."

"What?"

"Give me a name in Vegas."

"I can't. They'll kill me."

He was clearly terrified.

Drake contemplated. "If you give me a name, I'll make sure you have at least a twenty-four hour start before anybody in Vegas gets wind of anything. Your name will be kept out of it. If you don't cooperate, I can get your name plastered all over the front pages, because the race is getting lots of press. Then who'll be the long shot? If you like, I'll get you into the witness protection program."

"I'll…take my chances on my own. Okay. Give me a sheet of paper."

He wouldn't say the name out loud. It was as if he were afraid the room was bugged, although common sense said it wasn't. He wrote it down. Drake read it. The name looked vaguely familiar. At least it was a real person. Sterling wouldn't lie by giving a name of a real person who wasn't involved. That would be too risky.

Drake nodded to Sterling. "All right, you can start packing."

Sterling jumped off the bed and started fumbling with his pants and shirt. Melody joined Drake by the door, holding the piece of typewriter paper and the gun.

Drake put a hand on her shoulder and whispered, "Your reflexes are as good as ever. I'm glad you remembered our signal."

"As you said, it was reflex. The notes C, F, G, A, meaning 'He's got a gun.'"

"We never contemplated using it when such quick action was required."

"No. Your reflexes aren't so bad either."

Sterling scowled at them from the other side of the room where he was throwing clothes into his suitcase. "Are you going to give me back my gun? I may need it."

Drake chuckled. "I think we'll keep it as a souvenir of our night on the town in Solvang." He turned to Melody and whispered, "We need to get back to our motel. I think this is one late-night phone call Blade will enjoy."

CHAPTER 20

Today's run goes from the top of the hill on Route 1 near Gaviota to the top of the next hill, which is past Lompoc. That hill is almost comparable to the hill you climbed yesterday, so be prepared. The whole distance is on Route 1. Since it is a Monday, traffic should be lighter than it was yesterday, but be careful, especially on the narrow road until you get to Lompoc. After Lompoc, the road widens to four lanes with wide shoulders. The combination of the heat and the hill climb yesterday scrambled the rankings. We expect to see more changes after today's run. Remember to carry plenty of liquids and energy food with you. Watch for the watering places.

ሪ

"If there's anything worse than a steep uphill for a runner, it's a steep downhill."

Drake made this pronouncement as he and Melody made the long descent from their hilltop starting point. They had been wearing two-ply socks all along, but each of them wore an extra pair of socks today, expecting the downhill to be hard on their feet.

Melody looked at the last of the other runners disappearing around a curve in front of them. "Well, we're bringing up the rear this morning. It's just like old times."

"Not quite. We've moved into seventh place overall. We've finished first two days in a row. We must be doing something right. Six more days like this and we'll be in first place."

Melody laughed. "The Tom and Jerry and Phil and Brian teams are so far ahead of us that it's going to take more than a few good days to catch them, I'm afraid. However, I'm glad to see you so optimistic. I suspect we won't be finishing last today. Too much youthful exuberance can hurt the other lads. If their feet don't get them on the downhill, their knees will get such a pounding that bad things will happen."

"Don't forget the climb at the end of the run. We've proven to be the best climbing team. I don't know whether to thank Fred for putting the steep climbs at the end of the runs or not."

"There isn't any good time to do killer climbs like those. Although I'm sure Fred would help us if he knew how. He's got a stake in the outcome."

"Had a stake. Blade assured me that the noose was tightening on the Las Vegas bunch. They've been under surveillance for some time. The Sterling incident just means that things will move faster."

"Fast enough so that none of the runners get hurt, I hope. Do you think we should talk to Casey and have him cancel the race?"

Drake took a fast swig of Gatorade.

"Blade will let me know if there's still a risk. I think we should talk to Casey and fill him in, but in person, not on the phone. He's traveling around the state, campaigning. We're bound to run into him. When he finds out what happened, he'll probably can Fred."

"Good riddance."

"I need to have a little chat with Fred. I'm waiting until tonight because I promised Sterling he'd have a head start. Although, why I'm keeping my word I don't know. I also don't know whether Fred has any contacts in Vegas, himself, or whether it was all done through Sterling. He may be wondering where Sterling is right this minute."

"I'm wondering where Sterling is right this minute. Do you think he's on a plane to Brazil?"

"The girl from Ipanema must be looking pretty good right now."

"Did Blade tell you whether there's any new intelligence on the Malibu incident?"

"Nothing new, unfortunately. Casey is still agitating for doing something. He made another speech in front of a business group somewhere. Mentioned the land grab idea. At least he hasn't suggested attacking the USSR yet."

ᔓ

The first team they caught was that of Glen and Winthrop. Drake and Melody had an easy time catching them because the two were walking. Winthrop was walking very stiff-legged. As they approached them, Drake slowed down. "What's the matter?"

Winthrop grimaced. "My knees have locked up."

Melody nodded. "You took the downhill too fast. You'll have to walk it off."

"It'll take us all day to finish."

"Do you have anything better to do?"

There was nothing Drake and Melody could do for them, so they sped up. Drake was making mental calculations.

"Those two are right in front of us in the standings. I suspect that by the end of the day we'll have moved up another position."

"I'm going to eat some gorp—what Fred calls energy food. We're going to need all the energy we can find for the uphill."

ᔓ

The heat and the uphill climb were taking their toll again. Although Drake and Melody weren't running fast by any marathon standard, they had passed all the teams except Tom and Jerry and Phil and Brian during the ascent. They were gaining on those two teams, which were in sight. They figured to at least catch them by the end of the day's run. They shouldn't lose any time to them overall.

"This may turn out to be a three-team race," Drake said.

Melody nodded. "Don't count us out. Maybe we should have bet on ourselves."

ᔓ

Fred's only sign of nervousness was that he was smoking a cigarette. Drake knew that he smoked, but he usually did it in private because none of the runners smoked. Of course. And yet, Drake had once met a man in England who said he was a mountain runner, meaning that he ran up mountains such as Scotland's Ben Nevis, the highest peak in Great Britain at 4,400 feet. Drake was impressed, and then dumbfounded when he found out that the man smoked.

They were in Fred's room at the motel in Lompoc. Drake mentioned that he had talked to Sterling—he kept Melody out of it—and that Sterling had admitted his part in the betting. Fred took a drag on his cigarette.

"I hired Sterling to make sure that the runners followed the rules—and also to check up on them during the runs to see if anybody was in trouble. I didn't expect him to bet on the outcome."

Drake produced copies of the two letters from a folder.

"Sterling admitted he wrote the first letter, but he says it was at your insistence. We've proved that the second letter was written on his portable typewriter. He said you got it delivered it to the motel where we were staying."

Fred reached out his hand and took the two letters. He studied them for a long time.

"I love the broken English. I suppose he wanted you to believe that the writer was Russian or something. How did you say you found Sterling?"

"His fingerprints were on the first letter. They were in the FBI database. He's a known felon, and he's used the U.S. mail for extortion, among other sins."

"I wouldn't have hired him if I'd known that. So you tracked him to a motel in Solvang. Clever of you."

Drake didn't mention Peaches or Grace. Let Fred think he'd done it all himself. He waited for Fred to say something more. Fred reread the letters, as if trying to memorize them.

"You had Sterling cornered. Of course he's going to try to spread the blame. I can assure you that I and my staff didn't have anything to do with these letters."

Drake could prove otherwise, but he wasn't going to play his trump cards at the moment. "Anyway, Sterling's gone. Actually, fleeing for his life would be more apt. You never know what those Vegas folks are going to do."

Was that a shudder from Fred or just a noisy exhale of cigarette smoke? Whatever it was, Fred quickly gained control of himself.

"Drake, I want to thank you very much for bringing this to my attention. I guess I don't have to take any action on Sterling because he's gone. We don't really need him anymore. The rules have changed, and it's going to be easy to keep track of the runners on Route One, which we will be following for many miles. I apologize for the problems this has caused you. I trust that you won't be harassed again during the rest of the race."

"There's one thing more you should know. I asked Sterling why they bet on Melody and me since we were such long shots. He said all we had to do to win was to finish. The mob would take care of the rest. As I said before, they can get pretty nasty. Our good guys should have them neutralized soon, but I just wanted you to know what could have happened."

Fred's hand shook as he put the cigarette to his lips.

CHAPTER 21

After two very tough days of running, today will be a little easier. The run goes from the top of the hill past Lompoc to the top of the first (much shorter) hill after you cross the Santa Maria River, which is close to the border between Santa Barbara County and San Luis Obispo County. Be very careful on the steep downhill at the beginning of the run. It is steeper than the downhill during yesterday's run. Don't go so fast that you injure your knees. Again, since we will be inland all day, the weather will be warm. We will provide water along the way, but carry plenty of liquids.

ও

"It looks like everybody's learned their lesson."

Drake was referring to the fact that all nine teams were taking the downhill in one loose pack. Nobody was charging ahead. Several people had suffered knee problems from yesterday's run. Winthrop's were the worst; he and Glen trailed the other runners at the moment. Drake and Melody had passed them, overall, and moved into sixth place. They had also gained on everybody else except the two leading teams.

Melody changed the subject. "We've gotten rid of Sterling and, hopefully, the threat from Las Vegas. Fred hasn't admitted anything, but from what you've said, you scared him. He must think you're some kind of Superman to have dug up all that information while you were running."

"I don't think that Fred will be playing any more games with the boys from Vegas. They're out of his league as far as evil is concerned."

"So the question is whether we should be talking to Casey about all this."

"I've been giving that some thought. What would be our objective? To get rid of Fred? At least he's not bothering you and Grace. We would have a tough time proving anything without Sterling's and Grace's involvement. If we botched it, Grace could be without a job. If Fred is on the straight and narrow, maybe we shouldn't rock the boat."

"Maybe we could communicate better if you didn't use all those American clichés."

"Wasn't it your own Shaw who said we're separated by a common language? You can be my fair lady, and I'll teach you proper English."

"It'll be a bloody day in 'ell before you do that."

ꟿ

Drake wasn't expecting a knock on the door. He had gone through his evening ritual of bathing and stretching. He was tired after three hard days of running. He was happy with his performance, but he also had to get his rest to keep it up. He was dressed only in his briefs and was about to retire to his bed with one of Ian Fleming's James Bond novels. Spying through rose-colored glasses where the good guys were always good and the bad guys were always bad. He didn't want to get dressed if he didn't have to.

"Who is it?"

"It's Grace."

What the devil did she want?

"Just a minute."

He grabbed the first item of clothing he saw, a pair of running shorts, and pulled them on. Two weeks ago he wouldn't have been able to do that without feeling excruciating pain. He went to the door and opened it. Grace stood there looking beautiful in her standard costume of shorts and a Running California sleeveless shirt.

As he looked at her she was looking at him—at his bare chest. For a moment he felt what he supposed women felt when men stared at their breasts. The tableau couldn't have gone on for more than a couple of seconds, but it seemed longer. Then Drake remembered his manners and opened the door enough for Grace to come in.

She seemed to emerge from a brief trance when she entered the room. She didn't speak, and Drake felt it was his duty to break an awkward silence. "Where's Melody?"

"Oh, she went out for a drink with Tom and Jerry."

"And you didn't go because you don't cotton to runners."

"Something like that. Although they invited me. Can we sit down?"

The only chair had Drake's suitcase on it. He took a step toward it when she spoke.

"That's okay. We can sit on the bed."

It wasn't okay. She sat down beside him on the bed, so close that their bare arms and legs touched, generating something akin to static electricity. Drake was distinctly uncomfortable. He also felt something else he hadn't felt much of since the race had started. He tried to sound jovial. "So what can I do for you?"

"Nothing. Just sit with me and keep me company."

She glanced at his chest again. "Your bruise is all gone."

She reached out her far hand and touched him just below the breast bone. His muscles retracted a little in a reflex from being touched in a sensitive place. She hesitated. He couldn't make her think he didn't like her. "Sorry. Reflex. Like when the doctor hits you below the kneecap."

She gained courage and touched him again. Her fingers moved around his chest. Softly. Sensuously. "You don't have much chest hair."

"I shave."

A feeble attempt at a joke. What should he do? He didn't want her to stop. He didn't want her to continue. He did nothing.

She broke the silence. "I have the advantage over you."

Before Drake could guess what she meant, she reached down and pulled her shirt over her head in one fluid motion. As she tossed it on the chair, Drake was struck with the inane thought that here was proof she didn't wear a bra.

She smiled. "There. We're even."

She went back to playing with his chest. He sat frozen.

She spoke again. "Do I have to do everything? You can do to me what I'm doing to you. It would be nice to have somebody I like touching me for a change. Or you can just look. Your choice."

He did some of each. Her skin was silky. Her nipples reacted to his touch. He tried to come to his senses. "We shouldn't be doing this."

It sounded like one of the clichés Melody accused him of spouting. Grace apparently thought so too. "Yes, we should. Why not? Because of Melody? She's out with somebody else. You're not sleeping with her. Why shouldn't we enjoy each other? I know you like me."

To prove her point, she slid her hand down his front, finding out for herself. He was scared for the first time since he had been young. "I don't know if I can perform after all this running."

"Don't worry about it. We'll do what we can. Maybe I can help."

She could. Drake couldn't believe how strong he suddenly felt.

CHAPTER 22

DRAKE WAS STARTLED INTO WAKEFULNESS by the loud knocking on his door. His first thought, mixed up with his recurring erotic dream, was that Grace had returned. What time was it? It was dark outside. Drake clicked on the light beside the bed and looked at his watch. Almost 5:30. Morning.

He still couldn't shake the idea that it must be Grace. Was she upset about last night? He was naked; he needed to put something on. He grabbed his briefs from the floor and pulled them up. They would have to do. He opened the door, fully expecting to see Grace. Instead he saw Melody.

From the look on her face she must be steaming mad at him. How did she find out? She came into the room and closed the door behind her. She was shaking and breathing hard.

"Grace is dead."

Drake couldn't grasp what she said. "What?"

"Grace is dead."

Drake's legs wouldn't support him. He sat down hard on the bed. Grace was dead and he had caused it, although he wasn't sure how. He didn't want to know. He wanted to rewind the clock. But he had to know. "What…what happened?"

"Drake, she was murdered."

"When?"

"A few minutes ago."

Melody sat down on the bed beside him in the same spot Grace had occupied last night. She was still breathing hard, which was unlike her.

She never seemed to breathe hard, even while running. Drake finally understood what was happening. Grace was dead but not because of him. Melody was upset about Grace, not with him. Grace had been murdered. Grace with the silky skin. But how? Why?

"What happened?"

"Her alarm went off at quarter to five. It woke me. As you know, it happened before, so I was suspicious. She started getting dressed. I asked her where she was going. She said she was meeting somebody in the parking lot, but she wouldn't tell me who. She said it was okay; it wasn't anything bad, and she'd be back in a little while. I couldn't go back to sleep.

"She didn't come back. Finally, at five fifteen I couldn't stand it any longer. I got up, threw on some clothes, and went out the side door. At first I couldn't see much. The motel has several outside lights, and my eyes quickly adjusted to the dark. I walked around the parking lot. Nobody was there.

"Then I saw a shadow between two cars back in a corner away from the building. It was more than a shadow. It was Grace. She was on her back. I could see her face, lit by a spotlight like some sort of holy vision. I saw the hole in her forehead. I'm sure she was shot. I checked her neck for a pulse. There wasn't any. I ran around to the front of the motel and went in the main entrance. I yelled at the desk clerk to call the police. Then I came here."

An approaching siren told Drake that the police were on their way. Melody looked at him as if she were seeing him for the first time. "We have to get out there and show them where Grace is. Get some clothes on."

ೞ

"I wonder how many murder cases the sheriff's department gets here." Drake voiced his thought to Melody.

They were back in his room following several hours of confusion and trauma while the San Luis Obispo County sheriff's department carried out their initial investigation. It had taken some time for a detective and other specialized personnel to arrive on the scene following the arrival of the sheriff's officer. They were in a rural part of the county, some distance from the populated area surrounding the city of San Luis Obispo. The staff appeared to be doing a competent job. The initial finding was that Grace had been shot at point-blank range with a bullet from a small caliber gun.

Fred, Peaches, and the runners had been notified. They all reacted with shock and disbelief. Fred immediately cancelled the day's run and booked them for another night at the motel. The other guests were more or less inconvenienced, depending on how close their cars were parked to the murder scene. Some were temporarily blocked by police vehicles. The cars on either side of Grace's body were checked for blood and other evidence.

Melody said, "We need to catch our breath for a minute. I told the detective all I know, which, unfortunately, isn't much."

"I told him something that I also need to tell you."

Drake hesitated then blurted it out. "Grace and I were together last night."

To his surprise, Melody didn't show much of a reaction. "I suspected it. She refused to go out with me. She was gone when I returned. She came back a few minutes after me looking…well, looking like a cat who's been in the catnip. She's had her eye on you since day one."

"I figured the autopsy would show it, so I didn't want there to be any question. I also gave the detective the gun we got from Sterling. It hasn't been fired, so there shouldn't be a problem. I didn't want it to be found in a search."

"One reason I immediately ran to your room was because I had an irrational fear that you might have done it. But when I saw you, I knew better."

"I had no reason—"

"I know; I said it was irrational. You don't kill the cow that gives you cream."

"It was the first time…"

"And only, unfortunately."

They sat in silence for a minute. Drake tried to organize his thoughts. "The detective talked about a possible mugging. I don't think—"

"I told him several times that she was meeting somebody. She had no money on her. Her clothes weren't messed up. It wasn't a rape attempt or anything like that."

"The last time she went out early she met Sterling."

"Sterling's consorting with the girl from Ipanema."

"Which leaves him out of the picture. What about Fred?"

"What *about* Fred?"

"She had information that could get him fired."

Melody thought about that. "Possible motive. I don't think we want the local authorities looking into that."

"No. It's out of their jurisdiction. Maybe now's the time for us to talk to Casey." Drake had a pang of guilt. "Maybe we should have talked to him before."

"*If* Fred did it, we couldn't have foreseen it. Casey's on his way. He'll be here this afternoon. Fred told me that."

"Meanwhile, I'm going to call Blade and fill him in. I don't think the Las Vegas mob had anything to do with Grace's death, but since he's involved in the betting and also the Malibu incident, I want to keep him informed."

ᔓ

Casey was eating dinner with Drake and Melody in a restaurant a few miles from the motel so the other runners weren't apt to show up. He had suggested dinner when the two had requested an audience alone with him.

He talked to all the runners, giving his usual speech about how sorry he was, sounding sincere. It turned into a sort of memorial service; he said some nice things about Grace, and others did too. Melody spoke, but Drake couldn't bring himself to say anything.

Casey mentioned that he had talked to her parents who were, of course, shocked, but apparently they had been fearful ever since their daughter had decamped for the wickedness of California. They lived in New England and wouldn't get her body for some time because of the pending autopsy.

Casey had talked to the sheriff who would not try to keep any of them in town. The run would continue tomorrow. As he listened to Casey talk, Drake had to admire the fact that he took care of everything. Maybe he would make a good senator.

Casey read the wine list and selected the most expensive bottle. Melody agreed to drink some, a rarity for her. He turned to Drake.

"Will you join Melody and me in enjoying this California wine, or would you rather have beer?"

"I'm sure the wine is exquisite, but I think I'll stick to beer."

"A man of conviction. This race has been marred by tragedy. That makes me very sad. I'm hoping that the rest of it will come off without a hitch. I was in L.A. at a convention when I heard about Grace. Actually, I was at an early breakfast meeting and didn't get the word until sometime after it happened. My first thought was, 'Oh no, not again.' As I was driving up here, I tried to think whether better planning could have prevented either Grace or Harrison from dying, but the circumstances were so unforeseen."

"Grace is partly who we need to talk to you about."

Drake launched into his story, starting from the time when he had received the first letter. He had copies of the letters with him, which he showed to Casey. Casey paid close attention and asked an occasional question. Drake continued speaking off and on when not interrupted by the waitress, through the salad course and into the main course. He told about having a "friend in the service" who had helped with fingerprints and identified Sterling.

Melody talked about the threat to her mother and questioned whether Sterling knew anything about her mother. Casey agreed with that thinking.

Drake told about finding Sterling without mentioning the part played by Peaches. He said that Grace had admitted that she delivered the letters to the motels, at Fred's request. He didn't mention that Grace had accused Fred of sexual harassment. When he stopped talking, Casey took a sip of wine.

"I wish you had told me all this before. Of course, if wishes were horses… If I may try to net this out—Fred was apparently involved in a scheme to bet on the race. He may have a motive to kill Grace. Both of the people who can implicate him—Sterling and Grace—are gone. Your friends are taking care of the Las Vegas contingent, which eliminates the threat to my runners."

Casey took another sip of wine. "I will certainly speak to Fred, but not tonight because it's been a long day and I'm dead tired. I'm staying at the motel. I'll go back to L.A. tomorrow. It's going to be difficult to prove anything against Fred. I don't think Fred's the type to kill anyone, but you never know. Tell me immediately if you come up with any more evidence."

There was nothing more to be said on that subject. Drake asked Casey whether he had heard anything new about the Malibu incident.

"I have a feeling that something is going to turn up soon. Something that will make us realize that we can't just sit on our hands, fat, dumb, and happy, and let America be overthrown."

Drake and Melody asked him a few questions about what he meant, but he didn't come up with anything more except vague generalities.

ꟹ

"Casey was certainly correct about being tired. He almost drove off the road. If you hadn't yelled…"

Melody's voice trailed off. Drake was still shaken up.

"Avis wouldn't have been happy about having a totaled Lincoln Continental. To say nothing about our personal unhappiness. I'm glad for his sake that he's staying at the motel tonight. Also, I thought that his response to us telling him about Fred was rather tepid. I suspect he's not going to fire him."

"Let's see what Peaches has dug up."

They had left Casey making arrangements at the front desk. Melody knocked on Peaches' door. When it opened, Peaches gave a welcoming look to Melody and a neutral look to Drake. Maybe he shouldn't have come to Peaches' room, but Melody had insisted. They went inside but didn't sit down.

Peaches looked at Melody when he spoke. "I didn't find anything. I went through Fred's room very carefully. No gun, nothing incriminating."

Melody had asked Peaches to search Fred's room while Fred was out to dinner. She thanked him.

"I also searched the car and the bus. After Fred returned with the van I searched that. Nothing."

Fred had taken most of the runners to dinner in the van. Drake wasn't surprised. "He's too smart to leave a gun where it could easily be found. The sheriff's officers checked the bushes and the trash containers and didn't come up with anything. Wherever the gun is, it's well hidden."

Melody asked, "Did you get into any trouble with the detective for having a gun?"

Peaches shook his head. "It's licensed and everything. It hasn't been fired. I'm not a suspect. I wish I could help. Grace was a good girl. She didn't deserve to be killed. I said I'd protect her, and I didn't."

"It's not your fault." Drake had also been having guilt feelings. "There was nothing you could do. We don't know that it was Fred."

"We don't know that it wasn't."

There was obviously no love lost between Peaches and Fred.

CHAPTER 23

Today's run goes from the top of the first hill on Route 1 north of the Santa Maria River to Port San Luis, west of Avila Beach. You may take any route you like, but we recommend that you stay on roads the whole distance, as the beach is impassable in some areas and loaded with speeding dune buggies in the vicinity of Pismo Beach. Although you'll start on Route 1, you may choose to take local roads through parts of Oceano, Grover City, Pismo Beach, and Shell Beach.

ᘓ

"Casey and Fred didn't give us much time to mourn for Grace."

Drake was momentarily taken aback by Melody's statement, because she was less sentimental than most women, which was one of the things he liked about her. He knew she was deeply frustrated by the fact that they were leaving the scene of the crime without having any evidence as to what happened. Both of them felt the kind of guilt that comes from thinking they should have been able to save Grace, without knowing exactly how they could have done it. So Melody's emotions were understandable. Drake, himself, harbored a pent-up fury, which threatened to erupt.

"The damned race must go on, in spite of a rising body count. Nothing is as important as the publicity for California, or maybe it's the publicity for Giganticorp, or just maybe it's publicity for Casey's

Senate run, although I don't see how negative publicity like this can help him."

The newspapers had played up the story as big news, even though they had little in the way of facts to write about. But when did reporters ever let a paucity of facts get in their way? Several reporters had asked questions of Melody, since she had been rooming with Grace. Melody refused to speculate about what had happened, leaving them to make up their own theories or repeat what the sheriff's office said about a possible mugging.

Drake, the oldest runner, was asked a few generic questions, the kind answerable with a bland statement such as, "She was a wonderful young woman. I don't know why anybody would want to hurt her."

He was glad the men and women of the press didn't have enough insight to ask him penetrating questions. The liaison between Grace and him hadn't been leaked to them. Thank goodness. They had talked to the other male runners, trying to uncover a hint of a romance gone bad, but that attempt had failed.

Drake and Melody were taking their frustrations out on the road, running hard on the relatively level terrain, pulling away from all the runners except the ubiquitous Tom/Jerry and Phil/Brian teams, which they hadn't gained on except for the two days in which they finished first.

Melody voiced a thought that had been bouncing around in Drake's head. "Why don't we quit the race? This isn't fun anymore."

"Well, for one thing, we're being paid to run. A thousand dollars a day isn't chicken feed."

"Since when did you ever let money dictate what you did?"

"Since I've grown old enough to worry about my future. A few more days and I'll have enough money to buy half my own cabin in Idyllwild. Fifty percent makes a healthy down payment."

"I get the feeling you're half serious. All right, we'll stay in the race, at least for the moment, with the understanding that we'll try to dig up evidence on what happened to Grace. I think the murderer is amongst us and that his name is F-R-E-D."

"I'll have another talk with F-R-E-D."

"This time I'm going to join you. I want to look him in his piggy eyes when he goes into his music hall routine designed to obscure the truth."

ꞩ

"I have a message for you, Mr. Drake."

If there were any words in the English language that could get Drake's heart racing faster than those just uttered by the desk clerk at the Avila Beach motel, he didn't know what they were. The man picked up a folded piece of paper and handed it to Drake. He handed an identical sheet to Melody.

"Here's one for you, Miss Jefferson."

Drake and Melody cast alarmed glances at each other before they focused on the pages. Drake saw his name written in green fountain pen and knew that the writer was Fred. He unfolded the paper and read the beautifully written message.

"I'd like to see you and Melody in my room as soon as you get here."

It was signed "Fred." Drake's level of concern went down a few notches. Melody held her message up, side-by-side with Drake's. They were identical, except that hers stated Fred would like to see her and Drake. Melody looked from one to the other.

"It must be important if he wants to see us when we're hot, sweaty, tired, and bedraggled."

Drake quashed the impulse to say that at least Fred wouldn't be tempted to harass her. "Maybe he's trying to catch us off guard."

"But we're not off guard, are we? Let's go."

They obtained Fred's room number from the desk clerk and marched down the corridor to his room. He opened the door within a few seconds of their knock. The harsh odor of cigarette smoke issued forth from the room.

"Come in, come in. Thanks for coming so promptly."

Melody went into the room first and wrinkled her nose. "Your note implied that it was important."

"Yes. I'd like you to meet my new assistant for Running California, Charles Ortiz. Charles flew down from San Jose this afternoon. Charles, these are Melody Jefferson and Oliver Drake, but call him Drake."

They shook hands. Charles was a good looking young man, tall and thin. He had a high-wattage smile. But Drake was upset. This was what was so important that they had to do it unshowered? Meet Fred's new assistant? An assistant brought in when Grace's body was barely cold? He was tempted to say something sarcastic about the situation when Fred spoke again.

"Charles will be helping me with the race, as I said, replacing Grace." His voice actually broke a little when he mentioned Grace's name. Nice touch.

"Charles, go ahead and get yourself settled. We'll eat dinner together, and I'll bring you up to speed. I'll see you in a bit."

Charles beamed his smile on Melody and Drake, said, "It was nice to meet you both," and then left the room."

"Have a seat." Fred waved his arm to include a chair and the bed. "I'm sorry I only have one chair. Can I get you something to drink?"

Melody sat on the chair and sneezed, her nose irritated by the smoke. Drake sat on the edge of the bed, keeping his body straight. He didn't want to get too comfortable. In response to Fred's query about a drink, he pulled a container of Gatorade out of his pouch and sipped what remained of it. He didn't intend to give in an inch to Fred.

The seating arrangement didn't leave Fred much choice if he wanted to face them both. He leaned against a small dresser, folded his arms, and tried not to look awkward.

"I'm sorry to say that there's nothing new about Grace. I'm in touch with the sheriff's department. I'll let you know as soon as I hear something."

Drake decided not to comment because that might defuse the tension. He glanced at Melody. She was keeping a stone face, just as he was. Neither one of them was giving Fred any aid or comfort. They waited for him to continue.

Fred usually gave the impression of being able to handle any situation, but at the moment he looked distinctly uncomfortable. He wiped his face with the large handkerchief he carried, even though it wasn't that hot. His face was red. When he spoke again, he sounded as bad as he looked.

"Look, I know what you two are thinking. You think that I killed Grace. As God is my witness, I swear to you that I didn't do it. I may not always have behaved as well as I should have toward her, but I would never have killed her. I'm not that kind of person. I have my faults, but they don't include murder."

He stopped speaking, obviously wanting to say more but apparently worried that anything he said might make matters worse.

Drake was tempted to remain silent, but Melody spoke in a calm, unhurried voice, reciting facts. "Grace's alarm went off at quarter to five yesterday morning. The last time that happened she went to your room and you told her to go to the parking lot and pick up a letter for Drake. How do we know that's not what she did yesterday?"

"Because..." Fred stopped talking, went into deep thinking mode, and then tried again. "First of all, you have no proof that I had anything to do with those letters. Grace probably told you that story to get herself off the hook. I suspect she wasn't above feathering her own nest, if you know what I mean. You didn't get another letter, did you?"

Drake shook his head. "Grace wasn't in any position to be delivering letters."

Fred didn't want to be accused of murder, but he also didn't want to get fired for participating in a betting ring. Drake wondered whether Casey had talked to him about that. He still had his job. Trouble seemed to bounce off him. But then, he did have a resemblance to a ball.

Drake decided to try a different tack. "What's your theory as to what happened to Grace?"

Fred pondered that. "She obviously expected to meet somebody in the parking lot. That means somebody contacted her the day before, either by phone or in person. It would have had to be somebody she knew quite well. Knew and trusted. If it wasn't me and it wasn't one of you, it could have been one of the other runners. The roommates vouched for each other. Everybody was asleep. Peaches was the other person she knew at the motel. His gun hadn't been fired. Of course, he might have had another one."

Melody stared at him. "Are you accusing Peaches?"

"I didn't say that. You asked me what happened. I was just trying to examine the evidence."

Drake was about ninety-nine percent certain that Peaches hadn't had anything to do with Grace's death. Fred was trying to deflect the inquiry away from himself. There wasn't any sense in pursuing this further at the present time.

Drake stood up. "Melody and I are tired, dirty, and—as you've probably noticed—smelly. Please excuse us while we go get cleaned up."

Melody stood also, and they filed out of the room.

CHAPTER 24

Today's run goes from Port San Luis to Cayucos, north of Morro Bay. The first part of the run is free-form, meaning that you get to pick your own route. You can follow the road to the nuclear power plant that's being built, but be advised that the first part of it is very hilly and curvy. Once you get past the site of the power plant under construction, there are other small roads you can take. From Los Osos you can take South Bay Boulevard past the swamp and turn left into Morro Bay State Park. Take Main Street into Morro Bay and surface streets through Morro Bay, which is dominated by the picturesque Morro Rock. Stay off the part of Route 1 that is freeway, but get on it again before you reach Cayucos.

ൃ

"It's days like this that make me wonder why I ever got into this race."

Drake was panting hard running up the hill from Los Osos. He and Melody had determined that the road to the nuclear power plant was the only practical route after perusing available maps. Melody never panted as hard or sweat as much as the men, but she was struggling. Still, she tried to sound optimistic.

"It's days like this that separate the winners from the also-rans. If we can pick the best route, we may be able to gain some time on the others."

"If…at the moment it appears that everyone else is copying us."

Or vice versa. One of the maps Drake had gotten his hands on was a topographical map that indicated altitude changes. He motioned for Melody to slow down a little and let the other runners pass them. He had the topo map in his hand, folded to show this stretch of the road.

"The road switches back on itself and passes quite close to here at a higher altitude. There appears to be a path connecting the two sections. If we can find it and follow it without killing ourselves in the process, we may be able to cut off quite a bit of distance."

Several minutes later, the two plunged off the paved road onto a dirt path of dubious parentage. They ran on the hard, dry clay, trying to avoid ruts and fissures, between sections of dense and prickly brush that they didn't want to have to bushwhack through. After a few anxious minutes, during which the steepness of the terrain made them wonder whether they were headed in the right direction, they came upon the other section of the paved road.

They turned onto it, thankful for the firmness of the asphalt and the knowledge that they knew where they were and took a quick glance to the right before they ran to the left.

Melody said, "I don't see anyone."

"Since we didn't spend that much time on the shortcut, I think we can safely assume that we've taken the lead."

ᔕ

They still had the lead when they passed Diablo Canyon where the nuclear power plant was under construction. They ran across a cow pasture to connect with a road that went through Montana de Oro State Park.

Melody watched the placid animals watch them and tried to look for cow pies at the same time. "We've seen seals, birds, crabs, and cows today. I'm assuming that all but the cows are native to this area."

Drake laughed. "It's not the cows you have to worry about, it's the bulls. Although I suspect you won't find a bull in the same pasture with cows." He shifted his gaze to the blue water beyond the cliff. "If I'm not mistaken, that rock is called Lion Rock."

Melody looked at the large rock that did indeed resemble a lion. "What's that in the water next to it?"

"It's a boat of some sort."

They detoured closer to the cliff but kept running. Something didn't look right to Drake.

"That's a bad place for a boat. It appears to be a very rocky area."

"The way it's tilted, I suspect it's come upon hard times. It's a strange looking boat. I've never seen a boat that looked like that."

"It looks like a small submarine."

Drake flashed back to the day on the beach at Malibu. He vaguely remembered seeing a shape in the water that rapidly disappeared after the shells were fired. At least he thought he had seen a shape. Maybe it was his imagination filling in details. The Navy and Coast Guard still hadn't found anything. This place was remote enough that there was a good chance nobody else had spotted the boat if it hadn't been there long.

"I'm going to report this to Blade."

"Maybe there's a pay phone in the park."

"I'm not in any hurry to start World War Three. Let's wait until we finish the run. Especially since we've got an excellent chance of gaining on everybody."

Melody looked behind them. The closest runners were specks in the distance. "Anything you say, guv."

She had seen enough violence in her life to echo Drake's sentiment. She hoped that the boat would not turn out to be sinister. They angled over to the park road and continued their fast pace, determined to put more distance between themselves and the other runners.

ꟸ

Drake and Melody ate dinner in a Cayucos restaurant with several of the other runners. Nobody mentioned seeing the boat at Lion Rock, so the two didn't bring it up. Either the others didn't go close enough to the cliff to see it, or they didn't think it remarkable. Regardless, Drake and Melody didn't want to be the ones to start rumors.

They had moved into fifth place during the day's run. Although they had gained on the two leading teams, they were still far behind them in elapsed time.

Tom invited the two to join a card game in one of the rooms of the motel. Melody, who had lost her roommate and needed to take her mind off Grace, said she would sit in for a while. Drake was still following his nightly routine of bathing, stretching, and going to bed early. He excused himself.

The message light on Drake's telephone was flashing when he returned to his room. The message was to call a number collect. No name. Drake recognized the number as one belonging to Blade. He had talked to Blade earlier. Blade must be working late. Drake placed the call. Blade answered, repeating the number. The operator asked him if he would accept the charge from Oliver Drake.

Blade said, "Yes, ma'am."

The operator said, "Go ahead," and clicked off the line.

"Well, you old son of a bitch, you may be on to something."

"Always glad to be of service to my country."

"We haven't yet landed personnel on the objective, but we've got choppers doing flyovers and taking pictures. It looks like the real thing."

Blade was taking precautions in case somebody was listening in, so it must be important. How important, Drake wondered? "Is this going to start the big one?"

"Too soon to tell. Curious things going on. This place is remote, but not *that* remote. We think that it's only been there a short time, probably since last night."

"It was abandoned and drifted onto the rocks?"

"Unlikely, considering its location. Also, strange coincidence. You were present at the original incident. Now you're the one who makes this discovery."

"The other runners were present in Malibu. And any one of them could have made this discovery."

"True. But you've all got the same employer. I'm sending Slick up there. He'll meet you tomorrow."

"Not during the run. We can't afford to stop."

“You’re really into this thing, aren’t you? I fear for your energetic lifestyle. When I get the urge to exercise, I lie down until it passes. All right, Slick will meet you tomorrow evening.”

“I’m not sure where we’re going to stay—”

“Don’t worry your pretty head about that. I think we can probably find you. Don’t underestimate us.”

“I’d never do that.”

CHAPTER 25

Today's run goes from Cayucos to San Simeon (Hearst Castle) by way of Cambria, a lovely tourist trap. If you're up to it, we'll take a tour of Hearst Castle this afternoon. Stay on Route 1 the whole way, but be very careful. In some places there isn't any shoulder. Run single file on the left side of the road along the narrow stretches and keep a sharp eye out for cars. The good news is that the road is fairly flat. The altitude never gets much above 200 feet. Because it's Saturday, there will be weekend traffic.

ᔓ

WHAT THEY DIDN'T EXPECT TO see were hitchhiking hippies, off to commune with nature in the Big Sur where their troubles would vanish in a puff of smoke. The girls, ranging from twenty-something to teenage, wore long hair and long skirts with loose blouses covering bare skin and lugged bedrolls or backpacks. The boys had equally long hair, and except for their dress, it was sometimes difficult to tell one sex from the other from behind.

Most were headed north; they stationed themselves on the right side of the road, trying to grab rides with weekenders who had carloads of children. When a Volkswagen camper with flowers painted on the sides that wasn't already packed came along, it was like manna from heaven to them.

The runners and the hippies stared at each other as the former flashed by. They came from two different worlds, separated by a narrow strip of asphalt. Drake saw good looking girls and wondered what would happen to them if they were picked up by the wrong man. That made him speculate about free love. Which made him wonder when some of them had last washed, as he got a closer look at straggly hair and dirty clothes.

Melody interrupted his reverie. "If I were the mother of those girls, I'd lock them up until they were thirty-five."

"You're too young to be their mother. You're not even thirty-five, yourself."

"I'd lock myself up, too. I'm thinking ahead. I might get married some day, you know."

Married. Drake pictured himself being married once in a while, but never seriously. However, it did have its attractions, abundant sex being one of them. He decided to change the subject before Melody guessed his thoughts. "It looks like we're going to be running in a posse all day. No chance to excel on this road. We'll be on it for a long time."

"There will be other opportunities. We've moved up to fifth place. Who would have guessed that when we started out? At least we shouldn't lose ground to anyone."

In fact, several of the teams were lagging behind the group with various ailments affecting feet and knees.

Melody spoke again. "What do you think Blade's up to? Isn't this a job for the U.S. Army, Navy, and Marines?" She sang, "From the halls of Montezuma, to the shores of Lion Rock."

"Blade sees a conspiracy based on the fact that we were present at Malibu and also the ones who found the sub."

"So we're working for the Russkies?"

"Not us. Somebody at Giganticorp."

"Meaning Casey. He's the top dog. Why would he do that?"

"Who knows? Maybe he's an idealist."

"Idealists are fine as long as they don't actually try to do anything. You said that Slick is going to meet us at our motel, which I understand is in Cambria. At least he's not going to show up in his Porsche around the bend somewhere."

"I nixed that idea. This isn't like the first time when we were so far behind that stopping for a few minutes to chat with Slick didn't matter."

They were passing a house on the ocean side of the road with a sign that read, "This place dangerous to dogs, children, and reasonable people." The yard was strewn with junk.

Drake smiled. At least they were warned.

ꟸ

Drake and Melody were amazed at the magnificent buildings and the Olympian style swimming pool on the barren hillside above the sea. They were even more surprised at what they saw within the buildings.

Melody read the information brochure. "It says that Hearst collected items in hundreds of different categories. Including ceilings. I say, who in their right mind collects ceilings?"

They were gazing up at one of those ceilings at the moment, brought over in pieces from some medieval castle in Europe and reassembled in its current habitat.

"The man thought big. You can't deny that."

Drake and Melody jerked their heads down to the horizontal. There was no mistaking that resonant voice. Slick smiled easily at them from behind his dark glasses. They helped him take on the coloring of a tourist, along with a garish sport shirt and white sneakers. Only his powerful-looking arms and flat stomach gave away the fact that he probably wasn't driving one of those campers with the wide outside mirrors that the runners had to dodge all day, like a matador evading the horns of the bull.

Drake said, "I'm glad to see that you enjoy the finer things in life."

"Thought I'd absorb a little culture while I was up here. Let's stroll over to the pool."

They could talk outdoors without being overheard. There wasn't anything unusual about tourists chatting with each other. Among the Greco-Roman columns that surrounded the pool, they felt as if they had been carried back to an ancient age.

Melody couldn't resist asking about the topic that had occupied her thinking all day. "What did they find out about the boat?"

"Ah yes, you've been out of touch in your own little world. Well, it's going to hit the six o'clock news. What is being published is that it is indeed a miniature submarine, equipped to lob shells of the sort that destroyed the homes in Malibu. It appears that several such shells were fired by it."

Slick paused, prompting Drake to ask, "What isn't being published?"

"All of the written material in the boat is in Russian, including the signs that say, 'Watch your head.'"

"Why is that being suppressed?"

"The president doesn't feel that we have enough information to make it public. There's no sign of a crew, no sign of any enemy ship that might have come in to pick one up. The Navy and Coast Guard have the coast blanketed. The boat has suffered very little structural damage, and wasn't in danger of sinking. Too many things don't make sense."

"You mean the president doesn't want to start World War Three? That's novel. I was young at the time, but as I recall, Roosevelt was aching for an excuse to get into WW Two."

"Don't knock it. Wars hot and cold keep folks like you and me in beer and Porsches. Vietnam's not going to last forever. I know a little bit about your employment history. Both of you had top secret clearances. Which is why Blade authorized me to tell you this stuff. That and he needs your help."

Melody looked at the columns being reflected off Slick's dark glasses and wondered, not for the first time, what color his eyes were. "What does he want us to do?"

"You have access to Casey without arousing suspicion. He's the fair-haired child of the military, because he's got lots of brass on his board. Also, to give him credit, he's delivered weapons' systems on time, within budget, something not all our suppliers do. Of course, he's always looking for new markets. One thing he's developing is a mini sub, similar to the one we found.

"For several reasons, including the coincidence of you being present at both Malibu and Lion Rock, we think he's got a dog in this hunt, but we don't know what his game is. Anything you can find out would be appreciated."

Drake had a thought. "Any idea where the sub was manufactured?"

"It was built using the metric system, but the whole world uses metric except us. That's something we want to find out. Casey's giving a campaign speech on network television tonight at eight. Give it a listen. Maybe you'll get some clues."

Melody said, "We only see Casey when he decides to drop by, and we never know when that will be. He was just here because of Grace's murder."

"He likes Running California, and he likes you guys. He'll show up oftener than you think."

"Where did they take the sub?"

"It's being towed to Monterey, even as we speak."

Drake, newly money conscious, said, "You mentioned beer and Porsches. Is any of that going to filter down to us?"

"To be honest with you, since you're off the books, you may wind up with Green Stamps."

"So we're doing it for our love of humankind. Where are you going from here?"

"Thought I'd take a drive up the coast to Monterey. This rugged beauty turns me on."

ഗ

Drake and Melody ate together but not with any of the other runners, so that they could discuss their role as spies. Actually, double agents in a way, since they were being paid by Casey. They decided that because of the things that had happened so far in connection with Running California, this duplicity didn't bother them, but they didn't come up with any earthshaking plans either.

On their walk back to the motel, they passed a girl sitting on the sidewalk, wrapped in a blanket. She had long, blond, straight hair and a young, pretty face with tears running down her cheeks. She looked at them but didn't say anything.

Drake made a move to go back to her, but Melody grabbed his hand and pulled him away.

"Don't get involved. I say this for your own good. I know you want to help her, and I'm not going to question the purity of your motives, even though it's possible she might offer to thank you in a particularly pleasant way, but she can only bring you trouble. Besides, we're on a mission tonight."

The mission being to listen to Casey's speech. They went to Drake's room to listen to it together, so they could compare notes. Drake ran a cold bath for himself and even obtained a container of ice cubes from the motel dispenser and poured them into the tub. He had learned to almost tolerate the freezing water. He left the door to the bathroom open, which enabled him to hear the speech. Melody didn't object, but she also didn't volunteer to wash his back.

First they listened to news reports about the submarine. These were delivered with an urgency approaching hysteria. It was probably a good thing that no mention was made of the Russian writing found in it.

Somehow, Casey had wangled time on a national network, even though he was running for senator from California. When it was time for him to speak, a network anchor introduced him as the CEO of the company that was instrumental in the nation's military preparedness.

It was obvious from the start that Casey wasn't going to waste his time on California issues now that he had a national pulpit. He immediately started talking about the submarine. He said that the participants in Running California had gone past the spot where the boat was found on the same day, something that had not been mentioned in the news reports. He expanded on that.

"What if that submarine had still been manned? With its armament, it could easily have destroyed some of the cream of California citizenry, just as it killed one of our runners at Malibu, as well as destroying several houses. This is just the tip of the iceberg. There's more—information that has been suppressed by the administration, because it doesn't want to *worry* you unduly, but, ladies and gentlemen, this is information you need to know because it's a threat to national security."

Casey then told about the Russian writing in the sub. Melody wondered how he knew about that. Of course. His military connection. He was getting feedback on everything the military did. She had originally gripped the arms of her chair to keep herself from running into the bathroom and jumping into the tub with Drake, ice water and all. Now she gripped them harder.

She called to Drake. "Did you hear that?"

"Loud and clear. I think we know who our warmonger is."

Casey was just getting warmed up. He came close to saying that a president who didn't defend the country ought to be impeached. Then he talked about creating a buffer zone along the coast—land that would be owned by the government for security, with anti-missile batteries, but would also be a continuous beach during peacetime. Everyone would have complete access to the water everywhere. He was vague about the details.

Drake remembered that Casey had talked about this before. He must be serious about it since he was bringing it up again. Drake ran the water out of the tub and vigorously toweled himself off, trying to bring some circulation back into his frozen limbs. In spite of the discomfort, he had to admit that these baths were helping to keep him going. He threw on some clothes and came back into the main room just as Casey finished speaking.

Melody turned off the television set. "Apparently, he doesn't know that you were the one who spotted the sub. I'm sure he would have mentioned it if he did. That means what you tell Blade isn't getting through to him."

"Blade may be the only person in government who's not in his pocket. But I'm glad our spymaster isn't in cahoots with the person we're supposed to be spying on."

"His bringing up the Russian business when the president tried to suppress it is going to cause an uproar, or my name isn't Miss Marple. That's why I turned off the telly. Flying accusations give me a headache."

"How about that proposed land grab—taking the beach houses of the rich and famous, as well as the rich and not so famous? He's definitely trying to appeal to the masses—telling them they'll have full beach access. They really do now. They just have to work at it in some places."

"Your masses had better start connecting the dots and realize that if the government can take property from people along the coast, they can take property from people inland, as well. One of the reasons I like the U.S. is your strong private property laws, since property rights are mandatory for a free country."

"Unfortunately, we've also got something called eminent domain, which weakens the laws. If Casey can convince us that we're being attacked and land grabs are necessary for our defense, he might get away with it."

CHAPTER 26

Today's run goes from San Simeon to Gorda on Route 1. You'll leave San Luis Obispo County and enter Monterey County. The hardest part of the run is two hills after the county line that rise to over 700 feet. Then you'll dip down close to sea level before climbing to Gorda at 300 feet. Traffic gets lighter as you head north, but be careful, especially since it's Sunday.

ഗ

"DID YOU LISTEN TO CASEY's speech last night?" Melody addressed the question to Tom.

They were running in a pack again, at least for the moment. She suspected this would come to an abrupt halt later in the day when they started climbing the hills. The hills would separate, as she liked to think, the men from the women—or at least most of the men from one woman. The men would not fare well.

"Speech?" Tom was drawing a blank.

Drake raised his voice to include all the runners within earshot. "Did anyone listen to Casey's speech last night or read about it in this morning's paper?"

Apparently not, judging from the lack of response. Drake gave up and turned to Melody. "What we have here is a bunch of political apathetics."

"Unfortunately, what they don't know can hurt them."

Melody and Drake had obtained a San Francisco newspaper that spoke about the controversy Casey had caused by divulging information the president had repressed. The article mentioned that people in the administration were calling for Casey's scalp, saying that he had released classified information, but there was no proof given that it was actually classified.

The other side said that when America's security was at stake, people had a right to know everything. Some members of Congress praised Casey for making the information public. There were calls for an attack on the USSR. An editorial seemed generally favorable to Casey's idea for the creation of a buffer of land between the people and the ocean but said exceptions should be made for populated areas like San Francisco.

"What have we learned about our target?" Drake meant Casey, and kept his voice down so that the other runners wouldn't hear their conversation.

"He is ambitious, like Caesar was supposed to be—only I don't hear a Marc Antony taking his side and denying it."

"He isn't afraid of infringing on the rights of the populace, using national security as an excuse."

"Ever the excuse of those who would wield the power."

"You and I risked our lives fighting against this kind of tyranny. It looks like we're back in the business again."

ഗ

Gorda didn't have much of anything, including motels and restaurants. It did have, as Drake noticed, probably the highest gasoline prices in the country. He and Melody ate dinner with Fred and his new assistant, Charles.

Fred was beaming as they sat down at their table in the small, homey restaurant.

"Congratulations, you two. You're now in fourth place. Are you ready to take a shot at the lead?"

"Sure," Melody said. "I'm spending the evening casting spells on Tom, Jerry, Phil, and Brian to slow them down. It's a good thing I'm a witch."

"You gained a few minutes on both teams today."

Drake made a face. "At the rate we're gaining on them, we'll catch them in a month or so. But, unfortunately, we're almost out of time."

Charles spoke to Melody. "When I drove past you today on that first big hill, you were running away from the men. How do you do it?" His expression was a mixture of awe and admiration.

Melody didn't mind having male admirers, and if they were younger, that was all right too. Maybe she should sample some of that young stuff. After all, Drake had. She gave Charles her best smile.

"I tie their shoelaces together, but I leave enough play so that they don't notice it."

Drake didn't mind Melody having male admirers, but did she have to smile at Charles like that? They were here for a purpose. It was time to get to work.

He looked at Fred. "What did you think about Casey's speech last night?"

"I liked it. He said the things that had to be said. The first job of government is national defense. He'll make a good senator."

Melody's smile changed to an expression resembling cynicism.

"Spoken like a loyal employee of defense contractor Giganticorp. Who's going to take over when Casey becomes senator?"

"Not me, but we have a few candidates in mind."

"Do any of their names start with General?"

Fred laughed. "I can't tell you that. It's a military secret."

Drake's turn. "Do you agree with this buffer zone concept that means uprooting everybody who lives near the beach?"

Fred hesitated. "It's a radical idea, I admit. But…"

"Desperate times call for desperate measures. It's not the first time he's talked about that. I saw on TV that there have even been demonstrations in Malibu by those who want the rich people cleared off the beach. The comments of the demonstrators to the reporter made it sound more like a class struggle than a security measure. If I can't afford to live on the beach, then you can't either."

Fred shrugged and turned to the waitress to order a drink.

CHAPTER 27

Today's run goes from Gorda to Julia Pfeiffer Burns State Park, all on Route 1. The most challenging part of the run is the hill that rises to about 800 feet at Lucia, although the whole route is rolling with repeated gains and losses of 200 feet. Pace yourselves, take it easy on the downhills and carry plenty of liquids. There are a couple of drinking fountains along the route you can use to fill your water bottles. It's Monday, and traffic should be lighter than it was yesterday.

ശ

In spite of the fact that they were now in fourth place and had a shot at third, Drake was unhappy as they climbed the big hill. Not about the race, itself, but the events surrounding the race. Two people connected with the race were dead, including the beautiful Grace. Houses had been destroyed, the submarine that apparently had done the damage found, with evidence pointing to the USSR.

Panic had ensued, fed by the media. Some were accusing the president of doing nothing in the face of imminent danger to the U.S., and a drive to impeach him was taking shape. The president, although upset with Casey for talking about the Russian connection, maintained that the administration didn't have enough evidence to take any action. Russian officials denied any part in the incidents and were accusing the U.S. of heating up the cold war.

Casey was feeding the flames with his rhetoric, apparently for his political advantage. His proposal for a buffer zone along the coast was finding favor among certain groups of people, and the authors of a couple of newspaper op-ed pieces opposing it had been attacked as elitist and unpatriotic.

Drake and Melody were supposed to be collecting information on Casey, but that was hard to do when they were in the wilds of the Big Sur and Casey was off campaigning God knew where. Fred wasn't going to help them. Drake was feeling the frustration of watching negative events unfold in an escalating fashion without having any control over what happened.

Melody sensed his mood and tried to cheer him up. "We've proven to be the best team in the hills, of which we have plenty today. By the end of the day we may be in third place."

"What if we win the race and lose the war?"

"We're not at war yet. Don't count your battleships before they're launched. Enjoy the rugged but spectacular scenery we're running through. Live for the moment. Eat, drink, and make merry…"

"Maybe you're right. About this Merry. Who's she?"

Melody hit him.

Drake laughed. "Well, you've got Charles as a new conquest. We can add him to the growing list, which includes Tom, who's always inviting you for drinks and card games. And Peaches. Speaking of Peaches, since we don't have access to Casey at the moment, maybe it's time for you to have another talk with Peaches. He may know more than he's telling."

"All right, I'll do it. After all, I have to make sure that my conquests remained conquered. All this talking is slowing us down. Let's shut up and see if we can beat everybody up the hill."

ᔕ

Melody decided to dress up for her dinner with Peaches. She had invited him when she and Drake finished the run ahead of the pack and found Peaches waiting for them with the bus. He had been eating dinners alone or with Fred, but not with the runners. Melody indicated that it would be just the two of them. Peaches raised his eyebrows but accepted with no questions.

She was tired of wearing running clothes and sweat suits. She hadn't worn a skirt since the "Pageant of the Masters" way back in Laguna Beach. Even when going out for drinks with Tom and Jerry and a few other runners, she had dressed very casually. In addition, in spite of all the men around, she had been celibate. Other than engaging in a little kneesy with Tom in a bar, she hadn't done anything that would distress a nun.

She put on a miniskirt and a top with a V-neck cut down to here. Backless, it wasn't built to accommodate a bra, so she took the Grace approach and went without. She had no idea what effect this would have on Peaches, the stoic, but figured what the hell, I'm going to do it anyway.

Peaches drove them in the company car to a restaurant some distance from the motel. Both motels and restaurants were so sparse in this area that it was a wonder he knew where it was, but he did. He was the perfect gentleman, even holding her chair for her when she sat down.

Melody took off the sweater she had worn against the fog and chill that had rolled in late that afternoon and draped it over the back of her chair. Since she had chosen to wear this outfit, she wasn't going to hide it or what was beneath it. Since Peaches was wearing a suit, it was appropriate for her to be dressed up.

When the waitress came for drink orders, Peaches ordered iced tea—Melody obviously wasn't going to get him drunk—and she ordered a glass of wine. She pondered how to start a conversation.

She decided on an open-ended question. "What do you think about everything that's been going on?"

Peaches smiled a little and paused. "Casey really wants to be a senator."

That wasn't new or startling information, but Melody sensed there was more behind it.

"Has he been planning to run for a long time?"

"I think that's why Running California got started. He wanted to do something that would bring attention to himself. Fred told me they picked some of the runners very carefully. Tom because he won the Boston Marathon. Drake…"

"Because…?"

"Because of his father."

"Admiral Drake?"

"Admiral Drake is a good friend of Senator Leffingwell, the other senator from California. He's been in Congress for a long time. A word from him could help Casey's chances, according to Fred. Or even if he doesn't say anything negative about him it would be positive."

"Hmmm." Peaches knew more about politics than the runners, at least as far as Casey was concerned. Casey was playing all the angles. "When Drake got into that accident before the race started, it must have really upset Casey."

Peaches took a swig of iced tea and seemed to study the ice cubes in the glass. Melody sensed that he wanted to say something; she decided to wait him out. Finally, he put the glass down.

"On the day the race was scheduled to start, most of the runners had arrived at the border park. I remember that you were there. Drake was one of the few who were missing. Fred usually doesn't do anything physical that he doesn't have to, but he was pacing up and down like he was anxious about something. I didn't notice it so much then because I had just started working with him, but looking back I can see that it was abnormal behavior for him."

Melody tried to think back to that first day, but she couldn't remember anything that had happened before she had received word about Drake's accident. Again she waited for Peaches to continue.

"He kept looking down the road that came into the park. I figured he was just watching for the other runners. He was the one who spotted the fire."

Now Melody remembered. Although she had been some distance from Fred, introducing herself to the other runners, she had heard him yell. She turned and saw the flames shooting up, and her first thought was a fear that Drake had been in an accident. Uncanny, because she didn't claim to have psychic powers. But after not seeing him for six years, she didn't want anything to spoil their reunion.

Peaches continued, "Fred yelled for me to get the car. He had me drive as fast as I could. He kept swearing under his breath, like he knew what had happened. When we got to the taxi, the fire was so hot we couldn't get close to it. He said, 'Are they inside? Can you see if anybody's inside?' That's when Drake yelled from the field. He looked very relieved when he heard Drake's voice."

Peaches stopped again and took another drink of his tea. Melody was confused.

"So what do you make of this?"

"I think Fred knew the accident was going to happen."

"You mean he planned it?"

"He may have set it up, but it would have been Casey's idea. Fred wouldn't have done it by himself."

"But why? Especially if he wanted Drake in the race?"

Peaches shook his head. "I don't know. I've been over it and over it in my head, and I can't figure it out."

CHAPTER 28

More of the same today as you run from Julia Pfeiffer Burns State Park to Palo Colorado Road near the Carmel Highlands, all on Route 1. Early on, the route goes up to over 900 feet and then sharply downhill, bottoming out not far above sea level at the Little Sur River. Then up to 500 feet before falling again. This will be another test of your ability to run in the hills. Watch for traffic; shoulders are often narrow or non-existent.

ᘓ

"How does it feel to be in third place?"

Tom addressed this question to Melody. It was early in the run. Low-lying fog hid the water, and it was hazy enough on the road to keep the temperature cool. The teams were still closely bunched, but they were attacking a major climb. Melody knew from recent experience that by the end of the run, they would be spread out over several miles.

"It feels great; if you and Jerry would agree to walk today's route, it would feel even better."

Tom laughed. He and Jerry still held a substantial lead, and they had an annoying habit of dogging the heels of whoever was in first place during the daily runs and never losing very much ground. Not all the runners were as sanguine about the fact that Melody and Drake had managed to go from ninth place to third place in a short period of time. There were grumblings, especially since Melody was a "girl," but none of the runners had dared to say anything to her face. What could they say—that she had an unfair advantage on the hills because she was lighter? It wasn't as if she were attached to a helium balloon.

Drake, who was running a step behind Melody, touched her arm and motioned for her to fall back slightly.

"Are you going to fill me in on your dinner with Peaches? I expected you to come to my room last night."

"It was fairly late when we got back. I knew you would be going through your routine, and I didn't want to disturb you."

"How thoughtful of you. I take it you two hit it off."

"Yes, we did. Peaches is a gentleman, which makes him a member of a rare breed."

Melody was sure Peaches had enjoyed her company, although he hadn't tried anything, and except for wearing her most revealing dress, she hadn't tried to lead him on. However, she wouldn't mind causing Drake a twinge of jealousy. On second thought, she didn't know whether he was capable of that emotion. Maybe she should just tell him what Peaches had told her.

"One reason I didn't see you last night is because I thought you should be rested when I told you what Peaches said."

Drake was instantly all ears. "What did he say?"

Melody repeated the description Peaches had given of how Fred had acted before and after the accident and Peaches' thoughts about Casey's involvement.

"That bastard." Drake stumbled and almost fell. "So Casey didn't want me in the race, after all."

"If that's true, he changed his mind. But Peaches doesn't think it's that simple."

Melody told how Drake had been picked because of his father. Drake was livid.

"He's not only a bastard, he's a conniving bastard. I'm going to give him a piece of my mind."

"You may get the opportunity. Peaches thinks that Casey is in Monterey. We'll be staying in the Carmel area tonight. Carmel isn't far from Monterey.

ᔕ

Melody insisted on going along when Drake borrowed the company car and drove to Monterey. She was afraid of what Drake might do to Casey. They found out what hotel Casey was staying at from Fred, and after leaving a couple of urgent messages, Casey had called them back and agreed to meet them for dinner.

If Casey was concerned with what Drake wanted, he didn't show it as he escorted them into one of Monterey's finest restaurants after meeting them in the parking lot. Drake let him order the wine before he started talking.

"I want to talk about the accident that happened the day the race was supposed to start."

Casey nodded, apparently unconcerned. "You're fully recovered from that, aren't you?"

"Except for my back. I still have spasms; I'm always going to have to be careful of it. But I want to discuss how it happened. Everybody agrees that it was intentional. That being the case, somebody paid the truck driver to cause it. My contacts tell me that my previous employer had nothing to do with it. Any enemies I might have made in the world would have acted years ago."

"So what do you think happened?"

"One of my contacts has come up with something. All of the evidence points to one person."

"And that is…?"

"You."

Drake's eyes bored into Casey's. He was enjoying this, even though Casey had on his poker face.

"Me? Surely you jest. I'm paying you to be in this race. As they say on Perry Mason, what's my motivation?"

Drake shrugged. "Damned if I know. But then I never did understand all the ins and outs of politics. I think I'll have a talk with my father about this. He's a lot more politically tuned in than I am."

Drake continued to watch Casey. Did he see a slight change in his expression? Had he gotten to him? Casey shifted in his seat. Drake waited for him to speak. Casey took a deep breath.

"I have a confession. I really did want you in the race. When we approached you, you agreed to run, but not with the wholehearted enthusiasm of most of the other runners. I was afraid you'd fall behind and drop out. I needed a way to get you to stay. I decided to frighten you into thinking that someone from your past was trying to hurt you, and that the safest place for you was in the race."

"Frighten me? Hurt me? You damn near killed me."

"That was a terrible mistake. The truck driver was overzealous. I just wanted him to bump the taxi—to give you a warning. He didn't get the right message. Look, I want to make it up to you. Starting today, I'm going to double your per diem to two thousand dollars—a thousand apiece." He managed a smile. "I'm sure you won't have to mention any of this to your father."

It was concession time. Drake would be a fool not to milk it. "There's one other thing you can do."

"What's that?"

"Give Melody and me a tour of the submarine."

"It's off-limits."

"Melody and I both had top secret clearances, as I'm sure you know. You've got a lot of strings you can pull. It's not too much to ask. How about after dinner?"

Casey appeared to be thinking that over.

"You drive a hard bargain. I'll see what I can arrange."

Casey excused himself and went to a payphone.

ဟ

The boat was moored in a corner of the Monterey marina, surrounded by makeshift tarpaulins to hide it from the view of the common people, and guarded by armed sailors in uniform who patrolled the pier leading to it. Casey had apparently talked to the right authorities, because when he flashed his badge to the naval officer in charge, he was waved through, along with Drake and Melody.

Drake wondered what the officer thought about Casey escorting a man casually dressed in civilian clothes and a pretty, miniskirted blond. Melody's youthful good looks had gotten her into places when they worked together that would have been denied to somebody who aroused suspicions.

The boat looked larger than Drake remembered, but he had seen it from a distance. It probably could hold a crew of six, perhaps more. A makeshift gangplank had been extended from the pier to the boat.

Melody was glad she had worn flat shoes with nonskid soles. She and Drake had decided to attempt to find a way to see the boat up close, and so they were prepared. Even the short skirt was part of the plan. When they reached the boat, they had to descend a metal-runged ladder to the interior.

Drake said, "Let Melody go first so we won't be looking up her skirt."

Melody didn't wait for Casey's consent; she swung her foot onto a rung and climbed down as fast as she could. At the bottom she found herself in what must be the control room. The interior lights were turned on; it should be bright enough. She reached into her bra and pulled out a tiny Minox camera that she had used for her work in England. She had brought it to California because it was the only camera she owned.

She began snapping pictures as fast as she could, trying to photograph the instruments and the dials, and anything else that might be of interest. She kept an eye on the ladder. When she saw Drake's legs appear next, she continued shooting. Drake's head came into sight; he gave her an encouraging nod.

When Casey's legs appeared on the ladder, she stopped shooting and slipped the camera back inside her bra. When the rest of him followed, she smiled at him. "This is a lovely boat. But how do the men stand to live in here? Everything's so tiny."

It pained Melody to have to talk like a clueless female, but she had to keep Casey from getting suspicious.

"Submariners can't have claustrophobia."

Drake was inspecting what must be the periscope. "I understand that Giganticorp is developing a submarine similar to this. Can you explain what all this stuff is for?"

Casey could and did. He showed them how a pair of torpedoes were stored and fired. The gun that had lobbed the shells onto the beach was kept inside the sub and raised when it surfaced. They toured the sleeping quarters where you had to be good friends with your bunkmates. They saw a small galley. Drake was interested to note that any food that had been stored there had apparently been taken off the sub when the crew mysteriously disappeared. The crew hadn't left any clothing or other personal belongings either.

Casey's knowledge of the sub was so extensive that Drake became suspicious. Casey said he had been briefed by the people who had inspected it, because Giganticorp was also developing a mini-submarine. But his wealth of information went beyond that. There was almost a fatherly pride in Casey's voice when he talked about all the gadgets and technological wonders.

Drake distracted Casey so that Melody could take some more pictures. She managed to get a few, but she figured that the ones she had taken initially in the control room were the most important. When they exited the boat, Casey and Drake gallantly went up the ladder first, which allowed Melody to take more shots in the control room. She adjusted the distance control, trying to ensure maximum sharpness and duplicated some of her earlier pictures. She knew she'd better stop when she heard Casey's voice from above.

"Are you coming up?"

"Coming." Melody once more shoved the camera into her bra and climbed the ladder. "I wanted to take one last look. I've never been in a real submarine before."

Casey offered her a hand to help her from the ladder to the gangplank, although she didn't really need it. He gave her a patronizing smile.

"I'm sure you're more suited to life on a cabin cruiser, but it's always fun to see how other people live."

ଓ

Drake stifled a yawn.

Slick said, "Are we keeping you up?"

"Damn right. Don't forget—we have to run a marathon every day."

"Sorry. Somehow I figured that saving the country from idiots might be more important."

Drake had called Blade collect from a payphone as soon as they left Casey. When Blade heard about the pictures, he told them that Slick was still in the Monterey area and would meet them in thirty minutes.

He even had praise for Drake. "I take back every bad thing I've ever said about you. You've managed to gather more information than Slick has. The military is a tight organization, and it's difficult for outsiders like us to break into it."

"Credit Melody and her short skirt. Without her we couldn't have done it."

"I won't touch that line with a redwood tree, but give her my thanks. I always said she was too good for you."

Drake and Melody had parked on a residential street and waited for Slick's Porsche to park behind them. He had slipped into the backseat of their sedan where Melody gave him the roll of film. Then they filled him in on what they had observed on the submarine. He also seemed impressed.

"You two must have been a great team in England. What made you give it up?"

Drake and Melody took a quick look at each other in the semi-darkness, lit only by the dome light of the car and a streetlight fifty feet from them. Neither was inclined to say anything.

"All right, sorry I asked. I'll get the film developed tomorrow, and then we will see what we will see."

Slick glanced at a pad on which he had been taking notes.

"There's some good stuff here. I'm not exactly an expert on submarines, but we have people who are. They will be very interested in this."

Melody had a question for Slick. "Do you ever take off your dark glasses?"

"I'd take them off for you, honey. Maybe we should meet sometime without this bozo."

"Maybe we should."

CHAPTER 29

Today's run is scenic (as if they all weren't) and goes around the famous 17 Mile Drive. Enter the Drive at the Carmel Gate. There may be a quicker way to get there than following Route 1 as you get close to the Carmel Gate. Follow the 17 Mile Drive around the peninsula past Pebble Beach and Asilomar, always staying as close to the coast as possible, to the Lighthouse Gate in Pacific Grove. Work your way over to Del Monte Avenue. The run ends at the first intersection of Del Monte Avenue and Route 1 in Sand City.

ℴ

"It's a good thing we don't like to play golf. We might get seduced and stay here forever."

Melody had been taking in the beautifully manicured golf courses along the 17 Mile Drive, some of them set against the cliffs overlooking the ocean.

Drake snorted. "The first question I have is how much money is lost in golf balls that go over the cliffs."

"Spoken like a true nonbeliever."

"I think there's a fundamental difference between golfers and runners. Golfers make a big show out of having the right equipment and the right balls and the right lessons. Then most of them go out and stink up the course while riding in golf carts, which means that they don't even get any exercise. Runners are pure; they don't need fancy equipment. They don't put on a show. They just run."

Melody was laughing so hard that she had trouble running. "Don't let any of the golfers hear you. They'll beat you to death with their nine-irons. I wonder what they think when we run past."

"They feel a mixture of horror and pity, I'm sure. Just the idea that they might get sweat stains on their peacock shirts is more than they can bear."

Melody scanned the road in front and behind them. Every one of the runners was in sight. "It looks like we're having a group event today. Maybe we should have a picnic together on the rocks—practice our togetherness."

"There'll be a chance for individual initiative when we get to Pacific Grove. We'll be running on some side streets. Although it may just be the luck of the draw who picks the route with the fewest lights and traffic. Have you had any more thoughts on Casey?"

"He's certainly trying to buy your silence, at least as far as your father is concerned."

"I'm all for taking his money as compensation for my injuries, but I don't like his political methods. I don't like his agenda either—especially the land grab. I'm not going to vote for him."

"As long as you're in the run and you don't bad-mouth him to your dad, you may be giving him all the help he needs."

"There'll be plenty of time to expose him after the run is over."

"You hope."

ɞ

Drake's message light at the motel in Monterey was blinking. The motel was close to where they had met Casey last night. They could have stayed here both nights, since they had just run around the peninsula that contained Monterey, Pacific Grove, and Carmel, but had not advanced very far up the coast.

Running the 17 Mile Drive instead of bypassing the area on Route 1 had given them maximum exposure. Sometimes people they passed recognized who they were from their Running California shirts and cheered them on. Having them seen by the populace couldn't be bad for Casey.

The message was to meet Slick at a coffee shop in Monterey at six. It was within walking distance of the motel. This left them plenty of time to clean up. Drake called Melody's room to pass the information on to her.

ᔕ

When Drake and Melody walked into the coffee shop precisely at six, Slick wasn't already there. That was a surprise. They went to a booth in the corner and sat down. They sipped iced tea and waited while speculating what his news would be.

At 6:15 Drake started to get restless. "I don't want to sit here and starve while waiting for him not to show. Let's order dinner."

Melody, who had already checked the menu, made a face. "I think this is the original greasy spoon."

"You can always order a salad or something."

Drake wasn't as particular about the food he ate. They both settled for fish and chips since this was seafood country. After all, what can you do to fish and chips? Drench the coleslaw in too much mayonnaise and serve soggy chips. Melody remarked that at least they got the name correct, calling them chips instead of French fries.

"I see you started without me."

They were both intent on chewing mouthfuls of food and hadn't seen Slick approach the table. Drake almost choked on his fish. Melody put her napkin to her mouth to hide the fact that mayonnaise was dribbling down her chin. She recovered first. "We thought you'd fallen off the dock and drowned."

"No such luck."

Slick sat down next to Melody and smiled at the waitress who had bustled over to the table. He ordered a Coke. When the waitress asked whether he wanted to order dinner, he took a look at Drake's and Melody's plates and declined. He sat there perfectly at ease, not apologizing, watching them eat.

Drake said, "Who called this meeting?"

Slick fished around in an attaché case he had with him and pulled out some photographic prints.

"Interesting developments from Melody's pictures, pun intended. Blade wanted me to show you these, especially one." He took his time selecting a print from the pile. To Melody he said, "You're a pretty good photographer, shooting under less than ideal conditions—poor lighting and, of course, you didn't have all day to compose these. This one's a little fuzzy, but if you look at it through this magnifying glass…"

"I'll take all that as a compliment."

She took the print and magnifying glass from Slick. She studied the print for a few seconds.

"I took this on my knees because I saw something near the floor—near the deck, I mean—that caught my eye. It was in a shadow; I didn't know if it would turn out."

"It's good enough so we can tell what it is. It's the Giganticorp logo."

Melody recognized it now because it was on their running shirts: a caricature of a giant inside a letter G. She almost forgot to keep her voice down.

"My God. Are you telling me that Giganticorp built the sub?"

Drake had been impatiently waiting his turn. He reached across the table and more or less grabbed the photo and the magnifying glass from Melody. He peered through the glass until he had it focused on the photo.

"Unless someone's playing games, that's the Big G logo, all right."

Slick smiled smugly, now that he had their attention. "Some things are coming together. We've been able to get our hands on plans for a similar rig that Big G is supposedly just now developing, and there is an amazing resemblance to the description you all gave me."

A thought occurred to Melody. "The military have been studying the sub. Surely they must have seen the logo, too."

Drake said, "Surely they must have. Surely they and Big G are in bed together. It isn't unknown for us to sell weapons to our enemies. We've done it before."

Slick smiled. "You two must have used some kind of leverage on Casey to get him to give you the tour. I'm sure he didn't volunteer to do it. Either he forgot about the logo or figured he'd whisk you around so fast you wouldn't have a chance to see it."

Melody was still trying to figure out what happened. "Do you think Casey and his brass sold it to the bad guys without permission? What are they trying to do, start a war?"

Slick gave a head movement that was almost a nod. "That's difficult to substantiate, but we're working on it."

Drake asked, "Is Casey in hot water?"

"The president has requested that Casey go to D.C. for a little chat. He's flying tonight on the red-eye."

"Is there anything we can do?"

"Keep your eyes open. I suspect we don't know the whole story yet. Not everything jives."

Drake had been thinking about that. "Such as the disappearance of the crew of the sub without leaving behind any evidence as to who they were or where they went. They didn't get picked up by a larger ship, and they made no effort to scuttle the sub so it wouldn't be found. Besides, if there are no mechanical problems with the sub, why did they leave it behind?"

Slick did a full nod. "Good questions all. Thinking makes me hungry. I'm going to order a big piece of apple pie a la mode."

CHAPTER 30

Today's run goes from the intersection of Del Monte Avenue and Route 1 in Sand City to the Pajaro River at the Monterey County/Santa Cruz County line. Suggested route is Del Monte Blvd. to the Fort Ord Bike Path. Pick up the path where Del Monte crosses Route 1 again. Take the bike path to Marina, and then follow Route 1 through Castroville. Exit Route 1 at Jensen Road. Take Bluff Road, Trafton Road, and then McGowan Road across the river. There are no big ups and downs, except for a moderate climb at Zmudowski State Beach a few miles from the end of the run. What we're mostly testing today is your ability not to get lost.

ଓ

"I'LL BET YOU A NICKEL that Casey initiated the first threatening letter. He wasn't in on any betting; he was just trying to scare us into continuing the race. But it gave Fred the idea and he wrote the second letter on his own." Drake had come to this conclusion sometime in the middle of the night when he couldn't sleep.

"It was part of his effort to make sure you stayed in the race. That figures. Threats and incentives. Well, he's succeeded so far."

Melody wasn't sure whether they would do more good staying in the race or dropping out. One aspect of the problem was that she didn't know what part Drake's father played in this charade. Casey certainly didn't want Admiral Drake to know what he had done to Drake. Maybe it was time to speak to the admiral.

"Look, I know you and your father don't get along like strawberries and cream, but don't you think you should ask him questions about his relationship with Giganticorp? We know he's a friend of Senator Leffingwell, but there must be more to it than that."

Drake's father was his Achilles heel. He faced most situations with courage, but he had a hard time facing his father. He mumbled something and tried to think of reasons why it wasn't necessary to talk to the old man.

Tom and Jerry, who had been running a few feet behind them, pulled up beside them now that they were on the Fort Ord Bike Path and didn't have to worry about cars.

Tom grinned at Melody. "We're going to be staying in a populated area tonight where there should be plenty of bars. Would you like to go out and quaff a few? Although I know that in your case it'll probably be some diet drink. I never can get you drunk." He laughed.

"Since you're brazen enough to ask me in front of Drake, don't you think you should invite him too?"

"I didn't think he went out at night." He looked at Drake. "Don't you have to take an ice bath or something?"

"That's what happens when you get old. Listen, you children run out and play. Don't worry about me. As they say in show biz, break a leg."

"In show business that means good luck, but I have a feeling you mean it literally."

"How perceptive of you."

∽

Drake's hands were wet when he put through the phone call to his father from his motel room. He cursed himself for being a coward and hoped like hell that his father wouldn't answer. Maybe he was out drinking with his Army buddies. There must be a few old soldiers in Bakersfield.

"Drake."

Hearing his own name spoken in an authoritative voice always put Drake off, but he recovered. "Hi, Dad."

"Where are you?"

Not "How are you?" or "What's happening?" His father wasn't much on feelings and had never showed any interest in what he was doing.

"Near Santa Cruz."

"Hippie heaven. I hear everybody goes around naked there."

At least Drake had his attention. But he had to be careful what he said. He couldn't talk about the sub or anything classified, even to a retired admiral.

"I'm not sure about that; I'll let you know. The race is going well. Melody and I are in third place. Casey's run for the Senate appears to be going well, too. You probably know more about that than I do. I was wondering what you thought about Casey."

Silence at the other end of the line. It was a simple enough question. His father cleared his throat before he spoke. "Casey is the son I wish I had."

Now it was Drake who couldn't speak. He hadn't been expecting to be hit with a sledge hammer.

The deafening silence went on for several seconds before the admiral spoke again. "Casey has dedicated himself to serving his country. He didn't serve in the military, but if he had, you can be sure he would have been an officer, not just enlisted. He's built up Giganticorp from scratch, and now it's a key supplier of arms and weapons systems for the military. He's not a quitter. He didn't just work for a few years and then decide to hell with it and go off and live in the mountains. Now he's continuing his service to his country by running for the Senate."

Drake couldn't bring himself to say anything that wouldn't be the spark for an already flammable situation. Why had he listened to Melody? Melody, who was out doing things he didn't want to know about with Tom.

With a great effort Drake controlled his voice when he spoke. "I take it you're supporting Casey for the Senate."

"Damn right. He's the best man for the job. He's got voter appeal, too. Family man with a wife and kids. Never had any scandals. Sure, maybe he fools around a little now and then, but what the hell. Just proves he's a man's man."

A *divorced* family man with a second wife. And the other thing his father had said. "Fools around? Who does he fool around with?"

"When I was in Malibu, I mentioned to him what a nice piece of ass that girl—what's her name?—Grace, I think, would be. He smiles a cat-ate-the-canary smile and says yeah, I'm right. Turns out he's been bonking her in San Jose. Then he makes a face and says she started getting uppity and asking for things—promotions and stuff like that. So he sent her on the road with Running California. Say, didn't I hear on the news that she got killed by some mugger? Damn shame. What a waste."

Drake couldn't remember any other questions that he wanted to ask his father. He couldn't think. He couldn't speak. He hung up the phone without saying another word.

∽

Melody was surprised that Jerry wasn't with Tom when she met him in the lobby of the motel. Always before when they had gone out for drinks, both of them had accompanied her. She asked Tom about it. He told her that Jerry's hip was bothering him, and he was going to follow Drake's lead and take a cold bath.

It wasn't a big deal to Melody; Tom was easy to talk to, and they got along well. He was good looking, although his long red hair and slim build made him look a lot different than Drake. They went to an upscale bar where Tom had a couple of beers, and Melody matched them with diet drinks.

They chatted about the race. Tom joked that he and Jerry always had to keep Drake and her in sight so they wouldn't gain too much on them in the overall standings. Only it wasn't a joke. He talked about the cushy job he had in Redding with a car dealership, sort of a sponsorship that allowed him to keep running.

When Melody asked him how he felt about Casey's proposal to create a buffer zone along the coast, he shrugged. They didn't talk about the submarine or Casey's run for the Senate. If Tom was a barometer, none of the runners had an interest in politics.

They left the bar early. Melody paid for her drinks. She always made a point of paying her own way. They had borrowed the Giganticorp van because that was the vehicle that was available. When they got into the van, Tom suggested that they sit in one of the back seats and chat for a bit.

Melody knew that chatting wasn't what he had in mind. In a backseat they could sit right next to each other. But she felt itchy and went along with it. He put his arm around her and started kissing her. She went along with that, too. She hadn't done anything like that for some time, and he was a good kisser.

When he slid his hand inside her shirt, she went along with that because she was horny. It wasn't until he tried to unfasten her bra that she put a stop to it.

Tom looked upset. "What's the matter?"

"Sorry. I can't do this. I have to get back."

It was tawdry, too much like teenagers shagging in the backseat of an old car.

Tom argued; Melody refused. It occurred to her that she had the opportunity to do something to him that would knock him out of the race. Maybe break a bone in his foot. Justified mayhem. The idea sounded so funny to her that she burst out laughing.

Tom quickly slid away from her and looked hurt. "What's going on?"

"Nothing." Melody controlled her laughter. "Just a thought I had. It's not you. Here, give me the key, and I'll drive us back."

CHAPTER 31

Today's run goes from the Monterey County/Santa Cruz County line to Bonny Doon Road and Route 1. It's a longer run than usual, but everyone is in such good shape that it shouldn't be a problem. The challenge is to find the best route through Santa Cruz using a combination of San Andreas Road, Soquel Drive, and Mission Street to Route 1, or perhaps some combination of the Cliff Drives (East, West, Opal) that go closer to the beach. Hint: At some points it may even be advantageous to run on the railroad track (watch out for trains) to cross creeks and shorten distances.

ഗ

TODAY IT WAS PHIL AND Brian who were dogging the footsteps of Drake and Melody. The latter two had gained time on the former during the past few days. Phil and Brian still had a grip on second place in the standings, but that grip was not as tight as it used to be.

Tom and Jerry were nowhere in sight, having taken a different route somewhere along the way. Melody was sure she knew why. She and Tom had parted on less than cordial terms last night, and he was avoiding her. She was confident that she had made the correct decision about spurning his advances, because his absence didn't greatly bother her. Taking different routes could change the amount of time that separated their teams, for better or worse, depending on which team found the faster route.

Phil was complaining about Fred. "He hasn't given us a day off in forever, and now he expects us to run a long course."

Drake wasn't feeling sympathetic. "You have to be willing to endure a little pain for a million dollars."

Not to mention the per diem they were all receiving, although Drake and Melody received twice as much as the others and had been paid for a longer period of time.

Brian was one of the youngest in the race. "I'd like to spend a couple of days here in Santa Cruz. It's got tons of girls and topless beaches. I hear there's a viewing place call Peeper's Point. I hope we go by that."

"You sound just like my father."

The others looked at Drake, especially Melody, because of his tone of voice. He hadn't mentioned his conversation with his father to her yet this morning. She hadn't told him about her evening with Tom, either. She slowed a little, dropping behind Phil and Brian. When Drake dropped back beside her, she spoke for his ears only.

"I take it you talked to your father last night."

"Talk is too optimistic a term. Words were spoken, but I wouldn't describe it as a conversation." Drake couldn't speak of his father's statement about Casey being like a son to him. That was too painful. But he needed to bring up Grace, even though that also produced pain. "My father must be on chummier terms with Casey than we are, because he told me a story I haven't heard before."

"About Casey?"

"Yes. He told me that Casey and Grace had been having sex together."

"Grace? She never told me that. Do you think he was making it up?"

"One thing about my father is that he doesn't make things up. As one of his navy buddies once said, he is without guile. Which means he's also without tact, but that's another story. In any case, Miss Grace wasn't the innocent she appeared to be."

"As her roommate, I can tell you that she wasn't all that virginal. She had the hots for you from the start. I can't say I'm terribly surprised to hear about her and Casey. But it adds a new dimension to Grace's murder. What if Casey had her killed because she was threatening to make their liaison public? He's running for the Senate and can't afford to have a scandal like that brought out in the open."

Drake took a swig of Gatorade before he spoke. "I was thinking about it last night. If Casey hired somebody to kill Grace, it's going to be almost impossible for us or anybody else to prove it. But what if—"

"He killed Grace himself?" Melody's heart rate increased beyond that required by her running, and she slowed down to compensate. "Do you think that's possible? He said he was staying in Los Angeles and attending a convention there."

"Let me tell you a story. When I was in the army I was stationed for a short period of time at Camp Roberts, which is near Paso Robles, just north of San Luis Obispo where Grace was killed. I went to Los Angeles for the weekend to visit my mother. I was due back at Camp Roberts at noon on Monday. I figured I would be able to drive up Monday morning if I left early.

"My alarm didn't go off, and I overslept. By the time I woke up, it was a cinch I would be AWOL. However, I already had enough black marks on my record and didn't want any more. I decided I was going to make it. All I had was an old Chevy, not the Lincoln Continental that Casey was driving on the day Grace died, but I was the fastest thing on the one oh one that morning. I may hold the land speed record between L.A. and Paso Robles, with the possible exception of James Dean and his Porsche, although if I recall correctly, Dean drove up the inland route and hadn't made it to Paso Robles when he was killed."

Melody smiled. "I saw *Rebel Without a Cause,* and I suspect you liked Natalie Wood better than James Dean, but let's get back on track. Are you saying that Casey could have driven from L.A. to San Luis Obispo, killed Grace at about five a.m., driven back to L.A. where he received the message about Grace's death, and been able to claim that he hadn't received it earlier because he had been at a breakfast meeting?"

"Yes, and with time to stop for gas and coffee. It couldn't be much more than two hundred miles from the L.A. Airport to the motel where we were staying. Driving back he wouldn't have to slow down before

Santa Barbara, which has approximately four traffic lights on one oh one. He would have gone through there during early rush hour. Then it would be clear sailing until he hit the Los Angeles commuter traffic."

"No wonder he fell asleep when he was driving us back from the restaurant. All right, you've convinced me. How do we prove it?"

"We need to get hold of the record for the car he rented and find out how many miles he drove. It was from Avis, if I recall correctly. Although everybody is getting more and more automated these days, I suspect that each office has a handwritten copy of each rental agreement, including mileage. He would have rented it at the Avis office near the L.A. Airport."

"What are you going to do, call Blade and have his people look into it?"

"No. Even Blade would have to jump through hoops to get permission or a search warrant on this one. I have to do it myself. Phil said he needs a day off. That means all the runners need a day off. We're going to besiege Fred and get one tomorrow. We've got a good argument. There are only three running days left. We need a rest day so we'll be ready for a big finish. I'm going to fly to L.A. for the day."

"I'll go with you. You may have the beauty, but I have the brains."

"Fine. Let's catch up to Phil and Brian and plot our strategy for dealing with Fred."

CHAPTER 32

"How long have you worked for Giganticorp?" Melody asked Charles.

Fred's new assistant was driving the company car. He changed lanes to pass a truck. "It'll be a year in October."

"How do you like working for Big G?"

"It's wonderful. Great place to work. Interesting jobs, lots of opportunity for advancement…"

Since all the employees gave the same line, there must be some truth to it, Drake reflected. "How do you like Casey?"

"Mr. Messinger? I haven't had much contact with him, but when he sees me in the hall, he smiles at me and says hello. He must be a nice man."

Fred had volunteered to have Charles drive them to the San Jose Airport. After Fred agreed to give the runners the day off, he decided to send Charles to the corporate headquarters in San Jose on some errand, since they were so close, even though it was Saturday. This meant that Melody and Drake didn't have to rent a car or find some other means of getting to the airport.

Drake wondered whether they had exhausted Charles' fund of information about Casey.

"I guess Mr. Messinger travels a lot."

"I guess so. He seems to be gone most of the time."

"Are you aware of it when he's on a trip?"

"Naw. I work in another building. It's not my job to watch him." Charles laughed.

ᔓ

They flew T&A Airlines to LAX, so called because the stewardesses dressed provocatively, including wearing hot pants. Drake knew the rule about not ogling other women when you were with one, but he snuck surreptitious glances at the sexy young ladies, even while a small area in the back of his brain that he usually tried to suppress asked whether this was the correct corporate culture for a public company.

They had no luggage, so they walked off the plane directly into the Los Angeles summer sun. They boarded one of the Avis vans that circled the airport and arrived at the Avis lot a few blocks from the terminal within minutes. They wore their Running California jackets with the Giganticorp logos, thoughtfully provided by Big G. Drake wore a tie borrowed from Peaches. Melody wore a skirt, a blouse, and pantyhose. They strode confidently into the office.

They waited in line for an available agent. When it was their turn, they went up to the counter. The agent was a woman, so per previous agreement, Drake addressed her with a big smile.

"Good morning. We're with Giganticorp, the L.A. office. Our president, Casey Messinger, recently rented a car here. There were some questions about the rental, but, unfortunately, the invoice has been lost. We'd like to get another copy."

The woman went behind a partition and brought back a man who was evidently the manager. This time Melody repeated the story to him. When he heard the Giganticorp name, he seemed to become more alert.

"I'm Andy Teller. We at Avis appreciate your business. What was the date of the rental?"

"August eighteenth."

"Let me check."

They twiddled their thumbs while the man disappeared behind the partition. Minutes passed before he returned empty-handed.

"Our records are in a bit of a mess, but I couldn't find it. Are you sure it was the eighteenth?"

Drake hit the side of his head with his hand.

"You know what? We may have that wrong. It may have been the seventeenth."

The man disappeared again.

Melody said, "If we keep changing the date, he's going to get suspicious."

"Keep your fingers crossed." Drake suited action to the word.

The man was shaking his head when he reappeared. Melody said, "Do you keep track of rentals by customer? The president's name is Casey Messinger."

"We do that on the computer at the corporate office. We have to put in a request to get the information overnight. I could have it for you tomorrow."

"Too late. It's a shame, because Mr. Messinger really loves the service that Avis gives. He always tries to rent a Lincoln Continental."

"Did you say Lincoln Continental? We've only had one of those on the lot recently. We keep our records by car, too. Let me check that file."

More agonizing minutes went by. Drake remembered that one thing he didn't like about the spy business was the time spent waiting for something to happen—for example, waiting for the person under surveillance to make a move. When the man finally returned, he was smiling and carrying some paperwork.

"I'm glad you mentioned that it was a Continental. Mr. Messinger rented it on the eighteenth and turned it in on the twenty-first. I don't know why I couldn't find it the first time."

He handed Drake the copy of the invoice. Drake looked the sheets over quickly. The starting and ending mileage were recorded.

"Thank you very much. We knew that Avis would come through for us. That's why our corporate policy is to rent from Avis. We wouldn't rent from anyone else."

They both shook hands with Andy Teller and walked outside. Melody smiled. "Our corporate policy is to rent from Avis? We wouldn't rent from anyone else? When you get going, you really sling the bull."

"Hey, we got what we came for, didn't we? Now, onward to the Hilton. It's only a few blocks from here."

"Nice day for a walk. Or would you rather run to stay in shape?"

They walked. Casey had mentioned that he always stayed at the Airport Hilton in L.A. The hotel stood amid a number of others with familiar names to travelers, on the traffic-heavy Century Boulevard. Once inside, they employed the same strategy they had with Avis. Melody spoke to the male desk clerk.

In response to his "Good afternoon," she responded, "Good afternoon" and recited the story of Casey staying there and needing a copy of the paperwork. Fortunately, she now knew that he had probably been registered for three nights starting August eighteenth.

The desk clerk found the information and made a copy, all within five minutes. That was interesting, but not what they really wanted. Melody thanked him, thought for a moment, and then spoke again.

"When Mr. Messinger stayed here, he was very impressed with the service he received from one of your maids. He asked us to give her something."

Drake flashed a twenty-dollar bill.

"Do you know her name?"

"Unfortunately, Mr. Messinger never caught her name."

The desk clerk checked the room number on the bill and made a phone call. Two minutes later he hung up the phone in triumph.

"Her name's Cecilia. I'd be glad to see that she gets the money."

He held out his hand.

Melody said, "Mr. Messinger asked us to give her the money in person, along with his thanks. Is she working now? We don't want to take her away from her work, so we'd be more than happy to go to the floor she's on."

The clerk didn't see anything sinister about that. He ascertained Cecilia's whereabouts with another phone call and directed them to the fifth floor. They took the elevator.

They found her in one of the rooms changing the bed. She was young and attractive, although the gray maid's uniform didn't do anything for her. They knocked on the open door to gain her attention. When she looked up, Drake spoke, telling her they were from Giganticorp and how pleased Mr. Messinger had been with her service.

She looked surprised. "Mr. Messinger? Yes, he was here, but I not see him much. Wait." She blushed. "I see him when he was leaving. He ask me to come into the room. He give me a big tip." She pronounced it "teep." "Then he pat my ass and tell me I'm a good girl."

Melody couldn't restrain herself. "He patted your…ass? Weren't you offended?"

"If he give me a big tip, he can pat anywhere he wants."

Drake reached out the twenty to her. "He wanted me to give you this."

"But he doesn't get to pat anything," Melody said quickly.

Cecilia laughed and thanked them.

Drake said, "You mentioned that you didn't see much of Mr. Messinger when he was here. Did he actually stay here all three nights, do you know?"

"It is funny. The first morning when I come in to make the bed, I see that it has not been slept in. The second morning it is the same. I think he only sleep here one night."

Drake and Melody looked at each other. Melody smiled at Cecilia. "Thank you, Cecilia, for…giving such good service."

ᔕ

While they were waiting for their flight back to San Jose, Drake called Blade collect from an airport pay phone. He had left his office, but the woman who answered patched the call through to another number.

Blade came on the line. "Aren't you calling a little early? You're slipping. You didn't even wake me up. What are you doing, taking the day off?"

"Hardly. It's true we didn't run today, but Melody and I are in Los Angeles investigating the perambulations of our mark."

"Yeah? What did you find out?"

Drake quickly filled him in on what they knew and suspected about Casey's activities on the day of Grace's death. "He put five hundred miles on the car that aren't accounted for, even though we know he drove to San Luis Obispo once. That's enough mileage to cover a second trip there."

Drake also repeated what Cecilia had told them about Casey not sleeping at the Hilton until the third night of his reservation. "The second night he slept in San Luis Obispo. We know that. But the first night he apparently didn't sleep anywhere."

When he finished speaking there was silence on the other end of the line. Drake waited for Blade to say something.

He did after a ten second pause. "Sounds like you've got a good circumstantial case against our friend. Unfortunately, we can't convict on that. Even if an investigation showed that he was lying when he said he was attending a breakfast meeting around the time the girl was killed, that's still not enough. You haven't placed him at the scene or produced a weapon."

"If we can't convict him in a courtroom, we may do it on our own."

"Do *not* take any independent action. This is still a nation of laws, although it may not seem so at times. You two are doing a good job. Keep at it. But talk to me before you do anything foolish."

Blade's usually carefree manner had disappeared during that speech. Drake knew he was serious. He decided he'd better back off. "Well, the least you can do is to reimburse our air fare."

"What, and encourage you to flit around the country? It's a good thing you two are rich."

"By the way, how did our friend's chat with the president go?"

"He speaks softly, but he may be carrying a big stick. However, we can't make accusations about him without something to back them up."

CHAPTER 33

Today's run goes from Bonny Doon Road in Santa Cruz County to the intersection of Route 84 in San Mateo County near San Gregorio State Beach, all on Route 1. The terrain is relatively flat, compared to some of the hills you've seen in the past. Now that you're rested from your day off, it should be a day of high-speed running. You'll be close to the water and see lots of pretty beaches.

ᘓ

"THIS IS NOT WHAT I signed up for."

Drake couldn't tell who had uttered the complaint. The timbre of the voice behind him was changed by the headwind that was sapping the strength of the runners. It was also blowing sand in their faces, creating the illusion of being jabbed by hundreds of tiny needles. Some of the runners were trying to counteract the sand by wearing caps with the bills pulled low to protect their eyes, but sudden gusts of wind blew them off with regularity.

Drake, who was wearing dark glasses, turned to Melody who didn't seem to be affected by the elements. It was almost as if the wind and sand sailed right through her body without touching it. He felt a tinge of envy. "If we get any closer together we'll all have to get married."

"We're huddled like a herd of zebra on the Serengeti fending off a pride of lions."

Nobody wanted to take the lead and face the brunt of the wind and sand. As a consequence, they ran slowly with the lead changing often, the runners who were farther back being sheltered to some extend by those in front. Drake and Melody were content to stay with the group as long as they didn't get stepped on, because breaking away in the headwind would sap their strength at a disproportionate rate.

Because they were so close to the others, they couldn't talk about Casey. They had discussed him on the plane ride back to San Jose without reaching any conclusion as to what to do. Being quite certain that he had killed Grace and being able to prove it were two different matters. They felt frustrated and had an urge to become vigilantes, taking matters into their own hands, but as Blade had pointed out, they couldn't do that.

ಌ

Drake had barely entered his motel room when the phone rang. He was tired from running into the wind most of the day and didn't feel like speaking to anyone. After the third ring he figured he'd better answer it.

"Drake."

"Turn on the telly, channel seven." Melody's voice sounded urgent.

"Are we about to be hit by a meteor?"

"Worse. Just turn it on."

Drake hung up and clicked on the television set. When the picture appeared on channel seven, Casey's face filled the screen in glorious black and white. It took Drake a few seconds to understand what he was talking about. He heard the words "impeach the president" and "martial law," before he realized that although he didn't say it in so many words, Casey was advocating the overthrow of the government.

His pitch was that the U.S. was under attack by an unnamed "foreign power," and that this fact had not been acknowledged by the president who had attempted to hide the truth, leading one to infer that the president was in cahoots with the enemy. If the president refused to take action, it was up to the American people to defend themselves by enabling the military to take proper defensive measures. The country needed a strong leader in a time of peril.

Casey didn't say who this leader might be, but anyone watching the broadcast who bought what he was saying would come to the obvious conclusion. Casey mentioned his complete dedication to the well-being of his country, as exemplified by his design and production of weapons essential for the country's defense for the past twenty years. Almost tearfully, he said that he didn't want the efforts of all those who labored for peace at Giganticorp and in the armed forces to go to waste. In closing, he called for the country to unite, and without mentioning Winston Churchill by name, he paraphrased a few sentences from his "This was their finest hour" speech.

Drake angrily turned off the television set. What rubbish. Everybody would see Casey for the fraud he was. Twenty seconds later Melody burst into the room without knocking.

"Did you hear all that?"

Drake made a mental note to lock the door when staying at a Mom-and-Pop motel without automatic locks. "He's lost his north. He's gone off the deep end. Fortunately, nobody's going to go with him."

"Tom is."

Tom? Tom who? It took Drake a few seconds to realize that Melody was referring to Tom the runner.

"How do you know that?"

"He was in my room." Melody decided she'd better explain. "He was apologizing to me."

"For what?"

"For acting boorishly. What does it matter? The point is, he agrees with Casey. He was nodding his head and making comments while Casey was speaking. Tom is a smart, well educated man. If he agrees with Casey, how many other people are going to?"

Was it true that there were a lot of people who wouldn't see through Casey's naked grab for power? Who would be so concerned for their own safety that they would allow it to happen? Before Drake could reply to Melody, the phone rang.

"Drake."

"I'll be outside your motel in an hour, driving an inconspicuous Ford sedan."

There was a click and the line went dead. Drake stared at the receiver. Melody did too.

"Who was it?"

"Slick. He'll be here in an hour."

"That was fast. He must not be far away."

"Probably in the San Jose area. He's been investigating Casey, just like we have."

ေ

"Casey can't just mount a coup and take over the government. This isn't some fifth-rate country with flies and bribable officials. We have a constitution. The president is Commander in Chief of the armed forces."

Drake had a lot more he could say, but he didn't want to work himself into a state of apoplexy. Slick was driving them from the middle of nowhere to the middle of somewhere in the roomy Ford sedan. At least he didn't have his Porsche. With traffic momentarily clear in front of them, he glanced at Drake and Melody, both sitting on the bench seat beside him. "What you say is theoretically true. But what if…"

"What if what?"

"What if the armed forces don't obey the president?"

"That won't happen."

"What if the generals and admirals have an allegiance to a greater god?"

"You mean Casey? Why would they?"

Melody said, "Because the president is talking about ending the Vietnam War, or at least the U.S. involvement in it. He wants to downsize the military. Even if the Cold War continues, that doesn't get nearly the support of a hot war. The military may see a diminishing role for itself in the world."

Slick nodded. "If Casey can manufacture another war and scare enough people along the way, there's no telling what can happen. People may even support a temporary suspension of the Constitution."

Even though he was appalled at the idea, Drake knew Slick could be right. "Temporary usually becomes permanent."

Slick pulled into the parking lot of a restaurant. "My daddy told me never to eat at a place called Mom's, but when the alternative is starvation, I think we can make an exception."

In fact, the sign over the entrance read, "Mom's Café," and underneath it, "Good Food." The "F" was almost obliterated. It might just as easily have read "Good Wood" or even "Good Mood."

Once inside and seated, Drake asked, "What happens now?"

There was a pause as a waitress showed up and took their orders. They tried to order the least bad alternatives from a greasy menu. The place didn't have a liquor license, so Drake had to settle for coffee to drink.

When the waitress left, Slick spoke. "We need to discredit Casey with the American people. To that effect, we're leaking the story of Casey as a possible murderer, even though there's no proof. If we do it right, the press will eat it up."

Melody said, "What about the fact that Giganticorp manufactured the submarine?"

"That's a tricky one, although we've verified that they did make it. The accusation would be that they sold it illegally to the USSR, but we haven't been able to dig up any evidence that it actually happened that way, and we've got pretty good connections within the USSR. We need to do some more work on it. That's where you two come in."

"Can you leak that it was manufactured by Giganticorp and let the press run with it?"

"No, because it might backfire on the administration. The president could be accused of making deals with the enemy."

"Okay, what do you want us to do?"

"You..." Slick indicated Drake, "...have one of the best connections to the military."

"You mean my father? He thinks of Casey as his long lost son."

"Look, I know that's painful for you." Slick actually looked empathetic, if a macho man wearing dark glasses is able to look empathetic. "It can also help us. Admiral Drake knows—or can find out—things that you can't. The intelligence we're looking for is the whole story behind the sub and the attack."

Drake felt miserable. "My father doesn't confide in me."

"*Au contraire*. He told you about Casey's liaison with Grace."

Melody tried to come to Drake's rescue. "If we go to Bakersfield to see Admiral Drake, we'll have to quit Running California. That will blow our cover that gets us to Casey."

Slick smiled. "Blade doesn't want you to quit the race. Of course, you're getting paid to run also. There's nothing like receiving money from the enemy, is there, as long as it doesn't affect your judgment. We're in luck. I've found out that Casey is calling a meeting of the officers on his board for tomorrow to plot strategy. He's also asked Admiral Drake to come. He badly wants the admiral on his side."

"Where's the meeting being held?" Drake asked.

"Giganticorp headquarters in San Jose. Which is convenient because at the end of tomorrow's run, you'll still be south of San Francisco, within spitting distance of San Jose. I can furnish you a car and anything else you need."

"So all I have to do is somehow set up a meeting with my father when he's tied up with Casey, and then get him to tell me all of Casey's secrets."

Slick beamed. "You've got it in one."

CHAPTER 34

Today's run goes from the intersection of Route 84 and Route 1 to Thornton State Beach. Take Route 1through Half Moon Bay and continue to follow it until it becomes a freeway south of Pacifica. Follow surface streets to Route 35 (Skyline Boulevard). Follow Route 35 to Thornton State Beach. There are several interesting climbs, including one right at the beginning of the run, another after Montara, and a nice steep one at the end of the run. This is the next to last day of the race, so if you're going to make a move, it's now or never. Enjoy.

ഗ

THE HILLS ACCOMPLISHED WHAT THE wind and blowing sand yesterday hadn't been able to do: separate the runners. Drake and Melody had taken the lead on the hill at the start of the run and hadn't relinquished it. It gave them a chance to talk without anyone overhearing. Drake was trying to figure out how to contact his father.

"Even if I could reach him by phone, the chances of us having an intelligent conversation are nil."

"Then we'll have to go to where he is."

"You don't have to go. This is my job."

"I know how hard it is for you. The least I can do is give you moral support."

"If we just show up at Giganticorp, what then? I'm sure Casey has a full schedule planned for the troops, including dinner. We can't just cut my dad out of the herd."

"Maybe that's what we'll have to do. Now let's see if we can gain some time on the leaders."

ஐ

Slick picked up Drake and Melody near their motel in Daly City and drove them a few blocks to a rental car company. Their drive on to San Jose was complicated by the pre-rush hour traffic heading south out of San Francisco on Interstate 280. Drake grumbled as he had to slow down for a number of large trucks.

"Now I know why I chose to live in Idyllwild. There aren't any freeways there."

"We need to put a plan together on what to say to your father."

"If we even get to talk to him."

"We will. If necessary, we'll enlist Casey's help. He needs to stay on our good side."

"Does he? Not if he's already won Dad over."

Their discussion continued until they arrived at what was called the Giganticorp campus. It looked like a college campus. They drove in the main entrance between two square, brick posts with a sculpture of the Big G logo in dark metal standing on top of each one. Multi-storied buildings sat in isolated splendor in front of them, separated by large expanses of manicured lawn, dotted with carefully tended trees. The buildings were modern and not ivy covered, but they gave the effect of wealth and stability.

Signs with arrows pointed toward various buildings. Drake and Melody followed the direction of the arrows as they drove along the blacktop roads. A number of sprinklers came on as they passed one section of lawn, showering the grass and creating miniature rainbows with the help of the afternoon sun. They arrived at the administration building and parked in the ample lot.

They climbed the marble steps and went through the glass doors into a reception area that featured a round counter directly in front of them. Two men and a woman walked briskly past them wearing suits.

The woman's suit consisted of a blue skirt and jacket combination and a white blouse with a red sash instead of a tie.

Drake and Melody wore their Running California jackets. Drake wasn't wearing a tie, and Melody wore slacks. Drake felt under-dressed. A pretty young lady sat inside the circle of the counter. As they approached, she stood and greeted them with a bright smile. She asked how she could help them.

Drake said, "I'm Oliver Drake, and this is Melody Jefferson. We're part of Running California."

"Oh, yes." The woman's smile grew even brighter. "I recognized your jackets when you came in. Now I see that you look just like your pictures, except you're not in running clothes. It's so nice to meet you. I'm Thelma. We've been following your progress in the Giganticorp newsletter. A lot of us are rooting for your team. How did you do today?"

"Thank you." Drake turned on his smile. "We finished first. We're very close to the second place team, overall, within two minutes, I think. I don't know how the first place team did today, but we weren't within striking distance of them this morning."

"Good luck tomorrow."

"Thank you again. The reason we're here is because we heard that one of the participants in the meeting that's taking place is my father, Admiral Drake. We came to see him."

"Right. Let me call Mr. Messinger's executive assistant. Just a minute. Have a seat."

Thelma pointed to several chairs in a nook a few feet away. When Drake and Melody started toward them, Thelma sat down at her desk and made a short phone call they couldn't hear. Then she came out from behind the counter and walked over to them.

"Melinda is coming down to help you."

They thanked her. Thelma turned to Melody and started asking her questions about the race. It was obvious that her interest in their team was because of Melody. Several elevators stood in a row on the wall behind the round counter. Within a few minutes, one of the elevator doors opened, and a perfectly groomed, middle-aged woman with dyed blond hair stepped out wearing the skirt-and-jacket uniform.

She came toward them with her hand out.

"Hello, Mr. Drake, Miss Jefferson. I'm Melinda Gage. I'm very pleased to meet you."

Drake and Melody stood and shook hands with her.

"Congratulations are in order. I hear that you're only five minutes behind Tom and Jerry going into tomorrow's final run."

Drake was stunned. "Where did you hear that?"

"We get a report from Fred immediately after each day's run. Tom and Jerry got lost in the wilds of Pacifica, and by the time they sorted themselves out, they had given up a lot of time to you and the Phil and Brian team."

Melody was ecstatic. "I don't wish them any bad luck, but it's nice to have a shot at the big money."

Melinda smiled. "It will be an exciting finish, with three teams vying for the crown. Now, how may I help you?"

Drake suspected she already knew the answer to that. "We've come to see my father, Admiral Drake."

"Did he tell you he was going to be here?"

What should he say?

Melody spoke first. "When we heard about the meeting, we assumed he'd be here."

"Who told you there was going to be a meeting?"

Her tone was matter-of-fact, but her overall demeanor had chilled considerably. Drake was on his guard. "Can't remember. Did we get it wrong?"

"I'm afraid so. I'm sorry you came all this way for nothing."

"Is Casey, er, Mr. Messinger here?"

"Mr. Messinger is out of the office. But, of course, he'll be at the finish of Running California tomorrow. A big celebration is planned. You can talk to him then. Good luck tomorrow."

"Thank you."

Drake and Melody exchanged a quick look. Melody made a barely noticeable movement of her head toward the door. There was nothing more for them to gain here.

They thanked Melinda again and made as graceful an exit as possible. Once outside, they headed for the rental car. They climbed into the car, which was facing the front door of the building.

"What do we do now?" Melody asked.

"Maybe Slick had his information wrong. We should probably go back to the motel and get ready for tomorrow. Not to make too big a deal out of it, but we've got a million dollars riding on whether we win or lose."

"Let's check in with Slick or Blade first and tell them what happened. I saw some pay phones inside."

"Bad idea to go back in there. Melinda's already suspicious of us. In fact…who's that coming out the front door?"

It was a stocky man in a somewhat ill-fitting suit. Melody put their thoughts into words. "He's another Peaches, and I don't think he's a friendly Peaches. He's looking for us. I think he just spotted us."

"I think we're outta here."

Drake backed the car out of the parking spot and slowly but steadily drove away. They exited the Giganticorp campus and headed for a commercial part of town a few blocks away, stopping in front of a small restaurant. Once inside, Melody procured a corner booth while Drake went to a payphone and called the number he used for Slick collect.

The operator was told that Slick wasn't available. Was there a message? Drake said no. He gave the operator Blade's office number, hoping he was there.

Blade answered the phone by saying the number and accepted the charge before the operator could get the words out of her mouth. "I was hoping you'd call, you son of a bitch. Where are you?"

"San Jose." Drake outlined the problem in two sentences.

"This whole thing may be more serious than we thought. If they're holding secret meetings, that may mean something is imminent. Okay, here's what we think is happening. We think Casey wants to make some sort of important announcement coincident with the ending of Running California tomorrow. He's getting his generals in a row tonight. What you've just told us confirmed some other stuff we've learned. We don't think the meeting is on the Big G campus."

Drake was annoyed. "Then where is it?"

"Big G has a corporate hideaway in the mountains about thirty miles east of San Jose. They take their employees there to play bonding games and participate in other juvenile activities. Slick is headed there right this minute to find out what's going on. I talked to him just after he left you—unfortunately, too late to catch you. He's going to observe what he can, but he has to stay out of sight. He can't move in with guns blazing. What we need is someone who knows the players to infiltrate the meeting."

"Meaning me?"

"You're not on the payroll, and I can't order you to do it. After all, there's not much at stake here except the future of the United States of America and the free world."

Perhaps; perhaps not. There was *no* question that a million dollars might be riding on what he did tonight. "You're making this sound like the big time. If our man tries to take over, will people go along with it?"

"If they're scared enough, they will. The media have certainly been playing up the fear factor."

"How do you want me to proceed?"

"Don't do anything until we hear from Slick. Is there a place where you can get something to eat?"

"We're at a restaurant."

"Get some food inside you so you'll be prepared. I'm going to give you a number where you can reach me. Call it in thirty minutes. In addition, give me the number there."

Drake exchanged numbers with Blade and hung up. He had Melody move to a booth close to the pay phones, so if it rang he could answer it. He sat down opposite her and quickly filled her in, adding, "I'll go alone. We'll find a way to get you back to the motel. Maybe a taxi—"

"Belay that. I'm coming with you to make sure you get back safely. The run tomorrow doesn't start until ten, and it's a short one. We'll be there with bells on."

When Melody made up her mind about something, there was no use arguing with her. Drake mentioned that what they were doing could be dangerous, but she had faced danger before. It didn't faze her. They ordered dinner and ate.

In thirty minutes Drake called Blade. Blade hadn't heard from Slick and told Drake to call back in another thirty minutes. Drake and Melody ordered dessert. They talked about what they would do if they split a million dollars. The prospect wasn't real to them. Yesterday it had been almost out of reach. But on the hills today they had gained valuable minutes on both the teams ahead of them. Having Tom and Jerry get lost was serendipity. Maybe, with a superhuman effort tomorrow…

The pay phone rang. Drake stood and reached it in four long steps. He lifted the receiver and spoke softly.

"Drake."

"The meeting is in progress. Slick had to come back quite a distance to find a phone he could use. It's just your average ten thousand square foot rural retreat. He'll meet you near the entrance. I'm going to give you the directions on how to get there. Do you have pencil and paper?"

"Yes."

At least Drake had the back of the paper mat that had been set at his place at the table. He wrote down the directions with a cheap pen he always carried with him.

CHAPTER 35

Five minutes later they were in the car headed east with the dome light on so that Melody could read the scribbled directions. They started climbing through pine-scented woods. After a while they turned off onto a dirt road—stopped to verify that it was the correct dirt road—and then continued for a number of uphill miles.

"Slow down," Melody said. "That may be Slick's car ahead."

The car was parked on the other side of the road, facing them. The sun had set and it was dark in the woods. Drake pulled in front of the other car so that they could read the license plate using their car's headlights. Yes, it was the Ford that Slick had used to chauffeur them last night. Drake pulled around it and made a U-turn. He had to maneuver back and forth several times on the narrow road to complete the turn. He parked behind the Ford and turned off his lights. Drake and Melody got out.

Slick emerged from the Ford. The first thing Melody noticed about him was that he wasn't wearing his dark glasses, but it was too dark to see what color his eyes were. He stepped between the two cars to get off the road and pointed in the direction they had been heading.

"The entrance is two hundred yards from here. There aren't any guards at the entrance, but there are at least two inside the grounds. I got close enough to the building to look in the windows. Casey is there along with a bunch of grayheads. They were sitting around a big table. Dressed in civvies, of course, but I recognized your father and the Chairman of the Joint Chiefs of Staff from pictures I've seen. This is a high level meeting."

"How many are there?" Melody asked.

"At least a dozen, probably more. I'm sure I didn't see them all. It's your ballgame. How do you want to proceed?"

Drake said, "The only way this has a chance of working is the innocent approach. I'll walk up to the front door and try to crash their party. You two stay hidden. You'll be my backup."

Melody started to say something, but he glared her into silence.

"Hopefully, I'll get inside and start greeting people. 'Hi, Casey, hi, Dad, a little bird told me you were here. Thought I'd drop by and say hello. Can't stay long; got a race for a million dollars tomorrow, but maybe we can chat for a minute.'"

When he said the words out loud, he realized how lame they sounded. But what choice did he have? They walked along the road to the entrance. What impressed Drake was how dark it was. No outside lights shone on the grounds. Clouds covered the moon and stars. Slick had a flashlight, but he would need it more than Drake because he and Melody were remaining outside. Slick also had a gun, which he offered to Drake, but Drake knew that carrying a gun would be ineffective and counterproductive.

Slick pointed to a couple of lights faintly visible in the distance through the trees.

"Those lights are coming from the windows. You can follow the driveway. There are several vehicles, including a bus, parked along it. I heard two guards talking at one point, but I could barely see them. I didn't want to cause a commotion by taking them out, so I waited in the trees until they went away. Be careful when you're walking. It's dark as the inside of a whale's belly."

Drake's eyes were still getting acclimated to the dark. He could make out a few vertical trunks of trees but not much else. They decided that Slick and Melody would wait for thirty minutes. If Drake didn't appear by then, they would take whatever action they deemed appropriate.

Melody gave Drake a hug. "Don't do anything I wouldn't do."

"Not a chance."

Drake started walking slowly along the driveway, keeping his hands in front of him, feeling for real and imaginary obstacles. After a few steps he looked back, but Melody and Slick had already been swallowed by the night. The driveway was uneven gravel; Drake had to watch his footing to avoid twisting an ankle. Wouldn't it be ironic to run over 500 miles without injuring his legs or feet, only to have it happen here?

He wished he could see as well as he could smell the woodsy scent of the pine trees. It reminded him of hiking with his father when he was young. Those days were gone for good.

He didn't see the bus until he almost ran into it. Strange, because the dark was a gray color, not black, and he had the illusion he could see more than this incident suggested. He redoubled his caution. If he could just get inside where he could make contact with his father, he should be safe.

The driveway curved; he couldn't head straight for the lighted windows because tree trunks partially obscured his view of them, and he suspected that the ground among the trees was rough. He found one car and then another. He must be following the same route that Slick had followed.

Nothing blocked his view of the windows now. He could walk directly toward them. He saw people inside, but he was too far away to recognize anybody.

Suddenly he hit the ground. He had tripped over a rock and fallen forward so fast his hands had failed to protect him. Judging from the all-encompassing pain, he had hurt his head and just about everything else.

He lay on the ground for several seconds, trying to determine what parts of him were operational. He heard a noise and saw a light sweep over him. He rose to his knees but was blinded by the light, which was now shining directly in his eyes. The voice behind the light spoke. "What are you doing here?"

Drake was at a disadvantage. He couldn't see his questioner. He remained silent. He felt something running down his forehead. He must have cut himself. Blood was heading toward his eye. He reached for his pocket that contained a handkerchief.

"Don't move."

The man thought he was going for a gun. He raised his hands to show they were empty. Better to have blood in his eye than a bullet. The man spoke to somebody else. The second man appeared in the light of the flashlight. He walked up to Drake and roughly twisted his hands behind him one at a time, handcuffing them together.

"Get up."

Easier said than done. Drake rose slowly and awkwardly, feeling pain in both knees as he did. The man who had handcuffed him patted him down, searching for weapons. He grabbed Drake's arm and urged him forward. The other at least had the courtesy to shine the flashlight in his path so he wouldn't trip again. He walked slowly, not having his hands free to protect himself. He could see with one eye; the vision of the other was blurred by the blood. They escorted him around a corner of the building and down a dirt slope strewn with pine needles and the occasional rock.

One opened a door and then pushed him through the doorway. A light was turned on. Drake could see through a window that the guards had also turned on the outside lights. They were in what looked like a recreation room. It had wood-paneled walls. Drake saw a pool table and another for table tennis. He determined that this room was on a floor below the one where the conference was in session.

Drake turned and looked at his captors. They were big men wearing suits. The one holding the flashlight held a gun in his other hand. How many of these people did Casey employ?

A round table—perhaps for playing cards—sat along one wall with chairs surrounding it. The man without a gun turned around one of the chairs and indicated that Drake should sit in it. When Drake didn't move fast enough to satisfy him, he shoved Drake into the chair. Drake's handcuffed hands hit the back of the chair, but he repressed an epithet. He had to do something to even the odds.

"Okay, you can take the cuffs off now. I need to wipe the blood out of my eye."

The man peered at his forehead. "You'll live. You don't need to see."

It was time to play his ace. "I came here to see my father, Admiral Drake. He's in the meeting upstairs. My name is Oliver Drake. I'm part of Running California."

The men looked at each other. The one with the gun laughed and said, "Nice try, Jack."

"I'm wearing my Running California jacket."

"Any idiot can buy one of those things. They're for sale all over the place. I got one for my boy."

"My wallet is in my front right pocket. It has my identification."

The men looked at each other again. Drake was trying to use the tone of somebody in command. Men like these were used to taking orders. The man with the gun nodded to the other one who pulled Drake's wallet out of his pocket and checked his I.D.

"He's got a California driver's license, says his name is Oliver Drake."

The man with the gun looked at his watch and said to the other guard, "We're not supposed to interrupt the meeting unless it's really important. It's probably going to go on for another hour."

Drake couldn't wait an hour. The world as they knew it could end by then. "I've got information that concerns Mr. Messinger and everybody in that meeting. They need it now."

"I thought you came to see your daddy."

"That too."

The man with the gun looked skeptical, but he also realized that his job was on the line if he did the wrong thing. "Take off his cuffs and let him clean himself up. I'll go up and talk to Mr. Messinger."

With his hands free, Drake was allowed to use a bathroom that opened off the recreation room. He went inside and shut the door. It didn't have any windows, so he couldn't escape, even if he wanted to. He wiped the blood from his eye and forehead with a paper towel and examined his head in the mirror. The cut should probably have a couple of stitches, but it had pretty much stopped bleeding. As the man said, he would live.

He came out of the bathroom to find that the man without a gun now had a gun. They still didn't trust him. He tried to engage the guard in small talk but found that his supply of small talk was very small. Drake sat back down in the chair and waited for Casey.

In a short time he heard footsteps coming down the stairs at the other side of the room. Casey appeared, followed by the guard. Casey was dressed in sport clothes. He spotted Drake and came striding across the room.

"Drake, what are you doing here?"

"I heard my father was here, so I thought I'd come and say hello."

"What happened to your head? Did *they* do this to you?"

"No, I tripped in the dark."

"Sorry. I forget how dark it gets."

He spoke to the guard who had been watching Drake.

"Bennie, you can go back on patrol. Keep those outside lights on. We don't need another accident." And to the other one, "Artie, wait just outside the door and keep it open."

Bennie and Artie went through the outside doorway. Casey pulled one of the other chairs away from the table and sat down, facing Drake. Drake measured the distance to the stairs from where he sat and from the doorway. The doorway was closer to the stairs.

Casey said, "As you apparently already know, I'm holding a meeting here tonight."

"If I could just speak to him for a few minutes—"

"How did you find out about it? Did your dad tell you?"

"No. I…" Drake stopped, not having a ready answer.

Casey eyed him closely. "What are you doing here, anyway? You should be resting tonight. Tomorrow's the final leg of the race, and you've got a shot at a million."

"I thought this was more important."

Casey didn't ask the obvious incredulous question. He appeared to be mulling over what to say. Drake waited for him to speak first, which he did.

"I get the feeling that you're not wholeheartedly behind me."

"I don't like to see the Constitution trampled."

"I'm not here to have a constitutional debate with you, but as you know the founders of our country sanctioned rebellion in defense of freedom."

"Defense of freedom? You're overthrowing the government in the name of freedom?"

"Freedom from attack by a foreign power."

So many rebuttals came to Drake's mind that he was momentarily speechless. "Isn't that the job of our duly elected president and members of Congress? And another thing. You talk about freedom, and yet you advocate taking the property of everyone who lives on the coast."

"They will be compensated."

"But what choice do they have? What's next, taking everyone else's property 'in the national interest'?"

"Speaking of interest, it's in your interest to join us. I've got the top military brass here, including the Chairman of the Joint Chiefs. We're the winning side, Drake. By tomorrow morning, we'll control the government."

"The military is under civilian control. The president is the Commander in Chief."

"Starting tomorrow I'm going to be the civilian control. But don't worry. It's a bloodless coup. This will become the Western White House. I'm expecting you to finish the race. You'll collect your per diem, and you've got a shot at really big money. Besides, there's a place for you in my administration."

"Let me talk to my father."

"Sorry, there's no time for that right now. I've got to get back to the meeting. I'm going to have Artie keep an eye on you until the meeting's over. I suggest you rest in that reclining chair over there, try to get some sleep. After the meeting we'll get you back to your motel."

It couldn't be as simple as Casey said. Typically, overthrowing a government required lots of bullets and bloodshed. But if he had the military behind him… Drake remembered something.

"It's not a completely bloodless coup, is it? What about Grace?"

Casey looked surprised, then cunning. Finally, he shrugged. "There are always a few casualties along the way."

Casey stood up and walked toward the outside door. As soon as his back was turned, Drake stood and started for the stairs. He took several quiet steps and then accelerated into a run, slowed by knee pain. He saw Artie running to cut him off. Damn. The guard hadn't been napping. Artie must have played football, because he hit Drake with a solid tackle. Drake's knees hit the floor, exacerbating the injuries he had received from his previous fall.

Before he could move, Artie put the gun to his head.

"I liked you, Drake. I really did." Casey said the words to Drake and then whispered something in Artie's ear. Artie put a knee in Drake's back and handcuffed him while Drake listened to the clop of Casey's shoes as he ascended the stairs.

Drake said, "What happens now?"

Artie said, "In five minutes we're going outside."

Drake didn't have to ask where. Into the trees and far enough from the lodge that the people inside wouldn't hear a shot.

CHAPTER 36

"The lights have been turned on." Melody stated the obvious, partly to get Slick talking. He hadn't said two words since Drake disappeared into the dark. The spotlights were located all around the building and also along the driveway.

Slick grunted. "Don't know if that's good or bad for our boy. It's for sure he's made contact, though."

He looked at his watch with the aid of his flashlight. "Maybe I should go in there and see how he's doing."

Melody was having trouble waiting also. "We'll go in together."

Slick shone the flashlight on her feet. "Can you get around in those shoes?"

A typical male question. She didn't have sneakers on, but they weren't that bad.

"At least they aren't heels."

"It'll be easier walking with the lights, but we've got to take extra care. Stay behind me."

Melody was willing to do that. They approached the building, walking in the woods parallel to the driveway, so they wouldn't be illuminated by the lights. Slick was able to use his flashlight to keep them from stumbling over roots and stones. Nobody would see it; the other lights drowned out its beam.

The trees ended at a cleared area surrounding the building, which was set on a hill, sloping up to the right. Slick stopped when he came to the edge of the trees and surveyed the open space. The lit windows were directly across the clearing from them. They were closed against the cool air of an evening in the mountains. Melody could see people inside, but her view was limited. She couldn't tell whether Drake was among them. They didn't see anybody outside.

Slick pulled out his gun. "Do you know how to use this?"

It was a standard nine millimeter. Melody nodded. She had been trained in the use of small arms. He handed it to her.

"Cover me. I'm going to see if Drake's inside that room."

Before he could move, a man came around the corner of the building to the right and uphill from them, obviously a guard. He walked slowly along the wall, illuminated by the floodlights on the building. He passed the lit windows and was approaching the closest point to Melody and Slick.

Slick whispered, "Before, there were at least two."

They couldn't worry about the other one. Melody handed the gun back to Slick.

"I'll distract him and you can take him from behind."

She walked out of the trees, angling so it would appear that she had come up the driveway. She called to the guard, but not loudly enough that she would be heard inside the building.

"Excuse me, sir. Can you help me? I'm lost."

The man whirled around, his hand reaching inside his jacket. When he saw Melody, he paused and withdrew his hand without a gun.

"What are you doing here?"

"I'm lost. I saw your lights. I think I got on the wrong road."

"Come here."

Melody didn't move. She tried to look helpless. The guard approached her slowly, looking around for anyone else. Slick was still hidden in the trees. Melody turned her body so that the guard would have his back to Slick when he talked to her. The man was still wary, but he kept coming. Melody smiled at him.

"I knew you'd help me. I'm trying to get to San Jose. Do you know the way to San Jose?" She almost sang it.

"You shouldn't be here all by yourself."

He came up to her. Melody focused on his eyes, but with her peripheral vision she could see Slick come out of the trees. She stepped close to the guard and launched into a confusing story about where she had been and where she was going, speaking loudly so that the man wouldn't hear any noise inadvertently made by Slick.

Slick was just a couple of steps away when the guard sensed something and spun around, his right hand reaching for his gun. Melody grabbed his arm and pulled on it with all her weight. Slick hit him on the head with his pistol. The man went down in a heap. Slick pulled the gun out of his shoulder holster. The man moaned.

"He's just stunned. Put this in his mouth."

He handed Melody a handkerchief. She stuffed it into the mouth of the semi-conscious man. Slick produced a roll of tape. She securely taped the guard's mouth shut with pieces of tape handed to her by Slick, making sure he wouldn't be able to loosen the tape by moving his jaw.

Slick taped the man's arms behind him and then taped his legs together. He picked him up by the shoulders; Melody grabbed his feet. They dragged him into the trees and dumped him in the fetal position. He wouldn't be seen from the building. Slick handed the guard's gun to Melody.

"You can cover me with this."

The gun was similar to Slick's. Melody checked to make sure it was ready to fire. Slick took a look around; nobody else was in sight outside. He walked toward the windows, bending over so that he wouldn't be seen from inside. He peeked through the windows from several angles and then jogged back to Melody, still keeping his body low.

"No sign of Drake. Looks like business as usual. I saw Casey; he's doing most of the talking. There are several men in uniform, probably staff to the Chairman. I'll bet they're armed."

Melody said, "We need to get inside. The door on this side is adjacent to the room they're in. Too close to them, especially if Drake's not there. The building has several floors. If we go around to the right up the hill, maybe there's a door to the floor above them. I'd rather be above them than below them."

Slick approved the plan. Since no other guard had shown up, they headed up the hill in the cleared area. Melody wished she were wearing her running shoes. She was in danger of losing the ones she had on because of the rough ground, but she didn't say anything to Slick. Once they were past the line of sight from the windows, they followed a sidewalk close to the building. Walking on the concrete was easier. As they came around the corner of the building, they saw the door they were looking for. The window near it was dark.

Slick tried the handle. It was locked with a simple lock. He had a couple of thin metal strips attached to his key ring. He opened the door in less than a minute. They went inside and found a light switch by feel. A number of ceiling lights came on. The room was large, with all kinds of equipment in it, including blankets, bed linen, pots and pans, and other kitchen utensils. It had a stove and sink. There was also electronic gear of some sort. The room was furnished with a long table with chairs around it. Half a dozen cots were lined up along the far wall, made up for sleeping with military precision. Schematic drawings of what looked like a submarine covered another wall.

Melody was attracted to several manuals she saw sitting on a bookshelf. They looked familiar. She walked over to one and glanced at the cover. She gasped and opened it up.

"Slick. Look at this."

Slick ambled over and came as close to showing emotion as Melody had seen from him. "If I'm not mistaken that's Russian."

"This is identical to a manual Drake and I saw on the sub."

"Proof that Big G is dealing with the Russkies."

"Worse. It's proof that Big G made the attack on Malibu. This was a training room for the crew. They slept here; they studied here."

"Ah, the light dawns. Casey faked the attack to aid his quest for power."

"I remember now. A helicopter flew along the beach just before the attack. It must have been communicating with the sub, telling it when to fire to catch the tail-end of the runners. Killing one was acceptable to Casey, because it helped rouse the public to demand security."

"I wonder if those generals and admirals downstairs know about this."

"I doubt it. They're trained to defend their country, not attack it."

The only inside door leading from the room was to a bathroom. The training center was isolated from the rest of the building. Melody and Slick went back outside and continued around the building in a counterclockwise direction, looking for another way in.

CHAPTER 37

Drake walked slowly toward the doorway, trying to stall as long as possible. Where were Melody and Slick? He had lost track of the time. He had allowed this two-bit guard to get the best of him. Now he would die for the cause of freedom.

Millions of Americans had died for freedom already, but his was a useless death because Casey had won. He felt the pressure of Artie's gun in his back. Drake faked a limp to gain time and wondered how he could disarm Artie while handcuffed without getting himself killed.

He stepped outside into the cool night. At least the floodlights on the building allowed him to see. He took a step to the left toward the front of the lodge where Melody and Slick would be most likely to spot him. Artie grabbed his arm and roughly swung him in the opposite direction toward the lowest corner of the building.

Still moving slowly, Drake reached the back corner. Beyond and downhill from them were trees. They were headed away from the road and away from civilization and any chance for help. Drake glanced over his right shoulder, ostensibly to glance at his captor, and swept his eyes uphill along the back of the lodge, looking for a sign of Melody and Slick.

In that split second, he thought he saw a movement. He wasn't sure, and didn't dare look again, because he was afraid of directing Artie's attention behind the building. Even if it were a person, it might be that other guard on patrol.

Artie suddenly pulled him away from the corner, so that they were no longer visible from the back of the building, and directed him downhill in a slightly different direction. Even if what he had seen was some combination of Melody and Slick, if they hadn't seen him at that exact same moment, they wouldn't know he was here.

Drake whistled the same four warning notes that Melody had used to warn him about Sterling's gun in the motel room: C, F, G, A. Then in rapid succession he added the next four in the sequence: F, B flat, A, G. They had made up lyrics for the notes: "He's got a gun; this isn't fun."

Artie hit him on the side of the head with said gun, almost knocking him over, and growled, "Shut up."

Drake stumbled and wished his hands were free to help him regain his balance on the downhill slope.

ᔓ

"There's somebody down there." Slick spoke softly. Melody followed his gaze toward the downhill corner of the building; she didn't see anything. They had just been trying to look in a window, but it was dark inside. They were contemplating breaking the glass to gain entrance.

"It could be another guard. Stay behind me."

Slick moved silently downhill, keeping his gun in front of him and his body hugged against the wall of the building.

Melody heard the eight notes clearly in the still night. They sliced through her body like a scimitar. "That's Drake. He's in trouble."

She ran past Slick down to the corner of the building and looked around it. She saw two figures by the glow of the spotlights, heading downhill toward the trees. The one in front was stumbling, and it appeared that his hands were tied behind his back. Drake.

Slick came up behind her and looked over her shoulder.

Melody whispered, "A guard is taking Drake toward the woods. I bet he's going to shoot him."

Slick sucked in his breath. "We can't storm them, or Drake gets it. I'll go left. You go right. We'll approach from either side."

"Hurry."

Slick had to go uphill a bit to approach them from the left side. Melody's route was downhill; she went as fast as she could while making a minimum of noise and keeping a low profile. Fortunately, Drake and his guard were walking noisily. Drake was undoubtedly doing it on purpose.

She sped up as the two reached the trees, knowing that it would be more difficult for the guard to spot her now. How far was he going to take Drake before shooting him? Only far enough that the noise of the gun wouldn't alert the men in the meeting. It was dark in the woods, but the guard had turned on a flashlight. Melody worked her way toward its beam, being careful not to trip over a root, knowing that she and Slick had to act fast.

ဢ

Drake knew that the end was near. He had to take some action, not go out like a pantywaist. He was just about to try to knock Artie over when he heard the first two notes of the code he and Melody used. They came from close by on the right. He immediately dropped to the ground.

Artie swung his flashlight in the direction of the notes. Two gunshots came from the opposite direction. Artie swung the flashlight in a 180 and pointed it toward where the shots had come from. He fired in that direction as more shots came from there and behind him.

Artie grunted and dropped the flashlight, but he was still standing. Now Melody and Slick wouldn't be able to tell where he was. Drake could see by the peripheral light of the flashlight, now lying on the ground, that Artie was aiming the gun at him. He was going to make sure of his original objective.

The beam of another flashlight zigzagged rapidly toward them from the left, along with the sound of somebody crashing through the brush. It must be Slick. Artie whirled and fired toward the beam. There was a thud, and the flashlight disappeared. Another shot came from almost right beside them. Artie staggered as several more shots followed it.

Artie was still on his feet. Melody was having a problem aiming in the dark. Artie turned and was about to fire at Melody who couldn't be more than five feet away. Drake braced his arms on the ground beneath him and lunged upward with his feet toward where Artie's gun must be. He managed to kick the gun, deflecting its aim as Artie fired.

Melody was now right beside them. She put her gun to Artie's head and fired one more time. He dropped to the ground. She kept the gun aimed at him, but he didn't move. She carefully picked up the flashlight and shone it on his face. She spoke in a shaky voice. "I think I got him. He wouldn't go down."

She pulled Artie's gun out of his hand.

Drake said, "Good job. Are you okay?"

"Yes, and you?"

"Fine but handcuffed. I think he hit Slick."

Melody took the flashlight and went to find Slick. Drake struggled to his feet and followed her. Slick was lying on his stomach at the base of a tree with his head to one side. Melody knelt beside him and called his name. She put her fingers to his neck.

"He's still alive."

Drake said, "We have to get help. And tell the brass about this."

Melody shone the light on Slick's face. She noticed for the first time that he had beautiful blue eyes.

"I'll stay with him. Maybe I can help him."

Slick spoke so that they could barely hear him. "Go with Drake. Tell them about the training center."

"You need help."

"Go. Stop the craziness. Don't worry about me."

Slick lapsed into silence. Melody tore her eyes away from his face and stood up. She shone the light on Drake and saw his handcuffs.

"We need to find the key and set you free."

"Later. We've got to work fast. Let's get to the meeting."

She directed the flashlight ahead of them, and they carefully walked out of the woods. A trio of uniformed men, lit by the floodlights, came toward them from around the corner at the front of the lodge, waving handguns.

Drake said, "Drop your gun."

Melody was still carrying it, unconsciously. She let it fall to the ground.

The men spread out and covered the two. It was obvious that they were itching to shoot somebody. Melody raised her hands. Drake realized that they must be aides for the Chairman of the Joint Chiefs.

He turned so that they could see his handcuffs and spoke to the officer with bars on his shoulder.

"Casey's man just shot a government agent."

Melody pointed at Drake. "He's the son of Admiral Drake. The guard was going to shoot *him*."

The three looked confused. That could be dangerous. They needed to be won over. Drake tried again. "Casey's trying to overthrow the government with the help of the military. Giganticorp built the submarine."

That wasn't news. Melody interrupted. "Casey planned and carried out the Malibu attack. The USSR had nothing to do with it."

The three looked more confused. Melody continued. "The top floor of this building was used as a training center for the sailors of the submarine. They're probably all Americans, but we saw training manuals written in Russian to deceive us."

The soldier who was wearing captain's bars spoke. "Are you saying that Casey—Mr. Messinger—engineered this whole thing, and that there's no threat from the USSR?"

"That's correct." Drake was relieved that he had caught on. "We need to talk to your boss."

"Where's the agent?"

"In the woods. He's hurt bad. That direction. The guard is there, too. I think he's dead."

The captain turned to the other two soldiers. "Call for help. There's a phone in the rec room. Find the casualties and do what you can for them. I'm going to take these two to talk to the Chairman."

Melody gave her flashlight to one of the soldiers. She and Drake went up the hill, followed by the captain, and around to the front of the building. They went in the main doorway; they could hear voices coming from the next room—or rather, Casey's voice.

"…need for us to fill the void left by the government and provide national security, the first job of any government. If the president won't step up to the plate…"

CHAPTER 38

CASEY STOPPED TALKING AS THEY entered the room. A dozen heads swiveled to stare at them. The bodies beneath the heads were clad in civilian clothes. The captain spoke to one of them.

"Two men have been shot in the woods, sir. One is a Giganticorp security guard. The other is a government agent. Ferguson and Baker are calling for help and assisting them. The situation is under control."

The man the captain had addressed looked at Drake and Melody. "Who are these two?"

"We've got intelligence about the Malibu operation, sir. This is Mr. Drake. He's the son of Admiral Drake."

All eyes were on Drake and on his handcuffs. He must look a proper mess with the gash in his forehead and a lump on the side of his head.

The men were sitting around a long, rectangular table. Casey was at the far end. He glowered at Drake but didn't say anything. Drake spotted his father whose expression registered disbelief. Drake directed his remarks to the man the captain had addressed. He must be the Chairman of the Joint Chiefs.

"Melody and I have been working with undercover agents to get more information about the Malibu incident. One of these agents was just shot by Casey's guard. Casey told me this was going to be a bloodless coup."

Drake paused to let that sink in. "You're trying to protect the freedom of the U.S.A., which is admirable, but you're doing it in such a way that we, the citizens, will lose our freedoms. You've been led to believe that we've been attacked by an enemy power. The president wanted proof, but some decided that he wasn't doing his job. I'm here to tell you that the president is right."

Drake hoped that Melody knew what she was talking about. She almost always did. He parroted her words about the training operation in the building. Casey tried to interrupt him. The Chairman told Casey to shut up.

When Drake paused, the Chairman spoke. "Of course we're going to investigate the room you're talking about. This is a very serious charge. If true, it completely changes things—"

"If I may, sir…"

All eyes turned to Admiral Drake, including the Chairman's. "My son and I haven't always seen eye to eye. But I'm proud to say that there are at least two things we agree on. We both love our country, and we both tell the truth. If Oliver says that Casey is behind the Malibu incident, I believe him. I've had a sour taste in my mouth ever since I arrived at this meeting. I haven't been able to reconcile my respect for our founding fathers and the Constitution with what we were doing. I'm glad my son arrived to shock me back to reality. I will no longer have anything to do with what has been referred to as Casey's plan."

There were murmurs of what might be agreement from around the table. Casey was desperately searching the faces of the other men for support. Those faces were turned away from him. Drake decided to seize the opportunity. He addressed the Chairman. "Sir, I need to make a phone call. I have to call the boss of the agent who was shot."

"In Washington?"

"Yes sir, in Washington."

"Of course, the news will be relayed immediately to the president. Not yet, Mr. Drake. Before we do anything else, we're going to have a look at this so-called training room."

"General, I'd be happy to give you a tour of the room in question."

All eyes turned toward Casey. He had composed himself and projected his usual aura of confidence.

"Admiral Drake gave a very pretty speech about his son, and I'm sure what he said about Drake's veracity is correct. I, myself, have gained the utmost respect for him during the race. However, his information about the training room is incorrect. You see, Drake, himself, has never seen the room. He is relying on what somebody else told him—what is known in law as hearsay."

Casey paused. The silence was palpable as the assembled officers waited to hear what he would say next. Melody knew it would be difficult for her to get the attention of this roomful of testosterone-charged males. Seeing the training room for themselves would provide all the evidence they needed, especially the Russian manuals. Casey couldn't prevent that. What was his game?

Casey continued speaking. "Drake is correct in saying that this is a training facility. It is used for training the men who are testing the submarines Giganticorp is developing. I admit that we built the boat that was used in the Malibu attack. We lent it to one of our allies for testing. How it fell into the hands of the Soviets, I don't know. I was remiss in not reporting this sooner. I take full responsibility for this omission, and we will cooperate fully in any investigation."

Casey was trying to get himself off the hook by confessing to a lesser crime. As the officers rose from the table to walk up to the training room, Drake asked the captain, who was keeping an eye on him, if he could get his handcuffs taken off. The young officer shook his head. It would be a messy process since they didn't have the key. This was not the time.

Drake had to acquiesce to this, but he was determined to go to the training room. Casey was too slippery. He had fooled the officers so far. Drake eyed Casey as the latter rose from his seat at the head of the table with a half-smile on his face. Drake didn't like what he saw.

Drake and the captain trailed the others heading outside, except for Melody who was a step behind them. As soon as they were in the open air, Drake whistled all four lines of the tune he and Melody used as a signal, softly, so that only Melody and the captain could hear him: C, F, G, A; F, B flat, A G; C, E, F, G; E, A, G, F."

"What song is that?" the captain asked.

"Just a schmaltzy tune we sang when we were kids. 'The wind is free and so are we; we'll stake our lives on liberty.'"

ᔕ

Melody had no doubt about Drake's meaning. Casey had a gun. Apparently in his pants pocket since he was wearing a short-sleeved sport shirt. It must be small—Grace had been killed by a small-caliber bullet. Small, but at close range, deadly. Drake didn't trust the captain enough to tell him. Perhaps he was afraid the captain wouldn't believe him. They weren't convinced that Casey and not Drake was the enemy—yet.

As they walked uphill alongside the building, Melody lagged behind, trying to be inconspicuous. The captain didn't pay any attention to her. They rounded the corner; Casey had already unlocked the door to the training room and was leading the officers inside. Drake and the captain followed them. Melody stayed outside in the dark, against the wall, projecting her head past the door frame only far enough so that she could see Casey.

Casey had his back to her and was declaiming about the facility—pretending to tell how the training took place. He sounded believable, but then he always sounded believable. So far he had managed to keep everybody away from the bookcase containing the Russian manuals. But the men were starting to wander around on their own. It was just a matter of time…

Casey beckoned to the Chairman, indicating that he wanted to show him something. Melody saw him pull the gun, but it happened so fast there was nothing she could do. She was too far away. He put the gun to the head of the Chairman and told him not to move.

"Gentlemen, your attention please. I am holding a gun on the Chairman of the Joint Chiefs. Captain, kindly drop your gun belt to the floor and kick it away from you."

The captain looked stunned and did as he was told.

"Thank you. And thanks to the meddling of people like Drake, it appears that we can no longer work together. Fortunately, I am prepared for this contingency. Giganticorp has recently purchased a corporate jet, which is at this moment fueled and waiting at the San Jose Airport with a pilot standing by. I am a planner by nature, and I tried to plan for everything."

The other officers looked as stunned as the captain. Melody couldn't see the Chairman's face, but this probably wasn't his finest hour. He and Casey had their backs to the door. Drake spotted her, and his expression was calculating, but, handcuffed as he was, there wasn't a lot he could do. Melody was in the best position to attempt something, but she had to be careful not to get the Chairman of the Joint Chiefs killed. Casey spoke again.

"This is how it's going to play out. Drake's handcuffs are the ones used by my guards. Fortunately, I have a key to them." He reached into a pocket with his free hand and extracted it. "Colonel Kilgore," he indicated the smallest officer in the room, "you are going to take the handcuffs off Drake and put them on the Chairman. If anybody tries anything, the Chairman dies."

As this procedure was carried out, Casey explained that he was going to drive the Chairman to the airport. The plane was in a private area, and Casey could drive directly to it. The Chairman would be his passenger on the flight, which was to an unnamed country. If any planes were sent in pursuit of them, the Chairman would die. If they arrived safely, the Chairman would be sent back to the U.S.

The Chairman finally found his voice. "Don't worry about me, boys. Just get Casey."

Casey jabbed the gun against his head, making him wince. Of course the others wouldn't do anything to endanger his life. Casey had picked the correct hostage. Melody looked at Drake who now had his hands free. But what could he do? As Casey prepared to leave with the Chairman, he had everybody stand well away from the door and told them not to follow—or else. He had apparently forgotten about her. She was counting on it.

Melody made a gesture for Drake, indicating that she was going to try something. He gave an almost imperceptible nod and nudged the captain who was standing beside him. The captain saw Melody.

One of the officers spoke. "We'll make a deal with you, Casey. Just let the Chairman go."

Casey shook his head. "No deals."

As he and the Chairman turned around, Melody jerked her head back out of the doorway. Her muscles tensed. What if her actions got the Chairman killed? The Free World would stagger if this happened. But it would be worse if Casey managed to take him out of the country. In addition to the resulting international humiliation, perhaps Casey would decide not to let him return.

Melody counted the footsteps of the Chairman and Casey as they marched toward the door. They sounded loud on the wooden floor. She tensed her muscles even more. She would have only one chance. The Chairman came through the doorway first, followed by the gun to his head. Melody lunged, her timing almost perfect.

"Go," she shouted at the Chairman as she shoved the gun away from his head.

She tried to grab the gun out of Casey's hand but failed. His first shot went wild. He shook her loose, and she thought he was going to shoot her, but he had a bigger problem. Drake and the captain had moved when she did and were almost at the doorway. Casey heard the noise of their footsteps and swung around to face them.

His second shot hit the captain who was leading. He didn't get a chance to fire a third shot. Drake's momentum pushed the captain into Casey, and then Drake hit Casey like a Muhammad Ali punch, blasting him onto his back. Casey emitted a solid "ooof" as the wind was knocked out of him. Melody grabbed the gun from Casey's hand and pointed it at his head.

Drake sat astride him and spoke grimly. "Artie's not the only one who played football."

CHAPTER 39

Today's run ends the race. It goes from Thornton State Beach through San Francisco across the Golden Gate Bridge to the vista point at the north end. Follow Route 35 (Skyline Drive) into San Francisco County. Turn left on Great Highway and follow the coast past the Cliff House. You can improvise going through Lincoln Park (chance for some place changes here). You can take El Camino del Mar out of the park. Follow Lincoln Boulevard to approach the bridge. As you get close to the bridge, you can take Merchant Road to gain access to the bridge. Cross the bridge into Marin County. Enjoy yourselves. It's been a great race.

ᔓ

"It's too bad you didn't get a hug from your father."

They were running slowly, but they were running.

"At least he shook my hand and said, 'Good job.' He did hug *you*. So did the Chairman."

"Your father said some nice things about you in front of the Chairman. How many fathers do that for their sons? He'll make a good interim CEO for Giganticorp. I think they elected him because he's the only honest man of the bunch."

"He'll dispense with the mendacity, that's for sure. I gather that he's waiting for us at the end of the race, instead of Casey. That ought to get the media buzzing. He's probably already congratulating Tom and Jerry, the big winners. It's a nice gesture on his part, but I'd rather be met by dancing girls."

"What about dancing boys?"

"Boys, too, just for you."

The board of directors of Giganticorp, having a quorum present, had convened a meeting after things had calmed down. They had transacted two pieces of business. They had ousted Casey Messinger as chief executive officer of Giganticorp and elected Justin Drake to serve in his place until a committee with Admiral Drake at its head could find a suitable person to take the position in a permanent capacity.

Melody was still trying to absorb everything that had happened last night. "Casey showed a lot of hubris bringing the conspirators to the same building where he had trained the submariners. If Slick and I hadn't found that room, somebody else might have."

"I guess he felt that once he was President, or Dictator, or whatever his title was going to be, that it wouldn't matter anymore. He should be hanged as a traitor, but I doubt that's going to happen. Since he was captured by the military, I suspect that his real plan will be hushed up. It would show too much government vulnerability, and too many other heads would roll along with his. The official reason for Casey leaving Giganticorp will be, 'so he can spend more time with his family.'"

"He'll have to spend it on the private island he was about to fly to last night."

"He won't be allowed to live in the U.S., that's for sure."

"Do you think the president will replace the Chairman of the Joint Chiefs?"

"Definitely. But that happens quite frequently and won't raise many eyebrows. The generals and admirals present who are still on active duty will no doubt be taking early retirement. No heroes will emerge from this, but Slick should get a footnote in history. Even Blade was upset about him. It can truly be said that he gave his life for his country. And for me."

"If the guard hadn't made a lucky shot, Slick would still be alive…"

Melody's voice trailed off. She had to slow down even more because she was choking up. Their speed didn't matter, anyway. They were firmly entrenched in last place for today's run. She had found out one thing about Slick that she didn't care to share with Drake—his beautiful blue eyes. She pulled herself away from the image of those eyes as he lay dying and tried to concentrate on what Drake was saying.

"If you hadn't moved in and taken out Artie, he would have shot me."

"If you hadn't kicked his gun, he might have hit *me*. I thought he'd never go down."

Drake didn't want to talk about that phase of the operation anymore. They both could have been killed.

"You're the real hero for stopping Casey when he was kidnapping the Chairman."

"Casey forgot about me. Since he discounted my ability when we toured the submarine, I figured he might. But you and the captain kept him from shooting me."

"I'm glad the captain will be okay. The bullet basically bounced off his ribs."

Drake wasn't faking his limp. It was all he could do to keep running. "Sorry I'm such a mess today. My belly flop and the tackle by Artie ruined any chance we had at the million. Not to mention my tackle of Casey. My knees are killing me."

"My feet are sore from those damn shoes I was wearing. I keep telling myself that what we did was much more important than a million dollars."

"Thanks for trying to cheer me up. At least we're sure to collect on the per diem. With my father in charge, all the obligations of Giganticorp will be paid in full."

"You can buy your cabin in Idyllwild."

"And get away from people like Casey. If they're not going to hang him as a traitor, I hope the FBI nails his ass for Grace's murder."

"The Chairman said he would push them to investigate it. At least they've got a smoking gun now—"

"And a smoking executive assistant. I suspect that Ms. Melinda Gage knows secrets that would curl your hair."

"Thanks. I'm happy with my hair the way it is. But I'd like to see Casey put away in the U.S. equivalent of the Tower of London. Perhaps the Beefeaters would be willing to loan their guillotine to the Colonies to dispatch him. I'd volunteer to drop the blade on his neck."

"Speaking of Blade, he made a prediction. He predicted that Casey's life expectancy on his island would be about six months. I didn't ask any questions."

"That makes me feel a lot better."

"I never knew you were so bloodthirsty. You need a vacation."

In spite of his sadness about Slick and losing the chance at the big money and multiple aches from his fall, Drake suddenly felt good about the world. "It's such a fantastic day. I've never seen a day like this in San Francisco. It's a good omen."

They were running across the Golden Gate Bridge under a warm sun. The bright orange towers contrasted with the sparkling blue waters of the bay. It was a day in which anything was possible in a free country. Anything.

Drake turned to Melody. "Now that we've helped to save the world, we *both* deserve a vacation. We've already seen the coast. How about we go off into the mountains together?"

"'Will you walk into my parlor?' said the spider to the fly."

"Assuming that the mountains can be regarded as a parlor, I guess that's an apt analogy. Will you?"

"Anything's possible."

ABOUT THE AUTHOR

After spending more than a quarter of a century as a pioneer in the computer industry, Alan Cook is well into his second career as a writer.

The Hayloft: a 1950s mystery and prize-winning *Honeymoon for Three* feature Gary Blanchard, first as a high school senior who has to solve the murder of his cousin, and ten years later as a bridegroom who gets more than he bargained for on his honeymoon.

Hotline to Murder takes place at a crisis hotline in Bonita Beach, California. When a listener is murdered, Tony and Shahla team up to uncover the strange worlds of their callers and find the killer.

His Lillian Morgan mysteries, *Catch a Falling Knife* and *Thirteen Diamonds*, explore the secrets of retirement communities. Lillian, a retired mathematics professor from North Carolina, is smart, opinionated, and loves to solve puzzles, even when they involve murder.

Alan splits his time between writing and walking, another passion. His inspirational, prize-winning book, *Walking the World: Memories and Adventures*, has information and adventure in equal parts. He is also the author of *Walking to Denver*, a light-hearted, fictional account of a walk he did.

Freedom's Light: Quotations from History's Champions of Freedom, contains quotations from some of our favorite historical figures about personal freedom. *The Saga of Bill the Hermit* is a narrative poem about a hermit who decides that the single life isn't all it's cracked up to be.

Alan lives with his wife, Bonny, on a hill in Southern California. His website is alancook.50megs.com.